# A Noble Bargain

# The Bargainer Series

# A Noble Bargain

## Jan Sikes

Fresh Ink Group

Guntersville

# A Noble Bargain

Copyright © 2024
by Jan Sikes
All rights reserved

Fresh Ink Group
An Imprint of:
The Fresh Ink Group, LLC
1021 Blount Avenue #931
Guntersville, AL 35976
Email: info@FreshInkGroup.com
FreshInkGroup.com

Edition 1.0 2024

Cover by Stephen Geez / FIG
Cover Art by Anik/FIG
Book design by Amit Dey / FIG
Associate publisher Beem Weeks / FIG

Except as permitted under the U.S. Copyright Act of 1976 and except for brief quotations in critical reviews or articles, no portion of this book's content may be stored in any medium, transmitted in any form, used in whole or part, or sourced for derivative works such as videos, television, and motion pictures, without prior written permission from the publisher.

Cataloging-in-Publication Recommendations:
FIC014090 FICTION / Historical / 20th Century / Post-World War II
FIC045020 FICTION / Family Saga
FIC014030 FICTION / Historical / Romance

Library of Congress Control Number: xxx

ISBN-13: 978-1-964998-18-3 Softcover
ISBN-13: 978-1-964998-19-0 Hardcover
ISBN-13: 978-1-964998-20-6 Ebooks

# ACKNOWLEDGEMENTS

First and foremost, I want to thank my readers for insisting on a sequel to A Beggar's Bargain. It has been my pleasure to revisit the characters in that book while introducing new ones.

I wish to thank the staff at the Crossett Arkansas Public Library for their help in my research of the area and time period for this book. I'd be remiss if I didn't mention the wonderful people in Dade County Missouri who have been so willing to share this journey with me. All of their input enriches the stories and makes them more authentic.

I owe a huge 'thank you' to Gary Newell for his expertise and input on the mechanical operation of the Woody Wagon.

And, last but certainly not least, I am eternally grateful for the support of my daughters and grandchildren on my writing adventures. I am blessed beyond measure.

# CHAPTER 1

Music and laughter drifted around twenty-two-year-old Oliver Quinn as he tipped his paddy cap to a pretty young girl sitting alone on a bench against the wall. He'd had his eye on her since she'd arrived. It didn't escape his notice that she seemed to fold into herself, mostly staring down at her hands on her lap. Single lightbulbs hanging from the ceiling cast an auburn glow on her nut-brown hair.

The threadbare plain cotton dress and worn, scuffed shoes spoke of struggles that required no explanation.

The year was 1948, and in the small town of Crossett, Arkansas, local dances drew people from all around the area.

Young men showed up in their Sunday best, hoping to steal a dance and, if they were lucky, a kiss from their favorite girl. Old men came with jars of moonshine, looking for a good card game or perhaps a chance to jaw with their neighbors, while their wives gathered in close-knit circles to share the latest gossip or new recipe.

Folks in Crossett worked hard and played hard.

And Oliver did both.

He'd danced with almost every unattached girl since he'd arrived. He loved twirling them around the dance floor, dipping them at the end of the song.

After escorting his latest dance partner back to her parents, with a hand in one pocket, he sauntered over to the young girl he'd been watching. "Howdy." He gestured toward the crowded dance floor. "Care to dance?"

She glanced up, her face flushing bright pink, then quickly lowered her eyes, but not before Oliver glimpsed the most striking violet blues he'd ever seen. "Don't know how."

"Well, then." Oliver bowed at the waist. "Let me be the first to teach you."

"I..." She hesitated. "I can't."

Oliver followed her quick gaze to two boys around his age leaning against the opposite wall. "Miss, I can assure you I have the most honorable of intentions. Do I need to ask their permission?"

"No. Please." Tears pooled and her gaze widened.

"Your brothers?"

"Yes."

"Where's your ma and pa? I can ask their permission."

She jerked a thumb toward the back door. "Pa's out there, but he's in an awful mood, spoiling for a fight."

Oliver pulled off his cap and tucked it under his arm. "You got a name? If you don't tell me, I'm going to call you Violet. You have the most beautiful eyes I've ever seen."

"Name's Rose. You'd best be movin' along. My brothers are heading this way."

Squaring his shoulders, Oliver stayed rooted. "I'm not afraid, if that's what you think."

Her voice barely audible over the fiddles, guitars, and banjos, she pleaded, "Please go. Don't need no trouble."

Ignoring her quiet plea, Oliver leaned closer. "Rose, my name's Oliver Quinn, and I never back down from trouble. Seems to me you came to a dance, and what most folks do at a dance is, well—dance."

A rough hand on his shoulder spun Oliver around.

"Can I help you?" The question came from a young man with shoulder-length brown hair, dressed in loose-fitting overalls. A dark scowl creased his forehead.

"Don't reckon you can." Oliver pointed to Rose. "This your sister?"

The intruder nodded.

"Then you won't mind if I dance with her, will you?"

Shrugging his shoulders, the boy stuck his hands in his overall pockets. "Up to her, I guess. Just don't try no funny stuff."

Oliver turned back to Rose and held out his hand. "May I?"

She pushed to her feet and clumsily followed him around the dance floor. She held her thin body stiff under his hands, keeping a suitable distance between them, yet she still managed to step on his foot more than once.

"You're stubborn." She accidentally bumped into another dancer.

"Been called that a time or two." Oliver expertly guided her to the edge of the crowded area as the song ended.

With a hand on her elbow, he walked her back to the bench along the wall. "Thank you, Rose. That wasn't so bad, now was it?"

"You're a good dancer. Sorry I stepped on your toe."

"Never felt it." Before she could sit, he motioned toward the back of the building. "Say, would you like something to drink?"

Her eyebrows shot up.

"I don't mean liquor. I see they have a punchbowl back there."

"Okay. I guess."

Oliver took her hand and led her toward the long wooden table in the back of the hall laden with refreshments. "Two glasses of punch, please, Mabel," he said to a gray-haired woman behind the table.

He handed one to Rose. "I could use some fresh air."

"I can't go outside with you." She cocked her head toward the two, still leaning against the wall.

"You let me worry about them. I promise I can take care of myself." He took a sip of the fruity punch, focusing on her plump lips as she tasted hers. "You're awful pretty."

She choked on the punch and coughed. "No one's ever said that before."

"Then they must be blind." He pointed to the door. "Air?"

"My pa'll kill me if I go out there with you."

"Why? I can assure you I'm a decent person. I work over at the sawmill, loading lumber onto train cars. Live at home with my mother and two sisters. My mom works at the local bakery, and my two sisters are in school. I can provide references, if that's what it takes." He pointed to the gray-haired woman. "Mabel here knows me and my whole family. She can vouch for me, can't you, Mabel?"

The woman flashed a toothy smile. "Been knowin' Oliver all his life. No better person in the whole county."

"There. Feel better?"

"I'm not worth your time or trouble."

"Let me decide that. What or who in God's name are you afraid of, Rose? Why'd you come to this dance? Never seen you here before."

"That's 'cause I've never been here before."

Oliver pointed toward the door again. "Walk with me." He placed a hand gently on the middle of her back and ushered her through the wide doorway. Once outside, the crisp fall air prickled his skin, and dried leaves crunched beneath his scuffed lace-up work boots. In the distance, an owl hooted for his mate while crickets chirped and hopped under the single light that shone over the community hall entrance.

He motioned toward a fallen log at the edge of the tree line. "Let's sit. I'd like to know more about you, Rose." He brushed away dry leaves from a spot on the log and waited for Rose to sit before joining her. "You got a last name?"

"Name's Rose Blaine. Moved over here from Hamburg last month. My brothers are looking to find work. Why do you talk funny?"

Oliver chuckled. "My folks are from Ireland. Guess the accent has stuck with me. You haven't mentioned a mother."

She choked back a sob. "Ma died over four years ago. It's been hard ever since. She was the only one that could keep a rein on Pa. And now…"

Oliver sipped his punch. "And now, he's drinkin' hisself crazy."

"How do you know?"

"It's what men do when they lose someone they love. Seen it before."

"You got a pa?"

"He died when I was twelve. He got between a blade and a log at the sawmill and didn't make it. My twin sisters were just babies. Been us four ever since. I help support the family."

"That's good of you."

"Rose! Rose, you out here?"

She jumped up. "Over here, Harlan."

Oliver stood as the two boys approached.

Without a word, the one she called Harlan drew back his fist. Oliver easily sidestepped to dodge the blow. "I ain't doin' nothing disrespectful with your sister. Just talkin'."

"That ain't what Pa will think." Harlan angled toward Rose while the younger brother stepped in front of him.

"Harlan, don't."

Harlan shoved his brother aside. "Out of my way, Jack." He grabbed Rose's arm. "You ain't nothin' but trouble. You know Pa is in a bad way, and here you are makin' things worse."

She let out a yelp. "Ouch. Stop it, Harlan. Let me go."

"Hey." Oliver took a step forward. "You're hurting her."

Harlan whirled back to Oliver, his face a mass of fury. "Told you, Irish, stay away from our sister. Guess you don't listen too good."

When he took another swing at him, Oliver caught his arm midair and twisted it behind his back. "Told you I ain't lookin' for trouble. Just having a friendly conversation with Rose."

"And we told you to stay the hell away from her," Harlan growled.

"Look." Oliver released his arm. "Let's start over. I'm Oliver Quinn. I work over at the sawmill, and I'm a decent chap."

"Listen to him." Rose bit her bottom lip. "He's tellin' the truth. We was just talkin'. Besides, maybe he can help you and Jack get on over at the mill."

"That true? You lookin' for work?"

"Maybe." Harlan spit in the dirt and squinched one eye.

"I'm in tight with the foreman. Can put in a good word. Either of you had any sawmill experience?"

Jack fidgeted. "None to speak of, but we've lived in these Arkansas woods all our lives. Ain't scared of hard work."

"Come by on Monday, and I'll introduce you to Mr. Owen. Can't promise any more than that."

Jack stuck out his hand. "Sorry for the misunderstanding. We're new around here."

"So Rose said. No hard feelings." Oliver accepted the outstretched hand.

"Still, better git back inside 'fore Pa knows you're gone, Rose."

Oliver reached for her empty punch glass and smiled. "We were just heading back."

There was something about the fear reflecting in Rose's eyes that sent Oliver's protective instincts reeling. He'd bet his last dollar she'd suffered at the hands of her drunken father and maybe even the brothers. Call him old-fashioned, but there was never an excuse for a man to hit a woman or treat her unkindly. If anyone ever laid a hand on his mother or either of his sisters, there'd be hell to pay.

And as Oliver told Rose, he didn't back down from trouble.

Never had. Never would.

Rose hurried back inside, scanning the room for her father. She breathed a sigh of relief when she didn't see him.

Oliver Quinn seemed like a nice boy. No one besides her mother had ever told her she was pretty.

But why would a nice boy be interested in her? Her father was as mean as they came, especially after downing a pint of his special moonshine. He'd often bragged about killing a man with his bare hands after the man refused to pay for a delivery.

He thought nothing of laying a hand on her or her brothers for anything he considered an infraction. The bruises hidden beneath her clothes were the result.

No doubt he'd consider her dancing with and talking to Oliver Quinn a huge infraction to his strict rules.

At this rate, she'd die miserable and alone in their shack in the woods.

At almost eighteen, she felt old—old and tired.

Tired of being a whipping post, of doing the men's laundry on a rub board and cooking their meals with whatever meager supplies she could scrounge up.

But the beatings were the worst. Her bruises had barely healed from the last time. And all because she didn't get every tiny lump out of the gravy. God only knows what he'd do if he found out her secret.

Sometimes, her brothers tried to intervene. That's when things turned uglier. Fear that he would kill them one day kept her stomach in knots.

Glancing up, she spotted Oliver twirling a girl with long blonde hair across the dance floor. She liked the way his chestnut hair curled at the nape of his neck. But most of all, the kindness in his green eyes spoke volumes. And his lilting Irish accent reminded her of a bubbling brook.

He winked and flashed a wide smile that sent a flush to her cheeks.

A commotion from outside the building drew everyone's attention. Everyone but Rose. She knew. Her father was at it again. No telling who was the victim this time. He'd always had a mean streak in him, but after her mother died, his fuse was so short it was all but non-existent.

With all her heart, she wished she could take an ax and smash the whiskey still to smithereens, then escape from a life that choked and wrung every shred of hope from her.

There had to be something better out there.

As soon as she had that thought, it followed with another.

*But you're a Blaine, white trash, a nobody with no future.*

How many times had her pa spouted those words? Too many to count. Yet she dared to hold on to hope.

She sat unmoving as people rushed outside.

Her brothers would fetch her as soon as they could get Ezra Blaine loaded into the jalopy, which they jokingly called a car.

She hoped the sheriff wouldn't get involved and they could make a quiet exit, although she dreaded the trip back to their shack. Unless her father passed out, it would be pure torture.

Instead of following the others outside, Oliver made his way across the dance floor toward her.

"Your father, I presume?"

She nodded.

"Want I should take you home?"

"Oh no. That would be a disaster."

"A disaster? What do you mean?"

She twisted her hands in her lap. "He'll kill you."

# CHAPTER 2

True to their word, Jack and Harlan Blaine, dressed in worn but clean overalls with their hair freshly combed, arrived at the sawmill early on Monday morning. Oliver stuck his gloves in his back pocket and stepped off the platform, where he steadily transferred long bundles of lumber onto the waiting train car.

"You made it."

"Said we would." Harlan crushed out a cigarette, then shifted back to Oliver and stuck out his hand. "No hard feelings from the other night?"

Oliver shook his hand. "None on my part." He pointed toward a brick building with a faded red door. "Come on. I'll introduce you to Mr. Owen."

"We appreciate this." Jack fell in step beside him.

"Happy to help. There's plenty of work, if you're willing." Harlan's black eye kept Oliver from asking if they'd made it home from the dance with no problems. Obviously, their father didn't hold back his fists. It made him cringe to think about what Rose must have to endure. His dislike for Ezra Blaine grew. Regardless of a man's problems, he needn't take it out on his family.

No wonder Rose sat alone and kept to herself at the dance. He suspected a combination of shyness and fear had kept her glued to the wall. It made him appreciate his own family all that much more.

His mother seldom raised her voice. She didn't have to because the three of them, Oliver and his sisters, made sure of it.

Fiona Quinn worked at the local bakery, Millie's Pastry Shop, and could almost always be found with a flour-dusted apron tied around her ample middle. She freely gave smiles to everyone and generously shared the heavenly dishes she prepared with those who had less.

She'd instilled that spirit of giving in her children, along with a strong work ethic. Oliver had taken his first job at thirteen and still managed to excel in school and sports, especially baseball. He'd do anything to help ease his mother's burden of providing for the family.

Once Oliver made the introductions to Mr. Owen, he hurried back to the loading platform, thankful for a cloudy sky and cool fall breeze. Winter would be coming. But for now, he'd enjoy the pleasant transition from one of the hottest Arkansas summers he could remember.

As he loaded bundle after bundle of lumber, his thoughts drifted to Rose Blaine. He'd always prided himself on being able to read people. There was something special about her besides those violet-blue eyes that pierced right through him. She had intelligence that went beyond her family's social status, or lack thereof. And she had secrets. He'd stake a week's wages on that one. While the girls he knew in town were pretty enough, none of them turned his head. At least not since Ellen. He'd really thought Ellen was the one until she up and married the preacher's son. The pain of it taught him to guard his heart.

He reached for the next bundle, enjoying the rippling stretch across the muscles in his back and through his biceps as he hefted it onto the car.

Oliver looked like his father, a tall, sturdy Irishman built for hard labor and fighting. But he got his genteel spirit from the woman who'd given birth to him.

When Irish immigrants arrived in America, they found a less than enthusiastic welcome. Many resorted to fighting in the rings to put food on their family's table, and Oliver's father was no exception. That was until he landed a steady job at the sawmill.

While Oliver never cared for physical violence, he didn't avoid it and never quit once it started. He held close the memory of his father, Patrick Quinn. No better man had ever walked the face of the earth.

He encouraged Oliver to pursue his dreams. Said that's what America was all about. Was the main reason they left Ireland and immigrated here. More than anything else, Oliver loved baseball and until his father died, he loved playing with him. Now, he played on the Crossett Miller's team, and he was good. During off season, he played with some of the local boys. One day, when his mom and sisters could make it without him, he'd take a stab at the big leagues.

A few minutes later, Harlan and Jack exited the supervisor's office and disappeared inside the mill with Mr. Owen, leaving no doubt the man had hired them.

Good.

Maybe that would help ease the family's burden.

He looked forward to learning more about them. Noting no dinner pail in their hands, he made plans to share the bountiful food his mother sent him off with each day.

He had to admit to having a slight ulterior motive. Ever since Friday night, he'd given thought to courting Rose Blaine. And her brothers might help make that happen.

Focusing back on the tedious work, he grinned as he thought about how she'd clumsily followed him around the dance floor, careful to keep a distance. But he also remembered holding her delicate hand in his and how her striking eyes held such deep sadness. And though he'd never mention it, the purple bruise that peeked above her dress collar said she was no stranger to violence.

He wondered if she'd ever seen a movie or eaten in a cafe. Probably not. Being the first to expose her to things beyond a moonshiner's shack would be a pleasure. She obviously could use a friend.

Lost in thought, he jumped when the mid-day whistle blew.

Pocketing his gloves, he jumped down from the loading platform and grabbed his dinner pail from the front seat of his panel wagon. Then he went in search of Jack and Harlan.

He found them coming from the main entrance to the sawmill and waved. "Hey, fellas. Join me?"

Harlan ducked his head. "Wasn't expecting to get hired on the spot. Didn't bring anything to eat."

Oliver slapped him on the back. "Then, lucky for you, my mom always packs enough in my pail for ten men. Happy to share."

Embarrassment flashed across Harlan's face. "Don't need no charity."

"Speak for yourself, Harlan. I'm hungry." Jack stepped forward. "Thanks, Irish."

"Come on, Harlan. Let me share what I have. Got coffee, too."

Harlan reluctantly followed his brother and Oliver across the lot to a shade tree, where Oliver plopped down and opened his pail. He motioned. "Sit. Let's eat."

Jack wasted no time dropping to the ground. "Come on, Harlan. I know you're hungry, too. You missed breakfast this morning, just like I did."

Harlan sat on his haunches. "Reckon I could do with a bite."

"Great." Oliver took out half a loaf of Irish Soda Bread and broke it into three pieces, followed by a sausage link, cheese, apples, and peanut butter cookies. He handed each a generous portion. "See. Told you my mom packed too much."

Jack took a huge bite of bread, followed by cheese and sausage. "She does this every day?"

Oliver nodded. "Every day. I'm spoiled."

"I'll say. Our sister is a great cook. She feeds us good, except…"

Harlan punched Jack's arm. "Shut up, little brother. Irish don't need to know our business."

Jack rubbed his arm. "I was just sayin' she's a good cook."

Oliver chewed his food, poured coffee into the thermos lid, and passed it around. "Say, do you think your sister would go out with me if I asked your pa? I'd like to take her to The Wren to see a show."

"If you know what's good for you, you'll stay away." Harlan sipped the coffee, and his eyes hardened. "Pa don't cotton to strangers."

"He give you that black eye?" Oliver couldn't resist asking.

Harlan growled. "None of your business." He pushed to his feet and shoved the last of the bread into his mouth. "Come on, Jack."

"Come on, where, Harlan? You're being rude. This man just fed us. If he hadn't, we wouldn't have had anything 'til tonight."

"Sit back down, Harlan. Didn't mean to pry." Oliver pointed to the spot Harlan had vacated and handed him another thermos lid of coffee and a hunk of cheese.

Harlan dropped back to the ground but kept up his guard. "Thanks for the food, Irish. No more questions. Got it?"

"Got it." Oliver gazed into the distance. "Still, I'd like to court Rose."

Jack bit off a large bite of sausage. "She's shy."

"I could see that at the dance. But I have to wonder if she was more afraid than shy."

Harlan threw the rest of his food into Oliver's lap. "That's it. No more talk." He stalked off, leaving Jack and Oliver open-mouthed.

"Your brother's got a short fuse." Oliver passed Jack the bread Harlan had thrown.

"Yeah. Takes after Pa."

"And you?"

"I'd do anything not to be like Pa. I hate it when he goes into one of his rages. One of these times, he's gonna wind up killin' one of us."

Oliver cringed and fought against blistering anger toward the man. "He hit Rose, too?"

Jack chewed and swallowed. "He hits her, but not like he does me and Harlan. She's better at dodging."

"I'm sorry." Oliver meant it. His heart went out to shy Rose with the beautiful eyes and the two brothers.

"Nothin' to be sorry about. Not your problem. But if you're thinkin' Pa's gonna let you court Rose, you have another think coming. He won't hear of it." Jack finished off the bread and meat.

Oliver leaned against the tree trunk. "We'll see. I can be pretty stubborn when I take a mind to."

Jack chuckled. "You don't know Pa."

"No, I don't. But I can see that the three of you are scared of him, and that makes me even more determined. It ain't right."

"Maybe not, but he is our pa, and what he says goes."

"I understand that, but I have to tell you, Jack, I can't respect a man who hits his children, especially a girl. There's no excuse."

Jack ducked his head, and his ears turned beet red. "Shouldn't have told you all that. Harlan's gonna have my hide."

"So, don't tell him. I sure won't." He laid a hand on the boy's shoulder. "I like you, Jack." He passed the coffee. "Say, do you play baseball?"

Jack sipped the coffee. "Never had a chance to try it."

"I get a game together with local boys every weekend. You should join us."

"Don't know." Jack shrugged. "I'd like to, but can't make any promises."

"Good enough. It's a lot of fun. I love baseball. Someday, I'm gonna be good enough for the majors."

Jack whistled. "Big dreams. Had an uncle that played for the St. Louis Browns once upon a time, but didn't see them much. Don't reckon I've given much thought to the future. Just tryin' to make it through the days."

"Really? You had an uncle that played for the Browns?" Oliver leaned forward.

"Yes. Uncle Rube pitched for the team for several seasons. He's old now, though, if he's even still alive. Saw him briefly at my mother's funeral."

"Would that be Rube Livingston?"

"Yep. That's him."

"Wow, Jack. That's amazing. I'd give my eyeteeth to meet him."

"That ain't likely to happen. Him and my aunt live in St. Louis, but like I said, he may not even still be alive."

"Still. That's amazing." Oliver couldn't believe the unlikely connection.

By the time the dinner break ended, not a crumb of food remained in Oliver's pail. Tomorrow, he'd ask his mother for extra, knowing full well she'd happily give it.

What a contrast between families. One wrought with grief, anger, and violence—the other filled with love, laughter, and warmth.

That made Oliver a lucky man.

His heart broke for Rose and her brothers.

But what could he do?

His resolve to make things better for them doubled.

If only he knew how.

# CHAPTER 3

Rose tucked a stray hair behind her ear and bent over the metal washtub in the backyard. She had scrubbed her brother's bloody shirt until her fingers were red and raw. But it was Harlan's best shirt, and he'd need it. They certainly didn't have the money to replace it.

As the sun peeked over the treetops, Harlan and Jack had left for town, looking for work. The weekend's violence left raw, exposed nerves in her and both of her brothers. Things were changing. Harlan fought back harder this time.

An hour later, Ezra Blaine stumbled out of the back door of the small shack, adjusting his overalls on his bony shoulders. "Where's Harlan and Jack?"

She jumped at the sound of his voice and quickly put the washtub between her and the man whom she called her father. "Went lookin' for work."

"Dammit. Where's my coffee, girl?" He let out a growl. "I swear you're turnin' into a lazy good-for-nothin' just like every other woman."

She dried her hands on her apron. "I'll get it."

Ezra focused his bloodshot eyes on her. "Well, go. What the hell you waitin' on?" He fished a tin of rolling tobacco and a sleeve of papers out of his front pocket.

Her heart plummeted as she darted toward the back door. It was going to be another day of dancing around his foul mood. And with Harlan and Jack gone, there was no one but her to suffer the brunt of his rage. She fought to hold back tears.

There had to be a better way to live.

And things could get far worse. That scared her more than anything she'd suffered since her mother's death. This time, a life was on the line, even if it was a life she refused to acknowledge.

Her hands shook as she poured coffee into a tin cup. When the door slammed, she dropped the cup, spilling the brown liquid on the wood floor.

Before she could move, Ezra backhanded her, leaving a harsh sting on her cheek and a would-be bruise on her backside, where she collided with the edge of the stove. "Clean it up," he yelled. "I'll get my own damn coffee."

She cowered against the rickety cabinet until he poured the coffee and left, slamming the door behind him.

Grabbing a rag, she dropped to her knees, hot tears mixing with the brown liquid pooling across the uneven floor.

"Someday." She barely whispered the word, but it was a vow she meant. Someday she'd escape the hot temper and heavy hand of a man who'd gone completely off the rails.

It didn't help that he drank heavily of the moonshine he made. Truth be told, he swallowed any profits it might have produced.

And heaven forbid he ever find out what his partner, Amos Parker, had been doing.

Knowing her father, he'd blame her. She hated Amos, hated what she knew about him, and hated what he'd forced her to do. Nausea rose, and she ran for the sink. The sickness came more often. How long could she hide it?

Disgust and desperation clawed at her like a wild boar caught in an iron trap.

Harlan would probably blame her, too. Jack would have empathy for her, but he would never go against Harlan and their father. The consequences were too severe.

She was alone. Alone and scared.

If only her mother were still alive. She'd been the glue that held everything together. More hot tears flowed down her cheeks when she remembered her mother's tender smile and soft touch.

Once she emptied her stomach and rinsed her mouth, she fell back onto her knees and finished cleaning up the spilled coffee.

Squaring her shoulders, she drew in a sharp breath. Best to face whatever awaited and get it over with. Opening the back door, she called out. "Want breakfast, Pa?"

Ezra tossed the remainder of his coffee on the ground and blew out a stream of smoke. "Do folks in hell want ice water? What kind of fool question is that? It's mornin' ain't it?"

"I'll fix you some eggs and biscuits." She prayed that maybe food would ease his disposition a little. But dim hope was all but dashed when he stepped inside the kitchen and reached for the mason jar on the shelf above the sink.

The unscrewing sound of the metal lid grated on her teetering self-control. She focused on the eggs frying in the pan.

If only she could find the courage to run away again. But the beating she'd taken when Ezra had caught her had left scars that would never fade, both inside and out. If Harlan hadn't intervened, he might have killed her. Rage had blinded him to all rational thinking.

Ezra took a swig and leaned his tall frame against the cabinet. "Where did you say your brothers went?"

Without looking up, she replied, "Said they were going to look for work."

"Hmph." He took another swig.

She slid the eggs onto the plate and buttered two biscuits. "Here you go. If you don't need anything else, I need to finish the laundry."

He waved a hand of dismissal and dropped into a straight-backed chair at the rough-hewn table.

Making her escape, she was thankful for the distraction of soapy water and rugged ridges of the washboard.

It was getting harder to tolerate the man's sour disposition. If she was lucky, she might find some roots growing in the forest that would poison him and end his miserable life.

She almost laughed aloud at the ludicrous thought. If the rotgut he drank didn't kill him, nothing would.

In the next second, guilt washed over her. How could she have such horrible thoughts about her own flesh and blood?

No, she would never have the nerve to poison him. She did, however, have the guts to escape from the misery she lived in at the first opportunity.

But how?

She had no friends. Her pa had seen to that.

Her mother's sister, Aunt Katherine, lived in St. Louis, Missouri. She'd given Rose a sweet, sad smile and laid a kind hand on her shoulder at her mother's funeral. Unknowingly, she'd cast out a lifeline, when she told her she'd always be welcome in her home.

Aunt Katherine was Rose's only hope.

She'd miss Jack most of all. He didn't have the mean streak that Harlan seemed to have inherited from their father. Maybe she could convince him to go with her. Together, they'd have a better chance of surviving.

She sighed and scrubbed harder, acutely aware of the lilting birdsong in the forest and the soft breeze blowing through the trees.

It was almost as if she existed in two different worlds. One beautiful, the other ugly. And she was caught between them both.

As she rinsed the clothes, her thoughts turned to the young man who had asked her to dance Friday night. Oliver Quinn was handsome in a carefree, easy sort of way.

His green eyes sparkled with a joy for life that she craved to experience.

If she lived in a normal world, getting to know him better would be fun. He'd said she had beautiful eyes. No one around her ever handed out compliments. If only things were different. She tried to imagine what it would be like to do ordinary young people things.

But she lived in a vacuum that sucked the life from everyone and everything in it.

Ezra came out the back door, rolling a cigarette. "Goin' up to the still. Supper best be on the table when I get back, girl. Hear me?" He stomped off into the woods.

Rose knew exactly where the still was and how long he'd be gone. She'd been there several times when her father had insisted she and her brothers help with a new batch. Lifting the heavy bags of corn took every ounce of strength she had.

She turned back to the washtub and scrubbed with renewed vigor. At least she was alone, and that was the only time she felt safe these days.

Minutes later, her blood froze in her veins, and her taut nerves wound even tighter at the sound of a truck lumbering up the road toward their house. No one had to tell her who it was.

Amos Parker made regular visits. Her father made the moonshine, and Parker delivered the goods and brought back money. He'd bragged to her about stealing from the profits and how her pa stayed too liquored up to figure it out.

And when her father was off working at the still, he'd had his way with her. Her skin crawled, remembering his rough touch. He only took what he wanted and grunted when he finished, leaving her in a crumpled heap. Just the thought of his yellow-toothed grin and bulging belly made her gag. If she hadn't already thrown up her breakfast, she'd be retching again.

How she wished she could make herself disappear down a rabbit hole like Alice in Wonderland that she'd read about in school.

She jumped when the truck door slammed and glanced around for anything she could use as a weapon.

Amos pounded on the front door and yelled for Ezra. When no one answered, he walked around back. "There you are."

"Pa's at the still. You best go on up."

"That so?" Amos spit in the dirt. "What if I wanna see my favorite girl first?"

She took two steps backward and growled through clenched teeth. "I'm not your girl."

Amos grinned. "You wanna fight today? I like that even better." He rubbed his cock through his pants.

She grabbed the rub board and held it over one shoulder like a baseball bat. "Stay away from me. I'm warnin' you."

"You're warnin' me?"

Amos lunged for her, and she connected the board with the side of his head. "Don't come any closer. I mean it."

Rubbing the side of his face, he whined. "Now, Rose, you and me, we got a good thing here. Don't screw it up."

"I swear to you I'll tell my pa and Harlan if you touch me again."

The man cackled. "Go right ahead. Think they'll believe you over me? You know the answer to that."

Tears threatened, and she forced them back. She wouldn't dare let the despicable man see her cry, even if what he said was true.

He reached her in two long strides, and the minute he got close enough, she raised her foot and kicked him in the groin as hard as she could.

Not wasting a second, she darted into the safety of the forest like a frightened deer running on nimble legs.

Her heart pounded inside her chest.

Not today. Not ever again.

She crashed through the underbrush and ran until she reached Coffee Creek. In the distance, Amos yelled her name, followed by curses and branches breaking as he searched for her.

Huddling behind a thick growth of Loblolly Pine, she pulled her knees up to her chest and buried her face in her apron. Every beat of her heart vibrated through her body.

She ground her teeth so hard she feared they might crack.

Forcing her breath to slow, she struggled against rising nausea. "Quiet," she mumbled to herself. "Have to be quiet."

She lost all track of time, and at some point, dozed off. She awoke to dreams of a young, handsome boy with kind eyes the color of the forest, and hair that curled at the nape of his neck, holding her hand

and dancing across the forest floor. A tiny smile formed for the first time since Friday night.

Raising her head, she listened for any sound. Not hearing anything except for the birds and animals, she stood on wobbly legs and stretched.

Judging by the sun's position, it had to be near mid-day. She skirted the edge of the forest, working her way toward the house, prepared to dart back into hiding in a flash.

She watched the house for a while before circling around for a view of the driveway. Thank goodness, the truck was gone. She returned to empty her washtub water and then finish her daily chores.

The fact that Harlan and Jack weren't back yet had to mean good news. She hoped Oliver Quinn had kept his word and introduced them to his boss.

Even though it meant she'd be alone more with their father, they needed the work.

After she cleaned up her father's breakfast dishes, she made beds and swept the wood plank floors. All the while, she pictured what it would be like to live in a proper house with people who didn't fight, yell, or throw violent punches.

A safe place where no one hit her or violated her young body.

That would be like heaven.

Someday.

She just had to figure out how.

And the sooner, the better.

# CHAPTER 4

Over the next few weeks, Oliver continued to spend his dinner break with Jack. When they finished eating, they tossed around a baseball. Harlan occasionally joined them, but more often he huddled with some of the older men, most likely trying to peddle his father's moonshine.

In a random conversation, Jack mentioned how sad and downhearted his sister had been lately. "It's like she's given up on living." He shrugged. "I try to cheer her up, but really, there ain't a thing I can do."

Oliver rubbed his chin. "Jack, I'd really like to be a friend. Maybe take Rose to a movie or to get an ice cream. I want to ask your pa for permission."

Jack's eyes widened, and his eyebrows shot up. "Oh, hell no. Trust me. You do not want to do that."

"Rose deserves to have some fun. That much is obvious from what I saw at the dance and from what you've told me. So, help me out."

Jack jerked his cap off. "I don't know." He stared off into the distance and rolled a cigarette. "You have to understand Pa. He's not like other men. He's on the edge of a rage all the time. You comin' around to court Rose would only make it worse." He ran thin, calloused fingers through his dark hair. "He'll take it out on her. She's small and so thin. I'm scared he's gonna hurt her bad one of these days."

"Can't you say you're taking her into town? Maybe bring Rose and come and play baseball with us. Or better yet, the both of you come to my house for supper this Friday. Harlan would be welcome, too. My mum would be thrilled to have company."

"Maybe." Jack hesitated and sucked his teeth. "I'll see what I can do, but no promises."

"Good enough." Oliver slapped him on the back.

Leaning against the rough bark of a pine, Oliver contemplated everything Jack had shared. Things were way out of kilter with this family. No young girl should be so isolated. Everything his parents had taught him about kindness came to the forefront.

Learning about the girl's hardships, his mother would be extremely angry. She'd want to confront Ezra Blaine. For a lady, she had spunk, and she cared about the underdog.

So did Oliver.

That evening, he sat in the living room with his mother after his sisters had gone to bed. "Something terrible is happening to Rose Blaine and her brothers." He shared what Jack had revealed and what he'd seen at the dance. He finished with, "She didn't know it, but when I asked her to dance, I saw bruises near her collarbone. Lord only knows where there might be more."

Fiona Quinn listened quietly, then took a sip of tea and smoothed back her graying hair. "That's horrible, Oliver. No lass should have to live in such an unfit situation. Of course, they are welcome to have supper with us on Friday. I'd like to meet her and her brothers. Sounds like they could use a friend."

"Exactly. I feel that, too. I don't know everything that's happening out there, but I do know it's bad. And from what Jack said, Rose has lost all hope."

Fiona clucked her tongue. "'Tis a pity for such a young girl."

"I want to be a friend. I had hoped Jack would come in and play baseball with us on the weekends, but so far he hasn't shown up. Thanks for listening, Mum." He reached across and laid a hand on her soft, plump one. "I'm lucky to have you and my sisters, and we're happy together. If anyone ever raised a hand to you or them, I'd come unglued."

"Just like your father would. Patrick Quinn was never one to stand idly by if someone was being mistreated."

Oliver stood and stretched. "Guess I took after both you and him."

She took another sip of tea. "I have to warn ya, though. Folks don't take kindly to someone butting into their business."

He kissed his mother's forehead and strode across the spotless living room. "I know. I'll be careful. Going to bed. Keep your fingers crossed that Jack and Rose will come to town on Friday."

That evening, Jack and Rose sat alone after supper. Harlan had trudged off with their father to check on the whiskey still.

Rose crossed her arms in defiance. "I'm not going, Jack. I'm just not." The thought of it sent her heart racing and knotted her stomach.

"Why not? Oliver's a nice chap. He's been sharing food with me. Sometimes after we eat, we toss around a baseball. You think Pa or Harlan has ever done that with me? I like him. Comes from a nice family."

"Exactly. And we don't, Jack." She turned her back to hide the tears that sprang unbidden.

"Don't you want a chance to go somewhere nice for a change? Pa and Harlan will be gone with Amos on a run. No one will ever have to know. Just you and me."

She struggled to swallow past the lump in her throat. "Of course, I want a chance. I want to get out of here and live with Aunt Katherine in St. Louis. That's what I want. A meal with strangers ain't gonna change that."

"How do you know?" Jack touched her shoulder, and she flinched when he brushed against a fresh bruise.

"I just know, that's all."

"If you never give it a chance, then you'll just be stuck here and continue to be Pa's whipping post."

Whirling around, tears leaked from the corners of her eyes. "I'm ruined, Jack." She stomped her foot. "Ruined. Can't you see that?"

Jack's voice drifted softly across the ragged living room. "I don't know why you say that, Rose. You're the nicest person I know."

"You don't know everything."

"Please," he pleaded. "I don't ask for much, but I'm asking you to go with me as a favor." He stuck out his bottom lip. "Please."

"What if we get caught? What then?"

"So? Pa's mad all the time, anyway." He turned toward the door. "Well, I'm going with or without you. Oliver is my friend. Come along or not. It's your choice."

Rose sank onto the lumpy excuse for a couch as the front screen door slammed. She wanted in her heart of hearts to meet Oliver's family, spend time with him—to act like a normal young girl.

What if she got sick and threw up in the middle of the meal? She'd be humiliated and embarrassed. Or what if Oliver's mother and sisters didn't like her? She imagined every horrible scenario she could come up with.

Yet she knew Jack was right.

She swiped at her tears and squared her shoulders, then hurried out the door to find him sitting on the edge of the front porch blowing smoke rings. Dropping down beside him, she let out a long sigh. "Fine. I'll go with you just this once. But that's all I'll promise."

Jack crushed out his cigarette and gave her a quick side hug. "Once is all I ask."

"And if we get caught?"

Shrugging, Jack slung an arm around her thin shoulders. "It won't be the first beating I've ever had. You either. I'll take all the blame. Say I forced you to go with me."

Rose leaned her head against her brother's shoulder. "I couldn't let you do that. If we get caught, we'll take our punishment together. Or maybe we could run away, Jack. Go to Aunt Katherine's house."

She wanted more than anything to tell Jack her secret—to have an ally. But she couldn't bring herself to say the awful words. It was as if saying it out loud made it permanent and real.

Jack flicked his cigarette butt into the yard. "Rose, I'm only sixteen. They'd put us in jail if we ran away. Besides, I can't do that to Harlan."

"I know. Still, I can't help wishing."

Despite the apprehension, a stir of excitement rippled through her at the thought of spending time with a nice family. And to be honest, especially with a handsome boy who said she had pretty eyes.

Maybe Jack was right. Maybe somehow, Oliver Quinn would be her ticket out of this hellhole. God knew she needed rescuing.

The next thought all but strangled her. She was tainted, perhaps even cursed. What did she have to offer anyone?

Oliver had everything she craved.

A normal life without violence.

A loving parent and siblings.

A good stable job.

She had nothing except her honest heart and intelligent mind.

Thinking about her clothing options left little choice. She had one decent dress—the one she'd worn to the dance.

Otherwise, her wardrobe consisted of threadbare dresses that had belonged to her mother. Sometimes, she imagined she could still smell her mother's special scent, although she'd washed them many times over the years. Smaller than her mother, they hung like sacks around her slender body, even after she'd altered them. Yet, it was the last connection to the woman who'd given birth to her, and she clung to them like a tenuous, invisible thread of hope.

A longing stronger than anything she'd ever felt rushed through her. She needed a mother in the worst way.

Pushing to her feet, she left Jack sitting on the porch and hurried inside.

Another thought struck her. Perhaps the sight of the dresses increased her father's volatile tangents. Surely, they brought up memories of better times for him, which he quickly drowned in the liquor he made.

She'd never considered that before.

Still, nothing gave him the right to hit her, to leave cuts and bruises on her bony body.

She'd sew something new. And it would need long sleeves to hide the most recent telltale signs. Nothing she could do about the fading bruise on her cheek.

She had to rely on what she already had, but repurposing the dresses would at least give her a new outfit.

Maybe a skirt and blouse.

Her mother had taught her the art of sewing, and it had been a long time since she'd been inspired to get out needle and thread other than to mend tears and sew on buttons.

Time to put that talent to good use.

A foreign flutter of excitement surged through her. Rose stood in the middle of the floor and twirled around with a smile.

Rose Blaine had something pleasant to look forward to for the first time in forever.

Friday!

# CHAPTER 5

Oliver paced the floor on Friday evening, keeping one eye on the driveway in front of their modest wood-frame house. Where were they?

Jack had promised.

What if something had gone wrong? What if their father had caught them before they left?

His gut churned, and he tamped down rising anger toward Ezra Blaine. He tossed a baseball from one hand to the other, something he often did when nervous or deep in thought.

"Oliver, relax. They'll be here." Fiona Quinn wiped her hands on her apron as delectable smells wafted from the kitchen. "Supper's almost ready."

"What if they don't come?" Oliver gripped the ball harder.

"Son, there are things in life you cannot control. Focus on the ones you can."

Oliver's twin sisters, Margaret and Elizabeth, burst into the house. Their energy was boundless at fourteen, and they both possessed an undeniable zest for life. With light brown hair and brown eyes, Margaret favored her mother, while Elizabeth had darker hair and green eyes like Oliver and their father.

They threw their schoolbooks and jackets down on the bench in the hallway. "Something smells good, Mum," Elizabeth said.

"Girls, do you not remember we're having company tonight for supper? I was afraid I was going to have to send Oliver to fetch you from Gretchen's house." Fiona gave them her sternest look. "Now go wash up. They'll be here any minute."

"Sorry, Mum," they said in unison before hurrying off.

Pirate, Oliver's fox terrier, excitedly darted in wide circles around the yard, barking. Oliver ran to the window and whirled to face his mother. "They're here."

"Good." Fiona's face lit up with her sunny smile. "Now you can relax."

Oliver didn't wait for the car to stop before dropping the baseball, opening the door, and calling to Pirate.

When Rose and Jack got out of the jalopy, he hurried to greet them with Pirate trotting at his side, tongue hanging out. "You had me worried." He shook Jack's hand, slapped him on the back, and then turned to Rose. "I was afraid you'd backed out, or something happened that you couldn't leave."

The look on Rose's face told him everything he needed to know. She was as nervous as a cat in a room full of rockers, the fading bruise on her left cheek evidence of more violence. She leaned down and held her hand for Pirate to smell.

"Oh, and this is Pirate. He's friendly."

"Pirate?" Rose patted the little hound's fuzzy head.

"Named him that because of the black circle around his eye. Looks just like an eyepatch. He's a good dog, though."

Rose straightened and met his gaze briefly before ducking her head as if embarrassed. "Thank you for inviting us."

"My mum is thrilled that you've made it. She's cooked up a roast with all the trimmings." Oliver placed a hand on the small of Rose's back. "Come on in. Everyone's eager to meet you both."

Fiona Quinn held open the door. "Jack, Rose, I'm Oliver's mum. Please call me Fiona. We're not formal around here."

Pirate jumped onto the porch and sat on his haunches, his tail beating a staccato rhythm on the wooden planks.

"Thank you." Jack fidgeted and glanced at Rose. "We appreciate the invite."

Fiona waved a hand in dismissal. "Oy, 'tis nothing. Any friend of Oliver's is welcome here."

Oliver pointed to his sisters, who stood between the living room and a hallway. "Meet my sisters, Margaret and Elizabeth."

Both girls smiled. "Nice to meet you," they said in unison.

Oliver laughed. "They're twins and do things like that all the time."

Rose returned the smiles. "Nice to meet you."

A moment of awkward silence followed until Fiona spoke. "Please, both of you have a seat. Oliver, make sure our guests are comfortable while I put supper on the table." She motioned to Margaret and Elizabeth, and they disappeared into the kitchen.

Oliver pointed to the sofa and two overstuffed chairs at each end. "Mum will let us know when it's ready."

"Shouldn't I offer to help?" Rose fidgeted with the collar on her blouse.

"You could offer, but I can assure you she wouldn't hear of it. Company ain't allowed to help. It's the Quinn way." The purple blouse and full gathered skirt of a darker shade fit her slim frame much better than the dress she'd worn to the dance. Her soft brown hair fell around her face, framing those startling violet eyes. "You look lovely tonight, Rose. Don't you agree, Jack?"

Jack cleared his throat. "I reckon." His ears turned red.

Rose turned a bright shade of pink. "I'm right here, the both of you."

"Sorry. Didn't mean to make you uncomfortable." Oliver pointed again at the living room furniture. "Let's sit. Mum will call us when supper's on the table."

Jack dropped into an overstuffed armchair, and Oliver joined Rose on the sofa. "I hope coming here won't cause you any problems."

"Long as we're home before nine, we should be fine." Jack glanced around. "Nice place, Oliver."

"Thanks. It's home." Oliver turned toward Rose. "I really am glad you both came. I know the risk you took. Jack's told me some things."

She blushed again and whispered, "I'm embarrassed."

"Thank you for being honest. But please, you never have to feel that way around me. I mean it. Try to relax. No one will hurt you here, and we have no judgment."

Rose leaned back against the sofa and blew out a breath. "Your home is so warm and inviting and clean…" She paused and studied the family pictures arranged on the living room walls.

"It's the only place I can remember living." Oliver pointed to a black-and-white photo above the fireplace. "That's my father, Patrick Quinn."

"You look a lot like him," Rose said. "He has kind eyes."

Jack fidgeted in his chair. "Our pa always had a bit of a mean streak in him, but he didn't use to be as bad as he is now. Things really changed after our mother died."

Oliver didn't miss the wistfulness in Jack's voice. "Grief is a hard thing to get past. I was twelve when my father died, and the twins were only four. But I remember how the following days were so hard for all of us. He was our rock."

"How did he die?" Rose stared at the photo.

"Sawmill accident. That's why I work loading boxcars and not inside the mill. He got between a saw and a tree and couldn't recover." Just saying the words out loud twisted Oliver's gut at the memory.

Fiona interrupted the conversation. "Come on, everyone. Supper's ready."

---

Rose took in every detail of the Quinn household. It was exactly as she'd imagined it to be, and Fiona Quinn was the kind of woman who could make anyone feel at ease with her quick smile and sunny disposition. And despite the deep grief they'd experienced, they smiled and laughed.

It told her a lot that Oliver noticed her newly refurbished clothes. He didn't miss much. He'd ditched his customary paddy cap, and his chestnut-colored hair curled at the nape of his neck, the way she remembered from the dance.

The twins' joyful faces and sweet dispositions made her long for her mother more than ever. She doubted these girls had ever been hit out of anger and certainly never been subjected to the groping hands of a perverted man. She could easily imagine what Oliver would do if anyone touched either of them that way.

Fiona had set two extra chairs at the table and pointed to the empty one next to Oliver. "Rose, sit here, dear."

She put Jack next to the twins. Rose grinned behind her hand at Jack's discomfort. He'd never dated a girl and, even though he was sixteen, had more than likely never been kissed unless it was at a brothel. Jack had told her that Harlan had taken him there once and how it grossed him out.

But Oliver's sisters were both pretty. The way they giggled made her miss her teenage years. When had she gotten so old? She swallowed past a lump in her throat.

Fiona passed the first dish. "Help yourselves."

Rose dished out a small portion of meat, potatoes, and carrots when the platter reached her.

"That's not enough to keep a bird alive. Please, Rose, take more," Fiona insisted.

Self-conscious, she dished out another small portion, then passed it to Oliver. When his hand brushed against hers, she almost jerked it away. Nothing about Oliver resembled Amos Parker, but just the mere touch was enough to send her withdrawing.

The first bite tantalized her tongue and awoke all her taste buds. She couldn't remember when she'd had enough ingredients to cook a meal like this. As she ate, she took in the warm, inviting kitchen painted sunshine yellow with light blue trim. What a stark contrast to the dismal shack she shared with her father and brothers.

Conversation flowed with ease around the table. The twins talked about their classes and how hard they struggled to learn algebra.

Jack joined in with tales from the sawmill, while Oliver remained silent next to her.

Rose jolted when Fiona called her name. "Tell us a little about yourself."

Putting her fork down, she lowered her head. "Not much to tell, Miss Quinn…Fiona. I take care of the laundry and cooking while my brothers work."

"Please forgive me, my dear. I don't mean to put you on the spot. You're so quiet."

Jack rescued her. "Rose has always been shy. She sewed the clothes she's wearing and keeps our shirts mended." He forked another bite of meat into his mouth and chewed. "I'd say that's a talent."

"Well, of course it is." Fiona took a sip of water. "I've been trying to teach Margaret and Elizabeth, and they're learning, but I have a hard time getting them to sit still."

"Sewing is boring," Elizabeth declared.

"I find it relaxing." Rose picked up her fork.

"Maybe you'd have better luck teaching them." Fiona waved her fork in the air.

"I'd like that." The thought of spending time in this safe and warm environment made her tingle. But the odds of her pa allowing it took away the excitement as quickly as it came.

Besides, she couldn't forget she was in trouble. The kind of trouble that puts a black mark on any young single woman.

It was as if Fiona could sense her mood change. "Who has room for dessert?"

Jack's eyes grew wide. "Wow, Mrs. Quinn. You sure know how to put out a spread."

Fiona laughed. "Not Mrs. Quinn, Fiona, remember."

"Oh yeah. I forgot." Jack swiped the last drop of roast gravy from his plate.

"Oliver, can you gather up the empty plates?"

"Sure, Mum." He scooted his chair back and stacked the dishes in the sink while Fiona placed a three-layer cake in the middle of the table.

Rose gasped. "That looks delicious, Fiona."

"Well, dear, I work in a bakery, so I have all the ingredients I need. A lot of folks don't have that luxury, so I count us lucky."

"I can second that." Oliver placed smaller plates on the table. "In fact, I can openly admit we're spoiled."

"It's easier now that they've lifted most of the war rations. If I didn't work at the bakery, we would have a much simpler dessert." Fiona passed a knife to Oliver.

Rose marveled at how the knife sliced through the cake as if it were soft butter.

She soaked up the safe feeling. Whatever she had to face when she got home, this night was worth it.

And if luck was on her side, maybe she and Jack could get home before Pa and Harlan got back. Pushing away negative thoughts, she took a bite of the apple cake. It melted in her mouth, and she suppressed a groan. "This is the best apple cake I've ever tasted."

Fiona's smile lit up the entire room. "So glad you like it."

Jack took a huge bite and moaned out loud. "Best cake ever."

Everyone laughed.

By the time she finished, Rose was sure her stomach might burst, and she'd savored every bite.

That must be what the term 'cooked with love' meant.

Oliver laid a gentle hand on her arm. "After supper, would you take a walk with me? We've got a pond a little ways behind the house, and there's always a choir of frogs singing."

Rose's heart pounded. A walk with Oliver?

She glanced at Jack to see his wide, approving grin.

"I'd like that, but I didn't bring a sweater."

The twins giggled, and Fiona shot them a stern look. "You can borrow one from the girls."

"I'll get one of mine," Margaret offered.

"Thank you," she murmured. She'd always hold the memory of this night close in case she never had another one like it.

Maybe there would be more.

A girl could hope.

At least until stark reality came to call.

A hard rap on the front door sent Rose's heart plummeting. She let out a yelp and, out of instinctive reflex, jumped up, tipping over her chair.

# CHAPTER 6

While Fiona hurried to the front door, Oliver stood and placed a comforting hand on Rose's shoulder. "It's okay, Rose. I told you. You're safe here." He set her chair upright, but she remained standing. All color drained from her face, and she covered her mouth with a shaky hand.

Jack appeared to be frozen in place while Margaret and Elizabeth gasped.

Oliver strode toward the door, prepared for the worst, when a female voice stopped him. He breathed a sigh of relief. "It's Gretchen's mother. Everyone, relax."

A minute later, Fiona returned to the kitchen, waving a textbook. "I swear, Elizabeth, you'd leave your head somewhere if it wasn't attached. Your history book. You need to thank Gretchen's mum next time you see her."

Elizabeth put her hand over her mouth. "I'm so sorry."

"As you well should be." Fiona deposited the book on the kitchen cabinet.

Rose dropped back into her chair with a swoosh of air, and Jack shifted in his seat. Tension so thick you could slice it with a knife passed between them.

"Now, listen up, everyone. Here's what you're going to do." Fiona shook her finger. "Oliver, you and Rose are going on a walk. Elizabeth, you'll help me clean up the kitchen while Margaret sets up a game for us to play with Jack."

Elizabeth moaned. "Really, Mum?"

"No sass, young lady. Your absentmindedness caused poor Rose to be scared out of her wits." She turned to Rose. "Please accept my apologies."

"No apology necessary," Rose mumbled. "Sorry for overreacting. I'd be happy to help clean up."

"Sorry, lass, but that's not allowed in this house. Besides, it's Elizabeth's punishment. Maybe it'll teach her a lesson. And when you and Oliver return from your walk, we'll have a warm cup of tea before you leave."

"That sounds nice." Rose ran a shaky hand across her forehead.

"I really am sorry, Rose." Elizabeth stood and gathered empty cake plates.

"It's okay." Rose passed her plate.

"Alrighty then." Oliver pushed back his chair.

Margaret brought a sweater for Rose while Oliver donned his paddy cap. Thankful for his mother's keen insight and intervention, their newest board game would entertain Jack. The girls had been obsessed with playing Sorry since he'd brought it home a few weeks ago.

Now, with Margaret's sweater draped around her thin shoulders, Rose almost looked like a typical teenage girl, as the pink color returned to her face. Well, minus the greenish bruise still visible.

The minute they stepped outside, Pirate attached himself to them, trotting along, excited for an adventure. Oliver helped her over a small stone fence surrounding their backyard.

As Rose stepped across, she asked, "What's the purpose of this short fence?"

"None, really. It's just something Mum wanted to remind her of Ireland. I suppose it does help to keep some of the small critters out." He pointed to a tree just beyond the fence. "Used to have a treehouse up there. Spent lots of hours sitting above the world, watching animals and reading books. Do you like to read?"

"I did before my mother died. Now, I've got too many chores to do. Pa says reading is a waste of time that could be better spent working."

"Hmph. I beg to disagree. It's like traveling the world without ever leaving home."

Rose's soft words drifted across the cool night air. "I'd imagine you'd disagree with Pa on a lot of things."

"I 'spect you're right, but let's not talk about him unless you want to."

"I don't."

"Then tell me about yourself. What are your hopes, your dreams, your wishes?" Oliver put a hand on the small of her back and guided her toward the pond. Somewhere in the distance, an owl hooted, and Pirate took off to chase night varmints that rustled through the brush. A half-moon provided a smidgen of light and stars dotted the inky sky.

"Not much to tell. Gave up on dreaming a long time ago. And have too many hopes and wishes to list." She angled her gaze toward him. "You have no idea how lucky you are, Oliver."

"I think I do. I've always appreciated how hard Mum has had to work to keep us fed and a roof over our heads, especially after my dad died. We had some really hard times for a while. It makes me happy that I can take some of that load off her now."

"She's a wonderful lady. Her smile lights up the entire room, and her food—that was an amazing meal. Tell me she doesn't cook like that every day."

Oliver chuckled. "No, she doesn't. A lot of times, we have typical Irish fare or a pot of soup. Shepherd's Pie is one of my favorites. I must admit, she has a magic touch when it comes to cooking and baking."

"What hopes or dreams do you have? I can't imagine you'd want for anything you don't already have." Rose lifted her lovely violet eyes.

"Oh, I have dreams, big ones." Excitement crept into his voice. "I love playing baseball and I'm good at it. My dream is to play for a major team, if I ever get a chance. Maybe someday."

"An uncle on my mother's side of the family played in the major baseball leagues, but we didn't see them much. They live in St. Louis."

Oliver whistled, which brought Pirate running. "Jack told me about your uncle. I'd give my eyeteeth to meet him, just to hear stories. I've followed Rube Livingston's career and his famous knuckleball."

She lifted her chin. "We haven't always been the way we are now. Back when our mother was alive, life wasn't so bad, and we'd see family once a year around the holidays. But now…"

"I'm sorry, Rose. I hope things get better."

She cleared her throat. "What do you do after work every day?"

He picked up a stick. "Let's see. On a typical day, I come home, wash up, do chores, play baseball with anyone who is nearby, or play fetch with Pirate. I try to keep the twins focused on their homework, and sometimes I cook. Then, we all help clean the kitchen after supper. I keep things fixed up around the house. Mum says it's everyone's responsibility to help make a home."

Wistfulness crept into Rose's reply. "Sounds like heaven."

"Suppose it is. What's a typical day like for you?"

She blew out a long breath. "I do the laundry for the men, clean up after them, mend their clothes, and cook whatever food I have on hand." She paused. "Sometimes that ain't much." Her voice brightened. "But now that Jack and Harlan are both working, that should get better."

Oliver's heart wrenched. "You deserve more."

"Do I?" She lowered her gaze. "There's things you don't know."

"Then tell me."

"I can't," she whispered. "Let's change the subject."

He dropped his hand to his side. "What was the last book you read?" Anything to keep her talking.

"*Alice In Wonderland.*"

"Never read that one. What's your favorite of all?"

"I once read a library book called *The Little Prince*. That story took me to a different world, and I loved it."

"I read that one, and I agree. It took me to another world, but the messages in it were the best." He could sense her relaxing as they walked and talked. Good.

She gazed up at the sky. "Do you think there is other life out there like in that book? The Little Prince was from an asteroid."

"Who knows? All we know is what we have here. Reckon that's enough."

"I've wished a lot lately that I could escape to another planet. Life's been hard." Her voice cracked.

Oliver could only imagine. "Look. There's the pond. If we're quiet and Pirate doesn't make too much noise, the frogs will start singing. They heard us coming and stopped." A night bird flew from a nearby tree, flapping its huge wings.

Stars sprinkled across the velvet sky as they paused under the branches of an ancient oak.

In that moment of stillness, there was no ugliness, fear, or social boundaries separating them. They were simply two young people enjoying a casual conversation.

The frogs started their cacophony of night songs, filling the air and rising to a crescendo.

Rose shivered as a fall breeze blew through the trees, and Oliver tugged his sister's sweater closer around her.

---

Everything inside Rose screamed to spill her guts to Oliver. But she couldn't stand the thought of the disgust she might see in his eyes. Unlike her miserable, ugly one, he had a nice family, a lovely home, and an everyday happy life.

She trembled when she thought about the knock on the door. What if it had been Harlan or Pa? What then? No doubt Oliver would stand up for her, but he'd be no match for the two. And she preferred not to think about the punishment she and Jack would get.

When the frogs' chorus died down, Oliver picked up a rock and skipped it across the pond. There was so much she wanted to share.

But she didn't really know him. Or did she? He didn't appear to have any pretenses. And his family were some of the kindest people she'd ever been around.

Pirate bounded back out of the brush with a stick in his mouth, and she leaned down to pet him. "I had a dog once. He was a beagle and would set up a howl on a full moon. He got old and died."

"That's the problem with pets. We always outlive them. I've had Pirate for three years. He just wandered up one day and stayed. Don't know how old he is, but he's full of life. One of his favorite things is to play fetch. If I can't find anyone to play baseball with, I can hit the ball and Pirate will bring it back to me. The twins have a stray cat around here somewhere that they feed."

"Everyone in your family seems to be full of life. Your mother is so kind."

Oliver chuckled. "Oh, she's got an Irish temper, but it takes a lot to get her riled up. She's the strongest woman I know."

"We should probably be getting back. It makes me nervous to think we might not get home before Pa and Harlan."

"How about I drive you? I wouldn't mind at all."

Panic choked her. "No. You don't understand."

"I understand more than you think. If I can't drive you home, then I'll follow you and Jack to make sure you arrive safe."

Rose shrunk under his intense gaze in the dim moonlight. "That's not necessary. But I have a feeling you are pretty stubborn."

"Ask my mum. She'll confirm that. It's just that I care about people and don't like it when they're mistreated."

"I can see that. Thank you, but let's head back."

"Of course. I'm glad you walked with me. I'd enjoy showing you around in daylight sometime. Say, you ever been to a movie theater?"

"No, but I've heard about them."

"Let me take you to The Wren. They're showing a comedy and a western right now and I love both."

Panic mixed with excitement ran through her. While she'd love going to see a moving picture with Oliver, her father would never allow it. "That ain't likely to happen."

"We'll see about that. For now, let's go have a cup of Mum's special tea."

They walked in silence the short distance back to the inviting warmth of Oliver's home. Rose struggled to sort her thoughts.

If only things were different. If only she wasn't broken. Maybe not completely broken yet, but ruined. Her future held nothing but bleakness.

The only thing she had to look forward to was the day she could make her escape. But could she ever truly escape when she had an unwanted life growing inside?

Oliver whistled a tune while they walked.

What would it feel like to be carefree?

Gloom descended around her like a heavy cloak.

# CHAPTER 7

After they'd partaken in Fiona's special tea, Oliver followed behind Rose and Jack in his 1939 Ford Woody Wagon. He reflected on the night's events and the conversation with Rose. There was much she wasn't saying.

Maybe one day, he'd find a way to earn her trust. He'd hoped she would ride with him and they could talk more. But she insisted on staying with Jack, saying it wouldn't do for her to get out of a stranger's car if, by chance, her father was already home.

He couldn't imagine living under that dark cloud of fear. And while brother and sister openly stated their father hadn't always been this violent, there had to be an underlying pattern. A man didn't just turn bad overnight. But he didn't dare ask more.

About four miles from town, Jack turned off onto a dirt lane. While Oliver could only see what his headlights reflected, it was easy to tell this was a pretty remote and hidden area—not surprising for a moonshiner.

Another mile or so down a lane bordered on both sides by tall pines, a small one-story clapboard house came into sight. At first glance, it appeared to be abandoned with darkened windows and no vehicle to be seen. The outside of the house hadn't seen a coat of paint in many years, and the front porch sat lopsided. His heart broke for Rose. This was no life for a young girl.

Jack pulled to a stop and killed the engine.

Oliver left his wagon idling and leaned out the window. "Everything okay?"

Rose hurried over. "Looks like we beat them home." She leaned down. "Thank you and your family so much for a great evening."

"Let's do it again soon." He waved to Jack, who opened the front door and flipped on a single porch light.

"That would be nice, but don't count on it." She glanced around nervously. "We got away with it this time. Next time, we might not be so lucky."

"Well, at least you know where I live, and Mum said to make sure you know you are welcome there anytime, and so is Jack."

"Please tell her thank you for me." She straightened. "You better go."

Oliver waited until she was inside the house before he put the vehicle in reverse. All the way back to town, the starkness of the shack and the cloud of despair that surrounded it haunted him. Briars growing around the house made it all that much more unwelcoming. The crudely painted 'No Trespassing' sign nailed to the crumbling porch post left no room for doubt. Visitors were not welcome.

Life could be unfair sometimes, and Rose Blaine had more than her share.

One thing he knew for sure—he wanted to see her again.

---

Rose hurried to get out of her new clothes and into her faded nightgown. A single curtain separated her tiny corner of the house from the kitchen. Jack and Harlan's cots were a part of the living room, and her father occupied the only bedroom. At least they had indoor plumbing. The house they'd left behind in Hamburg didn't. She hoped she'd never have to use another outhouse as long as she lived.

What a night.

She fell asleep thinking of Oliver's easy way of conversing and his mother's delicious cooking, only to be jarred awake a couple of hours later by a thunderous crash.

Harlan's voice followed. "Come on, Pa, let me help you to bed."

"Get your hands off me." The words came out slurred.

She lay deathly still, barely breathing, waiting for what would come next.

Another thud vibrated the floor. "I said don't touch me."

"Just tryin' to help, Pa. Suit yourself."

She could picture Jack huddling in his bed, eyes squeezed shut, pretending not to hear. Tears leaked out of the corner of her eyes.

Harlan's boots hit the floor one at a time, and bedsprings creaked.

She waited. Maybe Pa would spend the night on the floor. Or maybe he'd eventually make it to his bedroom. She hoped for the latter and that he'd sleep late in the morning.

Being the weekend, the boys wouldn't go to work.

That meant they'd be working the still, and Amos would be coming for another load. She shuddered and buried her face in her cotton pillow that had long ago lost its fluff.

No matter what she had to do, he'd never touch her again.

She laid a hand on her stomach and tried not to hate what was growing inside.

---

Oliver stopped at a service station on the way home and filled up the tank. Outrageous that the price of gasoline had gone to twenty cents a gallon. He handed the station attendant three dollars and asked for a road map of Missouri.

As soon as he got home, he spread the map out on the kitchen table. Fiona peered over his shoulder. "Going somewhere, Oliver?"

"Just thinking, Mum. Rose and Jack said they have an uncle in St. Louis that used to play for the Browns. What I wouldn't give to meet him, even though he's old and hasn't played in years."

Fiona laid a hand on his shoulder. "I know how badly you want to play. And you have to know I would never hold you back, although I'd miss you terribly. You're a big help around here."

Oliver cocked his head. "The only way I'd leave you and the girls is if I truly had a shot at making some big money for you while living out my dream."

She hung her apron on a hook next to the door. "You never know what surprises life might have for you. I take it Jack and Rose made it home safely."

"No one was there." He glanced up from the map. "But Mum, the house they live in can hardly qualify as a house. It's nothing more than a rundown shack. It was a hard thing to drive away and leave them there."

"I understand," she said softly. "But some things are out of your control. Perhaps it would be good to pray about it. Only the good Lord above knows what's best."

"You better pray that I never get my hands on Ezra Blaine. I don't know that there'd be anything left of him."

"Oh, you don't have to tell me. I pray every day for us all, son." She kissed his cheek. "Don't stay up too long dreaming."

Oliver continued to study the map while his mother's footsteps faded. A nine-hour trip to St. Louis. He had to wonder if his Woody Wagon would hold up, although he kept it tuned and running like a top.

He couldn't deny the excitement that coursed through him at the thought of meeting a real baseball player. Even if Rube Livingston was old, he'd have to be full of glorious stories.

Maybe he could convince Jack and Rose to take a road trip with him.

Although, from everything they'd shared, the likelihood of their father letting them take off on a road trip with a stranger was pretty much nil.

Still, a man could dream.

He could almost see the stadium lights and hear the crowds cheering for their favorite team.

Yes. That was what he wanted to experience.

He'd keep practicing and getting better.

And if the good Lord saw fit, perhaps he'd get a shot at living out this dream.

# CHAPTER 8

Three days later, Rose leaned against the rickety excuse for a cabinet in the kitchen and stared out the window, barely breathing. She couldn't go on like this.

She shook from head to toe as icy fear flowed through her veins.

By accident, she'd stumbled upon her father and Amos in a heated argument. She'd simply gone to tell her father breakfast was ready. And when Amos drew back his fist, she knew things were going to get violent.

Now, branded in her mind, was the resounding crack of the fatal blow to Amos Parker's head. Not that she cared one bit that the man now lay dead in their backyard, but the level of violence her father had stooped to had her fearing for not only her life, but her brothers' lives as well.

And he'd seen her.

She'd witnessed the killing, and she'd heard every word. It was only a matter of time before he'd be coming for her.

She frantically glanced around the sparse kitchen for a weapon. When he burst through the door, she grabbed a butcher knife with shaking hands, and hid it behind her back. Though fear like she'd never known held her in an iron grip, she gritted her teeth and vowed to not go down without a fight.

Ezra's face twisted with rage when he barreled through the back door. He shoved her. "You whore. You dirty little whore." He sneered. "Walking around here pretending to be innocent while all the time you were pulling your britches down for Amos. Were you in on it with him? Stealing from me?"

She cowered, not daring to look at him. "I didn't pull my britches down, Pa." All control disappeared, and she screamed. "Amos raped me." Tears streamed down her cheeks. "More than once."

"You expect me to believe that?" He took another step toward her, his fists clenched at his sides.

"It's the truth." It was as if the weight of the butcher knife in her hand and the coolness of the wooden handle gave her strength, and she choked back more tears.

He swept a hand across a nearby shelf, sending dishes crashing to the floor. "Liar." He drew back his fist.

When he closed the gap between them, she raised the knife and pointed it at him, forcing her hand not to shake. "No more, Pa."

He threw his head back and cackled. "You ain't got the guts to use that. You're nothing but a piece of filthy white trash. Thank God your mother isn't alive to see what you've become."

She gritted her teeth. "Thank God my mother isn't alive to see the monster you've turned into. I will use this."

He lunged for her, and she plunged the knife into his bony side with every ounce of force she possessed.

His iron grip closed around her wrist and twisted, forcing the knife from her hand. A strangled scream left her throat when he sliced through her upper arm. A mix of blinding pain and desperation filled her.

He drew back his fist and punched her hard in the stomach. "I won't raise a bastard kid. You hear me?" He fastened his hands around her throat. She struggled against him, trying to kick him, but his long arms kept him out of reach.

Oh, God! She was going to die a horrible death. She reached behind her, grabbing for any kind of weapon.

What happened afterward became a blur. Ezra's face twisted with rage, blood streaming out of the wounds, and the deadly three seconds of complete silence as she fought to breathe spurred her into action.

Her hand landed on the cast-iron skillet, still warm on the stove with the eggs she'd cooked for him. When she swung it at his head with all her strength, the sickening thud of metal against bone, the stunned look on Ezra's face before he hit the floor, and the pounding of her heart that left her gasping for air were all her senses could recognize. She didn't stick around to see what happened next.

As she hurled herself over his prone body and stumbled out the back door, a scream lodged in her throat.

Oh, God! What had she done?

Blood ran down her arm and dripped off her fingertips, leaving splatters on her dress.

Amos Parker lay a few feet away, his head bashed in, unseeing eyes frozen wide.

Stark terror held Rose in its clutches.

Without pausing to think or to make a plan, she ran—ran like the wind, unconscious of anything except reaching her brothers. Her foot caught on a tree root and sent her sprawling. Despair clawed at her. She scrambled up, ignoring the stinging pain in her knee, and forced her feet to move. Once she hit the blacktop, her shoes pounded hard against the pavement, and she didn't slow down.

Oliver heard her screams before he saw her. Something was terribly wrong. He jumped down from the loading platform and took off with long strides toward Rose Blaine, who was running to beat the devil.

It wasn't until he got closer that he spied the blood. So much blood. His heart pounded.

"Rose!"

She fell into his arms, sobbing, trembling, broken.

He held her, not caring that she was getting him bloody. "What happened, Rose? You're bleeding. I need to get you to a doctor."

"I…I…I killed him," she stammered. "Oh, God! I killed Pa." Her knees buckled.

"Oh, Lord. Okay. Let's get you somewhere safe and sort this all out."

"Jack. I have to get to Jack and Harlan." Her voice rose to a level of hysteria.

"I'll get them." He pulled a handkerchief out of his pocket and wrapped it around her arm. He pointed toward his Woody Wagon. "Go wait in the car."

She trembled violently, and Oliver put an arm around her waist. "Easy. Lean on me. You're safe now."

"He killed him. I saw him." Her voice shook.

"Who killed who?" Oliver steered her toward the car.

"Amos. Pa killed Amos, and I saw it. Then he came after me."

"Shh. Don't talk about it. Just take some deep breaths and we'll figure this all out." They reached his car, and he opened the door. She got inside and collapsed against the back of the seat. "Don't move. I'll go get Harlan and Jack." Oliver jerked his paddy cap off and ran a hand through his hair.

She closed her eyes and whimpered, like a wounded animal.

Oliver's heart pounded in his ears. He'd been afraid the violence would escalate. Dammit! He should have stepped in regardless of all the warnings.

He rushed toward the sawmill, motioning to the foreman. "Something bad's happened at the Blaine place. I need to get Jack and Harlan."

The foreman nodded. "Wait here. I'll get 'em."

Oliver paced in front of the mill, trying to steady his breath and slow down his heart rate. Whatever happened, he wouldn't let Rose go back to that moonshiner's shack…ever.

Harlan and Jack strode out, questions in their eyes.

Harlan growled, "This better be good. Can't afford to miss any pay."

"It's Rose." Oliver pointed toward his car. "She's bleeding and ran all the way here. Says she killed your pa."

Jack punched Harlan's arm. "Told you shit was gettin' worse. But you refused to talk about it."

"Now's not the time to bicker." Oliver stepped between them. "Rose needs your help. Over there." He pointed to his car, and they rushed toward it.

Harlan reached her first and let out a rumble. "What the hell, Rose?"

She looked up at him with red-rimmed eyes, cradling her bleeding arm against her breast. "Pa killed Amos. Bashed his head right in. I saw him. Then he came after me."

Jack hurried around to the other side of the car and slid in next to her. He put his arm around her shoulders. "Tell us everything, Rose."

She wiped her nose on a handkerchief Jack passed her, then launched into a detailed account. "So, then, when Pa hit the floor, I jumped over him and ran here. That's all I knew to do. He…he was going to kill me, too."

Harlan leaned down. "Stay here, both of you. I'll go home and see what's going on."

Oliver put a hand on his shoulder. "Sounds like you might need the sheriff to go with you."

"Don't need no law. We handle our own problems." His eyes softened. "Can you take Rose to a doctor? Get her stitched up?"

Oliver nodded. "Just need to talk to the boss for a minute." He turned to Jack. "Stay with her. I'll be right back."

Harlan ran to their jalopy and cranked it while Oliver went to find his boss. He wished Harlan would go to the sheriff's office, but his major concern was for Rose. Not only was she traumatized, but also had a nasty wound.

As soon as his boss gave him permission to leave, he dashed back to the vehicle. Jack kept a hand on Rose's shoulder. Oliver sped across town to the Crossett Health Clinic.

He knew there would be questions, but he'd let Rose tell the doctor whatever she wanted.

Both he and Jack paced the floor when the nurse led Rose back to a room.

Jack ran a hand through his hair. "Shit! Shit! This has been brewing a long time. I should have done something."

Oliver clapped him on the shoulder. "Don't beat yourself up. Harlan should have been the one to step up, not you. Hell, you're just a kid."

Drawing himself up to full height, Jack grimaced. "Maybe so, but I knew. I knew it was getting worse. Guess I was just hoping things would change." His voice grew quiet. "What if Rose really did kill him? What will happen to her?"

"Let's cross that bridge when we get to it. Won't know anything until Harlan gets back."

Oliver wished he could offer words of hope.

But he couldn't.

All he could do was be there and offer to help.

His mother's words echoed. *Just like your father. Patrick Quinn was never one to stand idly by if someone was being mistreated.*

He squared his shoulders.

# CHAPTER 9

Oliver twisted his cap in his hands as he and Jack sat on hard wooden chairs in the lobby of the clinic. A good half hour passed before Rose returned, a bandage covering her upper arm. Pain and anguish etched her pale face, her frail shoulders slumped. The nurse accompanying her said, "Remember the doctor wants you to change the bandage on your arm every couple of days and wash the wound." She pressed a roll of gauze and tape into Rose's hand. "Come back in ten days and he'll take the stitches out. You were lucky you didn't slice through an artery. I hope you'll be more careful in the future."

Rose nodded and mumbled her thanks.

Oliver stood aside and Jack rushed forward to take her hand.

Once back the car, Rose got in the front seat with Oliver and Jack climbed in the back. He leaned forward. "What did you tell the doctor, Rose?"

"Told him I fell." She let out a sigh.

"And he bought it."

"Seemed to."

Oliver started the car. "I'd like to take you to my house until we get all this sorted, if you're willing."

"Not until we talk to Harlan. I have to know."

"I understand, but my mum would give me what for if I didn't offer." He steered toward the sawmill.

Silence filled the car.

Oliver pondered every option for the siblings. It all hinged on what Harlan said and did.

And they wouldn't know until he returned.

Rose leaned against the window and silently sobbed.

Oliver's heart broke for her and the direness of the whole situation. His mind flashed to the map of Missouri he'd picked up.

His motive for picking it up had been purely for selfish reasons. But now, that reason faded into the background as life's harsh reality set in.

There was still no sign of Harlan or the old jalopy when they reached the sawmill. Oliver parked and turned to Rose. "I think Jack and I should go back to work. Will you wait here in the car? Maybe lay down in the backseat?"

Jack put a hand on his sister's shoulder. "Please, Rose. Wait here for Harlan. It's not long 'til the dinner break and we can decide what we need to do then."

She nodded numbly. "I'll wait. I'm sorry for all the trouble."

Oliver paused before he opened the car door. "Rose, you have nothing to be sorry for. You did nothing wrong."

"I'm scared," she whispered.

"Of course you are. There would be something terribly wrong with you if you weren't, but everything is going to be okay."

"I wish I could believe that." She swiped at her tears.

Jack got out of the car and opened Rose's door. "You're tired. Lay down and rest while we wait for Harlan."

She climbed out and slipped into the backseat.

Oliver leaned in. "If anything happens, just honk the horn real loud. I'll be able to hear you."

"Thank you."

It took everything Oliver had to walk away and leave her alone and broken, but he had a job to do and she needed time to rest and to think. Surely Harlan would be back soon.

He grabbed his gloves from his back pocket, waved to the foreman, and jumped onto the loading platform as Jack disappeared back inside the mill.

Rose watched until Jack and Oliver disappeared from sight. Her arm throbbed where the doctor had stitched the wound back together. *Could have been more serious,* the doctor had said. If he only knew just how serious it all was.

Each time she attempted to close her eyes, she relived every vivid detail of the terror. She'd never be able to forget Amos Parker's sightless bulging eyes, and the sound of his skull cracking under the blow her father had delivered, or the smell of rotgut liquor and tobacco on her father's breath as he attempted to choke the life out of her.

Her hands instinctively went to her stomach. What if her father's blow killed the baby? Maybe that would be a blessing.

Her stomach roiled, and she shuddered.

She forced her breath to slow.

What if Pa wasn't dead? Then what? He'd come for her.

No matter what, she'd never return to the shack and his violence.

If only Harlan would come back. The not knowing tortured her like a wild, rabid animal caught in a trap.

She tried to focus on something else, anything else, but the scenes kept flashing by over and over.

At least she knew for sure Amos Parker would never lay another hand on her. He got his just reward. But her pa…that was another matter. She shouldn't be glad he could never hurt her again, but God help her, she was. If indeed he was dead.

Finally, she lay down on the seat and shut her eyes, focusing on breathing.

The monotonous sounds of the sawmill lulled her into a semi-sleep state, and she didn't awaken until someone knocked on the car window.

She bolted upright as Oliver and Jack slid inside the car.

"Didn't mean to scare you." Jack turned to face her. "No sign of Harlan yet?"

"No. It's been too long." She brushed her hair back and glanced around.

Oliver leaned over. "I hope you got a little rest."

"I tried. But I keep seeing the scenes over and over again. I wish I could erase it all from my mind." She stared down at her hands in horror and scrubbed them on her blood-spattered dress.

"It'll take time." Oliver opened his lunchpail. "Hungry?"

"Hadn't thought about it."

He passed her one half of a ham sandwich. "Here. I have too much."

She hesitated. "You sure?"

Jack winked. "You ought to see what Fiona sends him off with every day."

"You're lucky, Oliver." She bit into the soft bread.

The three of them ate in silence, keeping a close eye on the entrance to the sawmill.

"Harlan should be back by now." Jack stared out the window. "I've got a bad feelin'."

She did too, but it served no purpose to say it. "This waiting is killing me."

"He'll be back." Oliver passed her part of an apple that he'd sliced off with his pocketknife. "Just have to be patient. How's your arm feeling?"

"Throbs like crazy. But it'll be okay."

Jack pointed toward the road. "There's Harlan." He vaulted out of the car and waved.

Rose slowly opened the car door, anxious, yet dreading what her brother would have to say.

Harlan pulled to a stop next to them and got out, his mouth set in a grim line. He reached inside the car and pulled out two bundles of clothing. "Catch." He tossed them to Jack. "You and Rose need get out of here."

Jack caught the bundles. "What's going on, Harlan? You can't just toss us our clothes and tell us to go, then expect us not to ask questions."

"I'm sorry, Jack. I should've stepped in—for you and for Rose. Should've seen it coming."

Rose gripped Harlan's arm. "What happened? Is he?" She couldn't bring herself to say the word.

"Everything's going to be okay, but you and Jack have to git." He strode toward where Oliver stood at the side of the car. "Irish, I'll give you every cent I have if you'll take Rose and Jack to our aunt in St. Louis. I'd take them myself, but…" He pointed to the jalopy. "No way this hunk of junk would make it."

Rose fought against rising nausea. What was Harlan not telling them? She needed to know. It was too late to spare her. "Harlan. Tell me what's going on." She raised her voice. "I deserve to know. Is Pa dead?"

"It's better if you don't know, Rose." His gaze softened. "I have something of our mother's that I've saved for a long time. I want you to have it. Take it with you." He pressed a worn clothbound book into her trembling hand.

"What is it?" Rose didn't take her eyes off Harlan's face.

His voice cracked, and he cleared his throat. "It's a journal Ma kept. She gave it to me when she was dying, but I think it needs to be with you."

Oliver took a step forward. "Harlan, I don't want your money. I can take Jack and Rose to St. Louis, but you need to be straight with us."

Harlan ran a hand through his hair. "All you need to know is that my sister and brother are better off not being here and, like I said, I'll give you all the money I have."

"And like I said, I don't want your money."

Harlan turned to Jack. "Look after Rose."

Rose tried desperately to stop the stark terror rising inside her. "We'll do what you say, Harlan, but what are you going to do?"

He looked everywhere except directly at Rose. "Don't know. Might go back over to Hamburg or catch a freight somewhere. There's nothing here for any of us now. Get it?"

Those words answered her question. Pa was dead. But did she kill him? The need to know tore at her.

Harlan turned toward his car, and Rose grabbed his arm. She ground her teeth, stood toe-to-toe with her brother and poked his chest with her finger to emphasize each word. "I have to know. Did I kill Pa?"

Harlan simply answered, "No." He dropped his hands to his sides, and it was then Rose saw the raw knuckles and blood splattered on his overalls.

That one word suffocated her. While some part of her was relieved that her father was dead, the unspoken words made her ache for Harlan. What would happen to him? Could he go to jail? Was he lying to protect her? And yet the raw knuckles said otherwise.

She had so many questions, but Harlan had already started the jalopy and pulled away.

# CHAPTER 10

Her knees buckled, and Rose clutched her mother's journal to her chest. She sank to the ground, a moan escaping her throat.

Jack reached for her and lifted her back up. "You wanted to go to Aunt Katherine's and now we have a chance."

"Not like this, Jack. Not with Pa dead." She fought the rising hysteria. "Harlan as much as admitted to killing him. But what if he lied to make me feel better? Oh, God, Jack, I think I'm going to be sick." She leaned into the steady grip of his hand and drew in deep breaths, fighting the rising nausea, then finally giving in and vomiting on the ground.

"Don't torture yourself. You did nothing wrong." Jack patted her arm. "And don't read more into what Harlan said."

Oliver took a step toward them. "It's decided then. Rose, I'm taking you to my house while Jack and I finish out the day's work. Then I'll ask for some time off and we'll leave first thing tomorrow morning."

Jack tossed the bundles of clothing into the back of Oliver's Woody Wagon.

"My mum is still at the bakery, but I'll stop by and tell her what's going on."

"I'm so embarrassed." Rose covered her face with her hands.

"Stop," Oliver said firmly. "Accept that we want to help and I promise you my mother will not judge you. She'll only want to coddle you and fix you tea."

Jack patted her shoulder. "Go, get some rest. Me and Oliver will be there as soon as we finish out the day. He's right. We need to draw our pay."

"Let me just tell Mr. Owens that I'll be a little late coming back, then we'll go."

He and Jack strode back toward the sawmill and left her standing next to the Woody Wagon. She opened the front door and slipped inside, the remnants of Oliver's lunch still on the seat.

She hated that she would have to face Fiona. What would she tell her? The truth? A lie? Her stomach lurched. Through all of this she had forgotten—forgotten that a life was forming inside her.

What a mess she'd made of everything. Could she confide in Fiona? Should she?

After making quick work of putting Oliver's food back into his pail, she then rested her head on the back of the seat and waited.

---

Oliver called his boss aside. "Sir, something has come up and I'll have to be gone a few days. But I'll be back."

Mr. Owen squinched one eye. "Your mum and sisters okay, Oliver?"

"Yes sir. It's not my family. It's something else. But I promise you I'll be back as soon as possible. Please hold my job for me."

"You're a good solid worker, son. I'll keep it for you."

"Thank you, sir. And I have to take someone somewhere, then I'll finish out the day. I can work late if need be."

The older man clapped him on the shoulder. "Do what you need to."

"I appreciate your understanding."

Mr. Owen waved him away. "Hurry back."

Oliver wasted no time jogging back to the Woody. He'd let Rose tell Fiona as much or as little as she wanted. Mainly, he wanted to get her to a safe place where she could rest.

He opened the car door, noting immediately that she had cleaned up the food. "Ready?"

Rose nodded. "What do I tell your mother?"

"Tell her as much or as little as you want. She won't press you."

"I feel so awful to have brought all of this on you and your family."

He twisted on the seat to face her. "Rose, look at me." He waited until she raised her red-rimmed violet eyes to meet his. "You aren't bringing anything on me or my family. We want to help. Hell, I wanted to help the first night I met you and your brothers. So stop apologizing and let us do what we Quinns love the most…helping others."

Fresh tears sprung to her eyes. "You're all so kind. I'm not used to it."

He started the car. "Well, get used to it, 'cause you're stuck with us."

They didn't speak anymore as Oliver drove a few blocks to the bakery. When he stopped in front, he opened the door. "I'll be right back."

The conversation with Fiona Quinn was a short one. Oliver gave her no details, only that Rose had been injured and would be at the house when she got home.

He loved that his mother didn't voice her questions, even though her eyes held a million of them. He kissed her cheek and hurried back to Rose.

Another few blocks and he pulled to a stop at his house. Pirate greeted them both enthusiastically, yipping and running in circles. The pup had questions in his eyes, too. He knew the routines. Oliver never came home in the middle of the day.

As soon as they got inside the house, Oliver rushed to the hallway closet and pulled out a blanket and pillow. "Make yourself at home, please, Rose." He dropped the bedding onto the couch. "Maybe you can take a nap."

Rose stood in the middle of the living room, still clutching her mother's journal as if it were a lifeline. "Do you suppose it'd be okay if I take a bath? I feel so…so dirty."

"Of course it's okay. You might want to avoid getting your bandage wet." He pointed down the hall. "The bathroom is the second door on your left. Clean towels are in the cabinet."

She continued to stand still, as if rooted to the spot.

"Please, Rose. Make yourself at home. Mum will be here around three." He slapped his forehead. "Of course. Sorry. I'll be right back with your clothes."

He jogged back to the car and grabbed both bundles of clothing.

"Thank you, again and again," she said, as he dropped both bundles on the floor.

"And you're welcome again and again. I wish I could do more, that I could wipe this nightmare from your mind, but I can't." He wanted to hug her, but instead, his arms fell to his sides. "I need to change my shirt and get back to work."

"Of course." She waved him away. "I'll be okay."

Oliver hated driving away. He hated everything that had occurred over the past few hours, and yet another part of him couldn't help but be relieved that Ezra Blaine had met his end.

Now, if Rose could make peace with it.

Perhaps a road trip would be what both she and Jack needed.

A fresh start.

New beginnings that would allow Rose to thrive and discover who she really is.

And maybe, just maybe, he'd get to meet a real baseball hero.

Despite the horrific circumstances, excitement built as he hurried back to work.

While a part of him hated the delay of even a few hours, he had to fulfill his obligations.

# CHAPTER 11

Once Oliver left, Rose stood still, quiet solitude surrounding her. A glance around the spotless living room had her afraid to touch anything. She didn't belong here, where squalor and violence had no place. Or did she? Maybe it was something she'd deserved all along.

She stared down at her hands and even after washing them at the doctor's office, dried blood clung to her fingernails. Anguish and despair enveloped her. She desperately needed to wash the blood, dirt, and memories away.

And especially before Fiona arrived home. She couldn't—no, wouldn't let Oliver's mother see her in this state.

After she carefully laid her mother's journal on the coffee table, she reached for her clothes and trudged down the hallway where Oliver had pointed to the bathroom. A weariness such as she'd never known wrapped itself around her, making it almost impossible to force her legs to obey her command to move.

Every inch from her head to her toes hurt.

Within minutes, she filled the bathtub and sank into it, keeping her arm propped up on the edge. Her skinned knee smarted when the water touched it, as did the scrape on her hand. She stared at her dirty dress in a heap on the floor. She'd never wear it again. While she hated to waste anything, the ruined dress would go straight into the outside trash can.

She reached for lilac scented soap and scrubbed every inch of her body until her skin glowed a bright pink. With each soap bubble that popped, she let go of horrific scenes that flooded her mind. Nothing she could do now. What was done was done.

Did she regret her father was dead? Some small part of her did—the part that still remembered him the way he was before he went off the rails and the violence escalated. All it took to banish that regret was to relive his hateful words and the uncontrollable rage in his eyes. He would have taken her life, just like he did Amos Parker's.

She shuddered at the thought of her brothers arriving home from work to find her lifeless body beaten to death. And that could easily have happened if she hadn't fought back.

Lingering to soak a bit more after she'd finished scrubbing, she relaxed tense, sore muscles, and took deeper breaths.

By the time she got out of the tub and dried off, she felt somewhat more human. She donned a clean dress and rolled the bloody one up into a tight ball. A glance at the clock told her Fiona would be home in a couple of hours. She hurried outside and deposited the tainted dress in the trash, taking a minute to pet Pirate, who nipped at her heels.

The pillow and blanket on the couch beckoned when she walked back inside. She stretched out, then reached for her mother's journal. How strange that Harlan had kept it hidden all these years. She wondered if he'd ever read it.

Tears sprang into her eyes when she opened the book, and her mother's flowing handwriting covered the page.

*December 1, 1930*

*I gave birth to a baby girl today. She is so beautiful and has the prettiest violet-blue eyes. I'm naming her Rose Marie. Ezra even seems to be taken with her. I've never seen him hold anything so tenderly. Harlan is curious about his little sister and won't leave her side. Maybe Rose is the magic that will heal our fractured lives. Ezra is changing and I fear he is losing himself. Hard times can make a man's ego suffer. The Great Depression has affected all of us.*

Rose gasped and tears trickled down her cheeks. Even back then, almost eighteen years ago, her father had begun to lose his way. What had turned him? Maybe the clues were in the journal.

She closed the book, then her eyes, and gave in to the need to detach and drift into a safe, dark, warm abyss where violence had no place.

---

Oliver loaded the train cars with renewed vigor, stretching and releasing taut muscles as his mind whirled.

He'd never in a million years have imagined what this day would hold when he awoke this morning.

Mentally, he made a list of the necessities he wanted to pack for the journey. A spare tire for sure, a jack and lug wrench, a quart of oil and flashlight. While he didn't expect any trouble, it never hurt to be prepared. He trusted his Woody to make the journey. He'd always taken great pride in keeping his vehicle in tip-top shape. So far, it had never given a moment's worth of trouble.

He hoped Rose had taken his suggestion and made herself at home. No doubt, she was worn to the bone from all the adrenaline that had pumped through her body.

And once his mum got home, she'd take good care of her. What would Rose choose to tell his mother? If he was a betting man, he'd bet she'd opt for the truth, or at least some part of it.

Jack had to be struggling with all kinds of emotions as well. But Oliver admired him for bucking up and returning to work with the goal of collecting his pay.

Maybe all of this would work out for the best.

When the five o'clock whistle blew, Oliver still had stacks of lumber to load. He put his back into it and kept going.

Within a few minutes, Jack joined him on the platform. "Need a hand?"

"Sure. Thanks."

"No thanks needed. You really came to our rescue today and we owe you big time." Jack grunted as he struggled to heft a bundle of lumber onto the waiting car.

"Happy to help. You owe me nothing."

"Yeah, we kinda do. You're taking off work, using your car and money to take us to St. Louis. So, yeah, we owe you." Jack huffed out a breath. "What's your mum going to say?"

"She'll give us her blessing and load us down with food." Oliver grinned. "It's the Quinn way."

"But she'll miss you."

"Sure. But I'll only be gone a few days. It'll be okay, and Mr. Owen has promised to hold my job."

They continued loading the train car until the platform emptied. The sun lit up the western sky with brilliant hues of apricot and lavender. A chill filled the air when they headed to Oliver's home.

He pulled to a stop and got out, only to be greeted by an overly excited dog. Pirate ran and jumped, then ran some more, going from Oliver to Jack and yipping the whole time, barely stopping long enough to let them pet him.

Jack laughed. "He's happy to see us."

"Always." Oliver whistled and Pirate sat at attention at his feet. "They say the best reason to have a dog is that you'll always have someone excited to see you when you get home."

"Reckon that's true." Jack leaned down and scratched behind Pirate's ears, who promptly rewarded him with licks. "Someday I'm going to have a dog."

"I bet you will. Come on inside. Mum will be wondering why we're late."

Oliver opened the door to the smell of chicken frying.

Jack sniffed the air. "Dang, that smells good." His stomach growled in response.

"Mum. We're home." They followed sounds to the kitchen.

Rose sat on a stool, peeling potatoes, while Fiona turned over pieces of chicken in a deep iron skillet.

"Hello, boys. It's about time," Fiona said, flashing a warm smile. "Wash up. Supper will be ready soon."

Oliver cast a quizzical glance at Rose. She met his gaze, then lowered her eyes to the potato in her hand and bit her bottom lip. "You okay, Rose?"

She nodded, and Fiona spoke up. "Rose is doing just fine. Now go wash up. We have lots to talk about tonight."

"Are the twins home yet?"

"They're in their room studying. I sent them away so they wouldn't pester Rose. Would you look in on them and see if they have any books open?"

Oliver kissed his mother's cheek. "Sure. Come on, Jack. Let's go wash up and check on the girls."

Jack blushed. "Thank you, Mrs. Quinn, for having us."

She put a hand on one hip. "You're welcome, but how many times do I have to tell you to call me Fiona?"

He ducked his head. "Sorry, Fiona." He laid a hand on Rose's shoulder. "You good, sister?"

"Okay as I can be."

"I swear to goodness, I think they both need their ears cleaned out." Fiona removed a chicken leg from the skillet.

Oliver knew his mother well. They would have a group discussion after supper.

But she'd support them in every way.

That made him one lucky guy, and he knew it.

He stuck his head in his sisters' room. "You girls studying? Mum sent me to check."

Elizabeth closed a textbook and stuck out her bottom lip. "She sent us away. Said she didn't want us bothering Rose. That wasn't fair."

Jack poked his head around the corner and both girls said in unison, "Hi, Jack."

He grinned. "Hi, girls."

Oliver pointed across the hall. "There's the bathroom. You go first."

"Are Jack and Rose going to live with us, Oliver?" Margaret brushed her long hair back.

"No, they aren't. You ask too many questions. We'll have a family meeting after we eat and explain everything."

"Yeah, if Mum will let us stay."

"She will. You girls need to know what's going on. Supper will be ready soon."

"Okay," they said again in unison.

Oliver grinned. Their connection was uncanny and even though he should be used to it, still it caught him by surprise.

Jack came out of the bathroom.

"You can either wait in the living room or take your chances in the kitchen, Jack. I'll join you in a minute."

Jack nodded and strode down the hallway.

Oliver made quick work of cleaning up and found Jack leaning against the kitchen counter munching on a carrot while Fiona and Rose cooked.

He liked to see his friend comfortable in his home. And Rose had obviously relaxed somewhat under his mother's tender care.

But then his mum had a magic touch and could soothe the most troubled soul.

Again, Oliver thanked his lucky stars for a close-knit family.

He wanted the same for his friends.

Something told him they'd find it.

He remembered a quote he'd read somewhere.

*"A fire may burn you, but it will also purify you…"*

Beyond any shadow of a doubt, Rose, Jack, and Harlan had been through the fire.

Now, for the healing.

# CHAPTER 12

Rose appreciated that Fiona let her help prepare the meal. She needed desperately to feel useful…as if she belonged. She'd told Fiona almost everything. There were some things she wasn't ready to say aloud to anyone. And while she'd halfway expected the older woman to send her packing, instead, Fiona gathered her up in her arms and rocked her as if she were a small child.

That simple action had opened the floodgates for more tears. Surely the body only had so many tears to cry. She had to be nearing the bottom of that supply.

Then Fiona fixed her a cup of tea and sat with her. That Oliver's mother didn't pry or push for more information comforted her in an unspoken way. She'd shown Fiona her mother's journal and shared some of her fondest memories, one of them being working alongside her mother in the kitchen.

So, when Fiona went to the kitchen to start supper, Rose followed her.

"I'm making fried chicken tonight and will also make extra to pack for the trip tomorrow." Fiona opened the icebox. "Would you like to help?"

Rose set her empty cup on the counter. "I would love to. I need to do something to help me feel normal." She fisted her hands at her side to stop the trembling.

That was when Fiona had put her in charge of peeling a mound of potatoes.

They worked in comfortable silence. Then, when the twins got home, the noise level rose along with their boundless energy.

Rose tried to imagine what it might have been like to be a part of a family like this one. What a difference it would have made. She feared she might bite a hole in her bottom lip as she struggled to keep the tears at bay.

Once her mother died, her father only allowed her to attend school for another year, then he insisted she stay home and take care of the household.

How she longed to look in Elizabeth's history book or Margaret's algebra book. Maybe, once she got settled in St. Louis, she could return to school and at least get a high school diploma. But would a baby squash that dream? How could she go to school and care for a child? Renewed anger toward Amos Parker almost strangled her. He'd ruined every chance she'd ever have for a normal life.

She forced herself to push away those thoughts as activity swirled around her. The knots in Rose's shoulders and neck unwound somewhat, and she blew out a shaky sigh of release. It did her soul good to focus on anything but the horror the day had brought.

Then, when Oliver and Jack arrived, the house overflowed with conversation, delicious smells, and gentle feelings.

She finished peeling the last potato and diced them into cubes. When she scooped them up to drop into boiling water, she tripped, and the potatoes landed on the floor. "Oh, God! I'm so sorry." She shrunk back against the cabinet, raising a hand to protect her face, her heart pounding.

But Fiona only gave her an understanding smile and picked them up. "Rose, it was just a simple accident. No one is going to punish you here—ever. Do you understand?"

Rose let her hands drop to her side. "I...I don't know if I can ever get used to that."

Once she'd rinsed the potatoes and dropped them into the pan, Fiona laid down her fork and embraced Rose. "It will take time, lass. But in the meantime, be kind to yourself."

Melting under Fiona's hug, she whispered, "Thank you. What else can I do?"

Fiona pointed to the cabinet. "I usually make the girls set the table, but tonight I'd like it if you would."

Rose smiled through fresh tears. "Sure." She opened the cabinet and took out six plates.

Jack sauntered in, his hair slicked back and face pink from scrubbing. "It sure smells good in here, Fiona."

"Why thank you, Jack. Would you mind helping your sister set the table?"

Rose knew in her heart of hearts she was trying to make each of them feel at ease by giving them things to keep their hands busy. She handed the stack of plates to Jack. "You take these and I'll bring silverware."

Fiona pointed her meat fork to the cabinet drawer next to the sink. "In there. Thanks, kids."

When they finished and returned to the kitchen, Jack snagged a carrot from a tray. Rose started to admonish him, then stopped herself and leaned against the cabinet beside him. "You worked late."

He munched the carrot. "Helped Oliver finish clearing the platform since he missed so much work today helping us."

"How nice of you, Jack." Fiona loaded a platter with chicken, then stirred the potatoes.

"Thank you, Jack." Rose's words barely rose above a whisper.

He squeezed her hand. "We're in this together, sis."

A tear slipped out and trickled down her cheek. It was true. She and Jack would stick together and get through this nightmare.

Oliver stepped into the kitchen.

Fiona waved them away. "Okay, kids. Now, my kitchen is getting crowded. Oliver, you and Jack git on out of here and let us finish up."

Oliver chuckled. "I get it, Mum. Come on, Jack, let's go toss around a ball before it gets too dark."

Once they left, Fiona turned to Rose. "Never saw a boy who loves baseball more than my Oliver. He has that ball and bat in his hands every spare second he can find."

"Jack's never had a chance to play, but he's told me how he and Oliver have been playing at work after they eat."

Fiona grinned. "I swear he'd teach that dog of his to play if only the little fella had hands. Never seen anyone love something so much. I only hope he doesn't get disappointed."

They finished cooking, and Fiona called to the twins. "Margaret, Elizabeth, would you go get your brother and Jack? Tell them supper is ready."

As they sat at the table, passing around mounded platters of food, Rose looked at all the faces and swore to always remember this moment. No matter where life took her, she'd never forget the kindness the Quinns showed and the love they shared. That was the way life was supposed to be.

While she hated everything about what had happened that day, and especially the way it happened, a part of her understood the opportunity of a new beginning for both her and Jack.

She saw a new spark in her brother's eye that hadn't been there.

And maybe he saw a hint of that same spark in hers. Or he would eventually.

All she knew was that they now had a chance for something better.

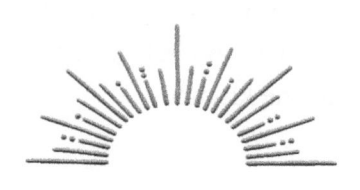

Oliver read his mother's face. He knew her so well. While she'd do anything to help Rose and Jack, she'd also worry about them all.

Once they finished supper and cleared the dishes away, Fiona cleared her throat. "Family meeting time. Everyone, sit back down, and that includes you, Jack and Rose."

She waited until they were all seated, then stood at the head of the table. "Rose told me about what happened today. My heart breaks over it all. But I understand that Rose and Jack need to get to their aunt's house. So, Oliver, let's hear what you have to say. Do you have a plan?" She sat down.

Margaret and Elizabeth both gasped in unison.

Oliver got to his feet. "I talked with Mr. Owen today and he assures me he'll hold my job. It's about a nine-hour drive to St. Louis. I figure we will divide it up into two days. And, unless you object, Mum, I want to spend a day in St. Louis to see the baseball park. Then I'll come straight back." He sat down.

Fiona stood. "Okay, it's settled. You'll leave early tomorrow morning. I'll make sure you have food for the road and extra blankets for camping. Oliver, you'll take the cots with you. Rose, Jack, do you have anything you want to say?" She dropped back into her chair.

Rose pushed to her feet. "Thank you, Fiona, for everything." A sob caught in her throat. "And you, Oliver." Her voice cracked. "You've gone above and beyond to help us. Just know that we deeply appreciate it."

"I second that," Jack chimed in.

Rose continued. "And please know that we'll repay you when we can. We don't cotton to charity, but don't have much of a choice right now." She faced Oliver. "If you'll take us to St. Louis, I promise you that you can talk with our uncle about how to try out for the baseball team. If he's alive, he'll help. That's my bargain, my promise to you." She settled back in her seat.

Oliver arose. "While that's a longstanding dream of mine, you don't have to make a bargain with me, Rose. I would take you regardless." He turned to his mother. "Mum, you know I'd never leave you and the girls in a lurch, so I'm going to give you half of the pay I drew today and take the other half with me."

Jack pushed back his chair. "I drew my pay today, too. I'll gladly leave some of it with you, Fiona. It's the least I can do."

Fiona waved her hand in dismissal. "Not necessary, boys. We will be just fine. All I ask, Oliver, is that you get them delivered safe and sound and hurry home."

"I'll keep that promise."

Margaret interrupted. "Can't Elizabeth and I go, too?"

"Of course not. Oliver doesn't need to have you two to look after and besides that, you're not missing school."

"But, Mum…"

"Not another word, girls. There's really nothing else to discuss. You all can get started early in the morning. Now, go listen to the radio or play a game."

"Okay, girls, you heard Mum. Go get the Sorry game and we'll all play." Oliver scooted his chair back.

Margaret jumped up. "I'll get it."

Fiona rose and motioned to Oliver to follow her. They stepped out the back door. Pirate bounded toward them.

"What is it, Mum?" Oliver bent over to pet the scruffy dog's head.

"I'm worried, son. I know Rose and Jack need to get away from here, but there is something else going on with Rose that she isn't saying. I just want you to be aware."

Oliver ran a hand through his hair. "I'd venture to say there's a lot she's keeping to herself. Jack's a pretty open book. He's got a good attitude."

"Just keep an eye on her, son. I have a feeling she isn't well."

Oliver embraced his mother. "Try not to worry. I'll get them to St. Louis safe and sound and be back home before you even know I'm gone."

Fiona swiped at tears. "Aye. I want to believe that, but a lot can go wrong on the road." She tiptoed and put both hands on Oliver's shoulders. "If anything happens, you can always get a message to me at the bakery."

"I know, and I promise. We'll be okay. I trust the Woody Wagon to get us to St. Louis."

She sighed. "And what if you get there and find out you can play ball? What then?"

"Then I will come home and we'll talk it out. I won't just abandon you and the twins."

"You're a good son, Oliver Quinn. Your father would be so proud of you, as am I."

He tweaked her nose. "Had a good teacher, Mum. Let's go play with the others and promise you'll try not to worry. I'll look after Rose and Jack. I'm responsible and if anything happens to delay my return, I'll let you know. Thank goodness the bakery has a telephone."

"Guess we'll eventually have to get one here at the house. Modern times are coming even to this little town." A worry line creased her forehead. "Lord knows it's an extra expense we can do without for now.

Oliver put an arm around her shoulders. "Let's go play."

Fiona wiped at her eyes and smiled, though her bottom lip trembled. "Lets. I love you, Oliver."

"I love you, too, Mum."

While Oliver couldn't squelch the excitement at the chance to see the baseball field where many of the games he'd listened to on the radio had been played, he didn't minimize the severity of the situation or how much his mother would worry until he returned.

He pondered for a moment about Harlan. Where would he go and what would he do, and what had really happened at that shack? The plumes of smoke he'd seen earlier in the day could only mean that Harlan burned everything…possibly including the bodies. What a horrible thing for a young man to go through.

Harlan had sacrificed everything for his brother and sister to have a better chance at life. And that raised his standing in Oliver's eyes.

He held the door open for his mother and followed her inside.

Tomorrow would dawn a new day for them all.

# CHAPTER 13

After a night of tossing and turning, filled with terrifying nightmares, Rose arose before the sun came up the next morning and groaned as sore muscles protested each movement. Her first reaction was panic and fear. It took more than a minute to remember where she was.

She'd made a bed on the couch and Jack had slept on a cot in Oliver's room. While there was no sound in the house yet, she got up and folded the ample blankets Fiona had provided. Everything came flooding back. Her stomach lurched. She was going to be sick.

As she tiptoed down the hall to the bathroom door, Fiona emerged from her bedroom dressed and ready for the day. "Good morning, dear. I hope you slept well."

"Can't say I did, but at least I rested." It was true. She'd slept very little.

"I'll put coffee on. Come to the kitchen when you're finished."

She nodded and rushed into the bathroom, hoping no one would hear her throwing up. How much longer could she hide her condition? None of it was of her choosing. Not that she wouldn't love to be a mother someday. Now was not that day. She wanted a chance to live, to get an education, experience new things and find happiness, maybe even someone nice, like Oliver, to love her.

It had been many years since she'd been outside Arkansas and a part of her couldn't help but be excited at the prospect of seeing something different. But then, she thought about Harlan, and wondered where he'd slept last night. She choked back a sob. Would she ever see her brother again? At least he knew where she and Jack were going. Maybe he'd even join them there at some point. She whispered a prayer for her brother. What he'd done yesterday showed a deep love she'd never realized existed. She swallowed hard.

After she splashed water on her face and rinsed her mouth, she ran her fingers through her hair and braided it. Then she hurried to the kitchen.

Fiona sifted flour into a bowl. "We have lots to do this morning, and I could use your help if you're up to it. I'm making extra biscuits for the road and we have plenty of fruit and cheese I'll pack, along with the leftover chicken from last night."

"What can I do?"

"How about you fry up some ham while I get these biscuits in the oven? Help yourself to coffee, if you wish."

Rose's stomach roiled, and she fought nausea. She wouldn't throw up again, no matter what she had to do. "Maybe just some water." She turned on the faucet and filled a glass.

"You okay, lass?" Fiona looked her up and down.

"Yes," she lied. "Just nervous." She reached for a skillet hanging over the stove and lit the burner.

They worked in silence for the next few minutes. One by one, Oliver, Jack, Margaret, and Elizabeth drifted in.

After breakfast, of which Rose only nibbled at, Oliver and Jack went to work loading the car and Rose helped Fiona prepare a basket of food.

By the time the sun rose, they had the wagon loaded down and everything was ready to go.

Rose hugged Fiona and the twins, then settled into the backseat while Oliver and Jack said their farewells. She swiped at her tears and bit her bottom lip to stop the trembling.

As soon as Oliver opened the car door to get in, Pirate rushed past him, jumped inside, and perched on the seat, his ears sticking straight up. Oliver called to him and whistled, but the dog turned his head, refusing to look at his master. He wasn't going to be left behind.

Finally, Oliver straightened and threw up his hands. "Looks like Pirate is going with us." He waved to his mother and sisters and got in on the driver's side while Jack took the front passenger seat.

The minute Jack closed his door, Pirate jumped into his lap and yipped. Jack laughed and ruffled his ears.

Rose leaned over the seat. "He's very determined. Want me to take him back here? There's more room."

"Nah. He ain't no trouble. I kinda like having his company." Pirate licked Jack's chin.

Oliver turned onto the main road. "Hadn't planned on bringing him, but reckon he has other ideas."

When he reached the highway, he turned north and sped up. "Might as well get comfortable. We've got a long way to go. Jack, there's a map in the glove box. Know how to read one?"

"Sure." Jack leaned over Pirate, clicked open the compartment, and pulled out the map. "You're prepared."

"Funny thing. That night after I had followed you home, I stopped for gas and on instinct picked up a Arkansas-Missouri map. Guess the idea of maybe someday getting to meet your uncle prompted me to grab it."

Jack opened the map and Pirate lay down on the seat. "Looks like we'll stay on highway 81 until we get to Pine Bluff."

Rose's stomach lurched. "Oliver, I'm so sorry, but can you pull over? I think I'm going to be sick." She hated to say anything.

"Of course." Oliver stopped the car.

She flung the door open and stepped out, then heaved onto the ground.

After wiping her mouth with the back of her hand, she got back inside the car. "Sorry."

"Nothing to be sorry about. Don't be shy about asking me to stop." Oliver pointed to the railroad track running alongside the road as he pulled back onto the blacktop. "Say, I know you haven't lived here long, but have you heard about the Crossett mystery light?"

Rose took a deep breath and leaned forward, resting her arms on the back of the seat. Oliver was obviously trying to take the focus off her. "What are you talking about?"

"It's real. I've seen it many times, and it's always right along this stretch of track. Rumors have it that a railroad worker got his head cut off in an accident and he's searching for it."

"That's horrible." Rose suppressed a shudder. She wondered if Ezra Blaine would haunt the last place he drew a breath. "You've really seen this light?"

"Yep. It's most always a green color and hovers two or three feet off the ground. It was first spotted in the early nineteen hundreds. I've tried to walk to it, but when I get close, it disappears until I move on, then it comes back. Lots of others have seen it, too."

"Spooky." Jack stared out the window. "Maybe if we come back for a visit, you can show me."

Rose's heart sped up at the thought of getting to come back to see Oliver and his family. She instinctively put a hand on her stomach. But could she stand the humiliation she'd feel to return with a baby in her arms? What would Fiona and the twins think of her?

She leaned back and closed her eyes, determined to keep the nausea at bay.

Somehow, things had to work out. Surely the good Lord had punished them all enough, although she couldn't think of what they had done to deserve it.

It was time for something better.

While she had no idea how it would all unfold, some deep part of her believed it would.

She desperately needed to hold on to that belief with every fiber of her being.

The whine of the tires beneath on the pavement and sun shining through the windows lulled her into a relaxed state. How long had it been since she'd felt that way? Years?

Oliver glanced in his rearview mirror. Dark circles under Rose's eyes contrasted with her pale face, and faint bruising was forming around her neck. Mum was right. Rose was not well, but then again, she'd been through hell.

Not only in the last twenty-four hours, but years. She wouldn't bounce back overnight.

Jack took it more in stride, but for Rose, the hurt went deep.

"We'll stop for gas and a break in Pine Bluff, if that's okay with you two."

"Sure." Jack folded the map and put it back in the glove box. "I want to pick up some tobacco. You don't smoke, Oliver?"

"No. Never had an urge to."

"Maybe I should quit. I just smoked because Pa and Harlan did."

"You're young. You'll figure it out." Oliver cruised along the narrow two-lane road, pushing the Woody Wagon to forty miles per hour.

But as soon as he settled in at a steady speed, Rose groaned. "Please pull over again, Oliver. I'm so sorry."

He pulled to a stop and shot Jack a questioning gaze.

Jack shrugged. "Probably just nerves."

"Probably." Still, Oliver couldn't help worrying about her. He could feel her humiliation.

He waited until she got back in the car, then got out and opened the back. "There's a canteen of water." He got back in the driver's seat, then handed the water to Rose, along with a clean cloth. "Wet this and put it on your forehead and drink some water. It might help."

"Thank you. I'll be okay." She refused to meet his gaze. "Let's go."

The pine scent and evergreen colors mixed with golden yellow of the hickory, and brown and orange leaves of the maples provided quite the panoramic view.

"I love the fall." Jack followed his gaze. "So colorful."

"Spring's my favorite, but guess that goes without saying, since baseball season kicks off in the spring."

The next time Oliver glanced at Rose, he was happy to see she'd curled up with a blanket under her head for a pillow, the wet cloth draped across her forehead. He couldn't tell if she was asleep, but at least she was resting. He wondered if he needed to find a doctor for her.

Pirate crawled closer and laid his small head on Oliver's leg. He reached down and scratched behind his ears. A part of him would welcome the little dog's company on the long trip back home.

His thoughts turned to the future. What if he got a shot at trying out for the majors? Would he be able to leave his mother and sisters? They depended on him.

And yet, he wouldn't turn down an opportunity. He'd figure out how to make it all work and still help his family.

Excitement thrummed beneath his skin.

It had been a long time since he'd taken a trip anywhere. He'd been locked into a routine of work, helping his mum, and playing ball. And not that he minded. However, the thought of seeing new places, different people and a big city had him humming with anticipation.

He'd be turning twenty-three in a few weeks.

His whole life lay ahead of him. He wondered if Rose and Jack might feel the same.

And while he couldn't deny he was attracted to Rose and would like very much to court her, she'd soon be in a different city and that possibility wouldn't be open.

Unless—unless he got to live part time in St. Louis.

Guess he'd have to wait and see how everything unfolded. Still, she was the first girl that had turned his head in a long time.

He rolled down a window and let the cool fall breeze brush across his face, loving the feeling of being alive.

Truly alive and full of hope, not only for himself but for the two people in the car that he now thought of as close friends.

He wanted only good things for them all.

Jack leaned his head against the window and dozed. Only the smooth purr of the engine and whine of the wheels filled the inside of the car.

Oliver steered between the lines and let hopes and dreams fill his head.

With a little imagination, he could hear the crack of the bat and roar of the crowd.

He pulled his paddy cap lower and shaded his eyes against the sun.

Life certainly had funny ways of turning on a dime.

And yesterday presented one of those unpredictable changes.

# CHAPTER 14

After pulling over twice more for Rose to throw up, Oliver stopped at a small grocery store in the next town they came to.

"Rose, I'm going to buy some saltines and a 7-Up to help settle your stomach. And if that doesn't work, then we need to think about trying to find a doctor."

"Mind if I come with you?" Jack ran a hand through his hair.

"No, of course not." Oliver handed Pirate over the seat to Rose. "Can Pirate stay with you?"

Rose ducked her head. "Sure. I'm sorry to be so much trouble."

"No trouble. I just want you to feel better. Ever had a soda?"

"I've seen them, but never had one."

"Then you're in for a treat. Come on, Jack." He hurried inside, remembering his mother's words about Rose not being well. She certainly wasn't. While he'd like to be making better time, Rose needed some help. At this rate, they'd never get out of Arkansas.

Inside the store, Oliver grabbed a box of saltines and paid for it, then dropped a nickel in the Coke machine. He called over his shoulder, "Jack, want a Coke?"

"Yes. But I can pay for it."

"You can get the next one." Oliver watched with a bit of humor as Jack eyed a pouch of rolling tobacco, then passed it up and bought a package of Beech-Nut gum instead. Good. He was too young to smoke, anyway.

Back in the car, Oliver handed the bottle of 7-Up and crackers to Rose. "Hope this helps."

"Thank you," she mumbled. Pirate sat on her lap and nuzzled her hand.

He backed the wagon out and turned onto the highway, sipping his Coke.

Jack took a swig from his bottle and groaned. "Only ever had this once when I went to town with Harlan."

"Well, I hope you get to have lots more, Jack. You're starting a new life."

"That's still sinking in. I keep thinking we need to get back home before Pa knows we're gone." His voice took on a dismal tone. "Don't seem real."

Rose nibbled on a cracker. "I know how you feel, Jack. But then all I have to do is remember Pa's fingers around my throat, choking me, and I know how real it was."

Jack turned on the seat. "I wish I could've prevented all of it. It's not fair to any of us, but especially to you. Don't think about it anymore."

"I'm trying. I'm worried about Harlan." Her voice cracked. "I wish I knew the truth. And I had to wonder where he might've slept last night. Hope he had a bed somewhere."

"Harlan can take care of hisself." Jack took a long swig from his Coke. "Focus on yourself and getting better. I've never seen you this sick."

She didn't respond, and Oliver glanced in the rearview mirror in time to see her swipe at a stray tear.

Time. It was going to take time.

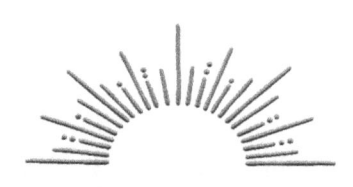

---

The bell rang when Oliver pulled across the rubber tube at a Magnolia gas station. Rose sat up and rubbed her eyes, and Jack straightened. Pirate stretched and let out a short bark.

"Where are we?" Rose asked.

"Pine Bluff. Need to gas up. This would be a good time to stretch your legs and go to the bathroom if you need to." Oliver rolled down his window as the attendant approached. "Fill it, please."

"Yes, sir." The young attendant unscrewed the gas cap.

Oliver got out of the car, and Pirate jumped out behind Rose. "Say, is there a park around here anywhere, mister?"

"Sure." The man pointed over his shoulder. "Up the road a couple of miles. Make a right on Lee Street and you'll find the city park a few blocks down on the left."

"Much obliged." Oliver picked up Pirate and walked a few feet away, then set him down on a patch of grass.

Thank goodness he hadn't had to pull over anymore after Rose ate the crackers and drank the soda.

And she'd fallen asleep. That was good. Although she'd cried out more than once in her sleep, no doubt plagued by memories replayed.

Jack got out and strode toward the restroom signs.

Once Pirate finished his business, he sniffed the ground and hiked his leg on every bush nearby.

A black and white police cruiser pulled into the station and Oliver tensed. They weren't that far from home. Could they be looking for Rose and Jack?

As if on cue, she walked back toward the car from the restroom. The police officer stepped out of his vehicle and stared at her. The minute she saw him, she ducked back inside the restroom, no doubt terrified. Oliver held his breath as the officer approached him.

"Nice looking dog you got there." The man adjusted his gun holster.

"Yes sir. He's a good dog, too. Anything I can help you with?"

"That girl with you?"

"She and her brother are traveling with me."

"What happened to her?"

"She had an accident." Oliver hated lying, but he had to protect Rose.

"Pays to be careful."

"That it does, sir." Oliver rubbed the back of his neck.

"Just came from working a domestic dispute down the road." He sucked on his teeth. "Always hate those. Never know who's telling the truth."

"I suppose that's true." Oliver angled toward the car and the officer followed him.

"You folks traveling?"

Oliver struggled to control his breathing. "Going to St. Louis."

"Be careful out there on the road. Lots of crazies running around these days."

"Yes sir. We will."

The officer motioned to the station attendant. "When you get done with this customer, fill me up, Delbert." He strode toward the men's room.

"Will do, sir."

Oliver blew out a quiet breath of relief. He could only imagine Rose's fear at the sight of the man.

The gas station attendant raised the hood on the Woody Wagon after cleaning off the windshield. He called to Oliver. "Say, mister, you're a little low on oil. Want me to fill 'er?"

Oliver joined him, looking at the dipstick. "Damn. I checked it before I left Crossett and it was full."

"These old cars use oil. Not unusual."

Still, Oliver couldn't shake a niggle of worry. The last thing they needed was car trouble. "Of course. Top it off and would you mind checking the tires?"

The young man tipped his hat. "Always do."

When Jack came out of the restroom, the police officer went inside. Oliver motioned to Jack. "Keep an eye on Pirate?"

"Sure thing."

By the time Oliver returned from the bathroom, Rose, Jack, and Pirate were back in the car. Rose sat low in the seat, her head barely visible.

He paid the attendant and slipped behind the wheel. Once he was out on the road, he glanced over his shoulder at Rose. "Seeing that cop had to terrify you. It did me."

"My heart stopped beating for a minute. I was sure he was going to arrest me." She chewed on a fingernail.

"He did ask what happened to you, and I told him you'd been in an accident."

Rose gasped. "Guess these bruises and bandage do raise a question or two."

"Anyway, he was just passing the time jawing with me. I don't know about you two, but I'm hungry. It's time for a bite of food. The man told me where to find the city park, but I'd feel a mite better if we get back out on the highway and stop somewhere under a shade tree."

"Sounds good to me. I'm hungry," Jack chimed in.

Rose remained quiet.

A few miles outside of town, Oliver pulled to a stop beneath the spreading crown of an old oak.

He retrieved the basket of food Fiona had packed, as Rose spread a red checkered tablecloth on the ground. And while Rose refused anything more than an apple, Jack and Oliver devoured the leftover chicken, tossing morsels to Pirate.

After they loaded everything back into the wagon, Rose touched Jack's arm. "Mind if I sit up front for a bit?"

"Nope. In fact, I was going to suggest it." Jack climbed in and stretched out in the backseat with Pirate tucked in next to him. "Don't forget we turn onto Highway 65 somewhere around here, Oliver."

"Thanks for reminding me. I might've missed it." Oliver glanced at Rose, who sat up straight on the seat and smoothed her worn dress. He was relieved that she seemed to feel better.

Hopefully, whatever had made her so sick had passed.

She deserved a break after all she'd been through.

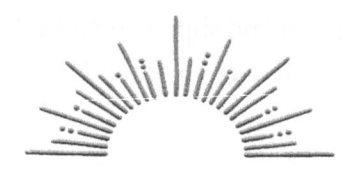

Rose glanced at Oliver and, for the millionth time, wished with all her heart that she was different. That she hadn't been violated and abused. He was such a handsome boy. More than that, he had a kind heart.

She hated she couldn't control the sickness. Her body rejected the new life as strongly as her mind did. Guilt washed over her. The baby was the innocent one. She should have done a better job of protecting herself, prevented it, but everything happened so fast.

Struggling to dismiss the memory, she shuddered.

"You okay?" Oliver shot her another worried glance.

"I don't feel sick anymore. I think the 7-Up and crackers did the trick."

"Glad to hear it. I was getting ready to hunt down a doctor."

"That law man really shook me up. I know Harlan said I didn't kill Pa, but how do I know he was telling the truth? Have you ever just wished you could rewind time and start over?"

Oliver slowed behind a farm tractor. "Can't say as I have."

Rose sighed. "I wish it with all my heart."

"What would you have done differently? Seems to me a lot of what happened was out of your control."

"Reckon that's true, but still can't help wishing and wondering."

They fell into an easy silence.

Oliver rolled down his window, and the breeze tugged at tendrils of her hair. "Tell me about this aunt where I'm taking you and Jack. Is she kind?"

"She and my mother were as close as sisters could be until Pa started twisting off. I think he was jealous of their relationship. But Aunt Katherine was always good to me and would bring me hair ribbons or a new doll."

"So they lived close by?"

"For a few years, but then they moved up to St. Louis when I was around seven."

"Was that when your uncle played ball?"

"No. He played years before then. He'd travel with the team and Aunt Katherine would stay home. I think that's one reason she wanted to live near us. They never had any children." She bit her bottom lip. "My pa never liked her husband, Uncle Rube. Said what he did was a waste of time. But I think he was jealous."

"Yeah. Lots of folks think playing ball is a waste of time." Oliver tapped the steering wheel. "But I can make more money in one season of playing in the majors than I can make all year at the sawmill."

Rose hoped her uncle was still alive—that she might help in some small way to make Oliver's dreams come true.

But what dreams did she have for herself? Only pipe dreams that would never manifest. Even if Aunt Katherine took her in and cared for her, she'd end up with a baby that would prevent her from returning to school and becoming the independent person she longed to be.

Her life was over in a different way than Ezra Blaine's.

A part of her wondered if he hadn't gotten off too easy.

That is, unless he burned in hell for an eternity, like the preachers stomped around and yelled about.

It'd be nothing less than what he deserved.

If she did have this child, she vowed it would never know any violence, even though it had been created by a brutal act. She'd protect it with her life.

Another thought stopped her in her tracks, and she drew in a sharp intake of breath. Oh, God! What if the child looked like Amos Parker?

Nausea rolled through her.

How could she learn to love something that came from such a horrific attack?

She scrubbed her hand across her face and leaned her forehead against the window.

Helpless. Hopeless. Heartsick.

But no matter what, she'd never give up. Her mother always used to tell her where there was a will, there was a way.

Rose Blaine had the will.

She just needed one tiny chance.

# CHAPTER 15

By evening, Oliver had grown stiff from sitting in the car for so many hours. He longed to stretch his legs and toss around the baseball with Jack. Thank goodness, Rose hadn't had any more sickness since they left Pine Bluff. Maybe whatever was wrong had passed.

For miles, after leaving the town, he'd watched in his rearview for the patrolman who had commented on Rose's bruises, and breathed a sigh of relief when he saw nothing.

He kept an eye out for the perfect camping spot somewhere along the road. There was still plenty of daylight left, but he was tired and could be sure his companions were, too.

As he neared Palarm Creek just past Conway, Arkansas, he slowed. He drove across the bridge, then pulled off the road and down a slight embankment. "This looks like the perfect camping spot. What do you think?"

"It's beautiful. And so peaceful." Rose pointed toward a giant hickory tree. "How about there?"

Jack put his arms across the seat and leaned forward. "It gets my vote. Wish we'd brought a fishing line. Bet this creek is full of fish."

Oliver steered toward the flat ground beneath the tree. "Bet you're right, Jack." He stopped the car. "Let's set up camp."

Jack hopped out of the car with Pirate on his heels. "How about I gather up some firewood?"

"That'd be great. Me and Rose can get things unloaded."

Oliver got out and stretched his arms over his head, groaning. "Not used to sitting for so long." His neck popped as he rolled his head from side to side.

Rose sauntered to the edge of the creek. "If it was warmer, a swim would be nice," she called over her shoulder.

"That it would." Oliver watched her for a moment before he opened the back of the wagon, and she hurried to help.

By the time Jack returned with arms full of kindling, Oliver had set up the cots for him and Jack while Rose unloaded the food. He'd insisted that Rose sleep in the wagon's backseat.

"What do you two think about fried potatoes and eggs for supper?" She lifted a cast-iron skillet out of Fiona's basket.

"And maybe some campfire coffee?" Jack dropped his load. "That is, if you are up to it."

Oliver stacked the kindling in a pyramid shape. "I'm happy to do the cooking if you want to rest, Rose."

Rose waved them away and rolled her eyes. "Stop treating me like I'm an invalid. I'm fine and I'm hungry. So, eggs and potatoes?"

"Fine by me." Jack whistled for Pirate, who'd disappeared into the brush along the creek.

The dog bounded out, with a stick in his mouth.

"Works for me, too." Oliver struck a match and held it to the kindling until a fire started. Then he blew on it until it caught, and stacked more small branches. "We need some flat rocks we can lay inside the fire for the skillet to sit on."

"I'll see what I can find." Jack tossed the stick for the little dog and hurried toward the edge of the creek.

While Oliver stoked the fire, Rose peeled potatoes. "Your mother sure knew what to pack for us. Do you go camping a lot?"

"Sometimes in the summer. We always enjoy it and there's usually fishing and swimming involved. My sisters love it. So, Mum has had plenty of experience."

"Think we'll make it to St. Louis tomorrow?" Rose dropped the potatoes into a bowl.

"With any luck, we should be there by midday."

"You mean if we can travel without having to stop so many times for me?" Her violet eyes held unspoken anguish.

"I didn't say that. We can stop as much as we need to." He sought her gaze, but she looked away.

"Rose, you do know you can talk to me, don't you? You've been through hell. That's not something you just get over in a day. I'm a good listener."

"I'm okay. Just gotta buck up. No other choice." She set her mouth in a firm line.

Jack returned with two large flat rocks. "These do?"

"Perfect." Oliver carefully placed them at the edge of the fire. "Once these are good and hot, they'll be ready for cooking." He stood. "If you're okay, Rose, me and Jack will go hit a few balls. I brought my bat."

She waved them away. "Go on. I'm fine."

While Oliver welcomed the opportunity to play, he couldn't help sending worried glances Rose's way while he placed three rocks to mark the bases.

She was keeping something to herself.

How did she go from being so sick to being okay?

It didn't add up.

The few times he'd ever had a stomach bug, it lasted for at least a couple of days.

He shrugged and tossed the ball to Jack, who hit it with a loud crack of the bat.

Oliver stretched his leg muscles and caught it midair, getting Jack out on first base.

Whatever was troubling Rose, he couldn't do anything to help if she wasn't willing to talk about it.

They switched places, and Jack pitched while Oliver swung the bat.

The second the ball connected with the bat, Oliver dashed toward the bases.

Crisp fall air filled his lungs making him feel alive. His powerful legs carried him in for a home-run while Jack chased the ball halfway down the creek.

"Safe." He called as he slid into home.

"That was a helluva hit, Irish." Jack wound up and threw another ball.

Oliver swung with all his might and the ball soared over the trees.

A splash left no doubt where the ball landed.

"I'll get it," Jack called, shucking his shoes and rolling up his pant legs. He yelped as the cold water hit him.

Laughing, Oliver joined him, with Pirate jumping in too. He let out a whoop. "Oh, that's cold."

"Wakes you up for sure." Jack leaned over and grabbed the ball. "Got it."

They both hurried back to dry ground, shivering, as the sun painted a brilliant portrait of golden and orange hues across the skies turning the fall leaves into glistening gold.

Oliver slapped Jack on the back. "You're a good sport."

For a moment, Oliver reflected on his family and wondered what it would be like to have a brother like Jack. He liked his easy-going attitude and even temper. He couldn't be more opposite from Harlan.

Whatever awaited Jack and Rose in St. Louis, he hoped it would turn out even better than they hoped.

Lord knows, they deserved it.

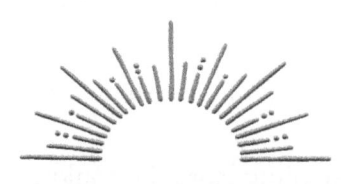

---

Watching the two boys play, Rose couldn't help but smile. She and Jack needed a break from the trauma. When Pirate shook and sprayed them both, she chuckled, then returned to her cooking. A part of her longed for that kind of carefree play—for a friend she could talk to and laugh with.

When had she gotten so old?

The pungent smell of burning hickory tickled her nostrils.

While she'd cooked many times over a campfire, the challenge was always to keep the fire hot enough, but not too hot. Oliver had done a good job of stacking the kindling. She added a small log to the fire and sparks flew, sending a plume of smoke toward her. Her eyes watered and she coughed.

With laughter from the boys in the background, she sat cross-legged by the fire and gazed at the brilliant hues of the fall leaves decorating trees on both sides of the creek. So beautiful. So untouched by ugliness. She sighed and stirred the potatoes.

While they cooked, she wiped out the crock bowl and got six eggs out of Fiona's basket. She marveled at the careful way the woman had packed a dish towel around the eggs to keep them from breaking. If only there was a way to wrap a dish towel around herself to keep from breaking.

Then, to her surprise, she unwrapped a fairly large piece of ham. That would be the perfect addition to the meal.

The sun slipped behind the trees and slowly night sounds came alive. It was as if one world ended and a new one began, much like her life at the present time.

The aroma from the campfire, coffee boiling, and potatoes cooking teased her nostrils, and her stomach growled in response. She needed food.

Oliver and Jack rejoined her as darkness descended.

"Smells good." Jack plopped down on one of the cots and reached for a blanket, shivering. Pirate promptly jumped up beside him and whined. Jack wrapped the blanket around them both.

"It'll be ready soon." She lifted out a portion of the potatoes. "It was fun to watch you and Oliver play. I can't recall seeing you and Harlan play since Mama died."

"Yeah. Things got heavy. Wasn't Harlan's fault. Too much got put on him."

Oliver leaned over the fire and held his hands toward the warmth. "Jack's going to make an outstanding baseball player."

The mention of Harlan brought a deep sadness over Rose. Where was he tonight? Did he have anything to eat? At least he had a little money, and that brought a measure of comfort.

Within the next fifteen minutes, she finished cooking their dinner and dished food out onto tin plates.

"This is a surprise. Didn't expect ham." Jack took a big bite and washed it down with coffee.

"You can thank Fiona for that." Rose handed Oliver a plate, then filled one for herself. She took a bite and savored the flavor. Yes, she needed food. Now, if only she could keep it down in the morning.

Once they'd eaten their fill, Oliver took the plates down to the creek and washed them. Rose added a larger log to the fire. She wrapped a blanket around her shoulders and sat on the edge of the narrow cot.

Jack headed into the bushes with Pirate on his heels, and Oliver sat down beside her after putting the clean dishes back into the basket. "That was a delicious meal."

She ducked her head. "Wasn't nothing."

"Glad to see you eating. Feeling better?"

"I told you I'm fine." She didn't mean to be sharp. Oliver was just being kind.

"Don't mean nothing by it. Just concerned."

Jack stomped back through the brush and moved his cot closer to the fire before lying down. He wrapped the blanket around him and picked up the dog. "I'm turning in. Have a feeling we'll be leaving early in the morning. Good supper, sis."

"Glad you liked it. Goodnight, Jack." Rose stood. "Figure you'll be wanting to turn in, too." She faced Oliver, noting the tired lines around his eyes.

"In a little bit. Would you sit with me for a while longer?" Oliver poked at the fire, causing sparks to fly into the air.

Her breath caught in her throat. "Sure, I guess."

He patted the cot. "Sit. Need another blanket?"

"I'm okay." She tugged the soft wrapping closer around her shoulders and perched on the edge.

They sat in silence for a long minute.

Jack's soft snores filled the air. It had always amazed her how quickly her brother could fall asleep.

"I know you probably don't want to talk about it, but Rose, something's eating at you. And it's making you sick. I can't say that I know what to do to help, but I can say that I'm a good listener." He blew out a breath.

She stilled, her heart pounding. Did she dare? She opened her mouth twice, but no sound came out beyond a sigh. "I...I" She paused. "I can't say it out loud."

Oliver leaned forward, seeking her gaze. "Why not? What can you not say? Do you not trust me?"

"It's not that."

"Then what?"

She fought to slow down her breathing. Dropping her head into her hands, she whispered, "I'm pregnant."

Oliver's gasp spoke volumes.

She jumped up and ran to the creek, unable to look at him. Unable to face the disgust that must be in his eyes.

Tears flowed, and her cheeks burned with humiliation.

She sensed him before he said anything. "Rose. I'm so sorry."

"Not as sorry as I am." She forced herself to look at him, surprised to see only pity in his eyes. Maybe he didn't hate or judge her.

"Come back and sit with me. Please. Let's talk." The gentle arm he placed around her shaking shoulders was like a healing balm.

Stumbling beside him on numb legs, she returned to the spot she'd vacated as the tears continued to flow. "I'm so ashamed."

Oliver snugged the blanket around her shoulders. An owl hooted in the distance and nocturnal animals rustled through the underbrush. "Please tell me everything. I promise I won't judge."

While she told him about the attacks, Oliver tensed next to her.

When she stopped talking, a growl left his throat. "Bastard. Good thing he's dead, or I'd be obligated to kill him."

"So, that's what the sickness is." She paused and swiped at her tears. "It comes every morning, and it's nothing I can control." She fought to steady her voice. "I only hope Aunt Katherine won't turn me away when she finds out." She brought a shaky hand to her forehead. "I tried to fight him, Oliver. I really did, but he was stronger."

"I'm sure you did. And Rose, none of it is your fault. You are a victim. Does Jack know?"

She shook her head. "I've told no one."

Oliver was quiet for so long, she feared that he'd say nothing more. "What if I marry you? I could give you a home and the baby a name."

She sucked in an audible breath. "No way. I won't be responsible for ruining your life, too. You have your dreams, your plans. A wife and child don't fit in those."

"Yet, I would do it to give you stability and a home. We can turn around right now and go back to Crossett. I would expect nothing from you. You'd only be my wife in name."

She clutched his arm. "You're serious."

"I am." He tucked a stray hair behind her ear.

His selfless offer shook her all the way to her core. She jerked her hand away and stared into the inky blackness. "Thank you for offering, but the answer is no. I cannot, no…will not do that to you. I have to handle this on my own. Besides, I can only imagine what your mother and sisters would think of me."

Oliver leaned toward the fire. "I can assure you that Mum would support you one-hundred percent. She'd understand. Rose, it's not your fault. You were attacked."

She stared into the fire and twisted her hands on her lap. Her voice dropped to a whisper, "I know I should be ashamed for thinking it, but I keep hoping something will happen…you know, to the baby." She glanced up. "What kind of person does that?"

Oliver stilled beside her and a moment of silence passed. Finally, he spoke. "A girl who is desperate for a life." He scooted closer. "Can I hold you?"

She nodded and sighed when Oliver wrapped his strong arms around her. "I'm sorry for voicing my wish for the baby to disappear. I should never allow myself to think or say such things."

"No apology necessary. Just know there are lots of single mothers raising children. My mother is one. Of course, she had my dad until the accident."

"Thank you, Oliver."

"For?"

"For being so kind."

"You're welcome."

She laid her head on his strong shoulder and listened to the crackling fire and rushing water. "I'd dreamed of going back to school and getting my high school diploma, but now that might not be possible."

"You never know how things will turn out. But I'm glad you trusted me enough to tell me."

"You and your family are the kindest people I've ever known."

"We're just people. Nothing special."

"I beg to differ. The love you all share is special. I used to know that kind of love." A sob caught in her throat. "I miss my mother so much. She would have protected me."

Oliver rubbed her arm. "I understand. Try to think positive. Somehow, everything will work out."

She relaxed against him and a weight lifted off her shoulders.

While embarrassment and shame still overpowered her, a certain relief came from finally telling someone.

To say the words out loud.

To not be completely alone with her heavy burden.

# CHAPTER 16

Oliver lay awake staring up at the stars twinkling against the inky night sky long after Rose had gone to sleep. Cicadas chirped and nocturnal animals foraged through the underbrush looking for an easy meal. Water rushed around rocks in the creek, creating a soothing rhythm.

The fire crackled and sent a spray of sparks, followed by a stream of smoke into the air as a log collapsed.

What she'd shared shook him to the core. Had he said the right words of comfort? He had to admit her statement about wishing the baby dead shocked him. Yet, he understood.

The abuse she'd endured and now the burden she carried was more than anyone should have to endure, especially a girl so young and alone. It was obvious she'd never confided in her brothers. And he couldn't help wondering how long the abuse had gone on. He didn't dare ask and dig deeper into her wound.

His offer to marry her and give the child his name was one he'd follow through, should she change her mind, or her aunt turn her away.

It certainly was not in his plans—not by a long shot. Still, someone needed to help her. He could provide a safe place for them to live.

But what about his dreams? Could he give them up that easily?

None of it seemed fair.

He blew out a long sigh.

Barring any trouble, they should reach St. Louis tomorrow.

*Guess it's best to wait and see how it will all play out.* But if life offered no other options, and Rose would agree to it, he would marry her.

He could easily imagine his mum's reaction. Of course, she'd want to help Rose. But it would change all of their lives.

Finally, he forced his brain to shut off and closed his eyes. Tomorrow would be a long day.

---

Oliver awoke the next morning before the sun came up. Rose was stirring the fire and adding logs to the dying embers.

He sat up and ran his fingers through his hair, then reached for his cap. "Mornin', Rose."

She jerked around. "Mornin'. I was trying to be quiet."

"Don't apologize. It's time to get up. You okay?"

She nodded. "So far." Her nut-brown hair hung down her back in a long braid, and she had the blanket wrapped tightly around her shoulders.

"That's good. Maybe today will be better." He slipped on his boots and stood. "I hope you don't regret confiding in me last night."

She avoided his gaze and poked at the fire. "I sorta do. But then again, it was a relief to tell someone. I did a lot of thinking after I went to bed and I need to stop hating this baby. It's not the baby's fault, and it's selfish of me to wish it away."

"It's not selfish. It's a normal reaction, but I'm glad you are making peace with it. You're right. None of it is the baby's fault." He laid a hand on her shoulder. "Another option would be to put it up for adoption when it's born. Then you could go on with your life."

"I thought about that." She glanced up. "I will see."

"How old are you, Rose?"

"Seventeen. I'll be eighteen the first of December."

"So young to be saddled with such heavy burdens."

"I don't want your pity, Oliver."

He cringed at her sharp tone. He hadn't meant to offend. "What do you want, Rose?"

"A friend would be nice."

"That you have." He nudged Jack. "Rise and shine, sleeping beauty."

Jack groaned, and Pirate stretched, then hopped down.

Oliver scratched behind Pirate's ears. "Looks like I've lost my dog."

Rose poured water into the coffeepot. "Maybe Pirate knows Jack needs him more than you do right now."

"Could be. Animals have a special sixth sense."

Jack slipped his feet into worn brogans and yawned, stretching his long arms over his head. "Man, I slept good. Can't remember the last time I slept under the stars."

"Good for the soul." Oliver kneeled beside the fire and blew on the embers. "If it's okay with you both, we'll have a quick breakfast and get on the road. With any luck, we'll be in St. Louis tonight."

Jack ambled off into the bushes calling over his shoulder, "Coffee will do me just fine."

Rose rummaged through Fiona's food basket. "I found banana muffins. Would that work for breakfast?"

"You bet." Oliver stepped back when the fire took hold. "It'll be hot enough to boil coffee in a few minutes and we can fill up my thermos." He laid a hand on Rose's shoulder. "Don't be shy about asking to stop if you need to."

"Thank you." She laid her hand on top of his for a brief second, then reached for the enamel coffeepot and set it on one of the flat rocks.

"Any ham scraps left from last night?"

"A few. Want I should give them to Pirate?"

Oliver whistled, and the terrier came running. "That would be great. Gotta feed the little guy."

Before the sun fully arose, they had the wagon loaded, and fire extinguished. Rose chose the backseat again, and Oliver handed her the water canteen and a clean rag. Jack rode up front with Pirate perched between them as Oliver pulled out onto the blacktop.

"Say, if you get tired of driving, Irish, I could rest you a spell. I'm a pretty good driver." Jack patted Pirate's head.

"Thanks, man. Appreciate that." Oliver shifted gears and settled into a steady speed. "I want to stop in the next town and get Rose another 7-Up."

Jack twisted on the seat. "You still sick, Rose?"

"A little. Not as bad as yesterday."

Oliver caught her eye in the rearview mirror. "Regardless, a little 7-Up can help prevent more nausea."

Jack swiveled on the seat and looked from one to the other. "There's something you two ain't tellin' me. I can feel it."

"Not my place." Oliver stared at the road ahead. "Up to Rose to tell you what she wants."

"Rose?" Jack was hanging over the seat. "What's going on?"

"Nothing, Jack."

He settled back against the seat, grumbling. "Could've damn sure fooled me. But if you don't want to tell me, that's your right."

She folded her arms across her chest. "I don't."

"Fine," Jack huffed.

Oliver cast a side glance at the boy. "How old are you, Jack?"

He straightened in the seat. "Sixteen. Be seventeen come spring."

"You and Rose are both so young to be facing what you are. What do you want to be when you grow up?"

"Never gave it much thought. Reckon I'd like to go back to school and get an education. Or maybe I'll just live off the land and not be tied to anyone or anything." Jack rubbed his chin. "I wanna know what it feels like to be free."

Rose cleared her throat. "Oliver, can you pull over?"

"Of course." He angled to the side of the road.

She lurched out and emptied her stomach.

As soon as she got back inside the car, Jack turned and shook his finger. "Now, you're going to tell me what's going on, or I'm getting out of this car and walking to St. Louis." He blew out an exasperated sigh. "I thought we were in this together, Rose."

Tears trickled down her cheeks, and she ducked her head. "I don't want to tell you."

"Why?" He put a hand on Oliver's arm as he shifted into first gear to pull back onto the blacktop. "Not yet. I'm not moving another inch until I know what's wrong with my sister."

Oliver took his foot off the clutch and let the car idle. His heart broke for her, knowing how difficult it would be for her to say the words. Yet, it was her choice.

When he caught her glance in the rearview mirror, he nodded, hoping to give her courage.

She covered her face with her hands and sobbed. "I hate it, Jack. I hate it."

"Hate what, Rose?" Jack fairly hung over the seat.

She raised her tear-stained face and yelled, pounding her fists against the car seat. "I'm going to have a baby. That's what's wrong." She paused and her voice cracked. "And that's what I hate." She covered her face with her hands. "And that's what I didn't want to tell you or anyone else."

Jack fell backward as if punched. He sought Oliver's gaze. "You knew?"

"Just last night."

He turned back to his sister. "Who? And please don't tell me Pa or Harlan. I couldn't take that."

"No." She wiped her face with the wet cloth and took a sip of water.

"Then who, Rose? I'll kill the bastard."

"He's already dead," she said flatly. "Pa done killed him because he was stealing from him."

With a shaky hand, Jack jerked off his hat and raked his fingers through his hair. "Shit! Amos Parker?"

She nodded, then raised her chin. "I fought him as hard as I could. Really, I did. You have to believe me."

"Shit! Shit! Shit!" He turned around and crumpled against the seat.

"I'm sorry. Sorry about all of it. I shoulda' told you the first time he attacked me." She whispered, "I was scared. Said he'd tell Pa I seduced him, and Pa would've believed him. You know how it was. He blamed me for everything anyway, and I would have gotten another beating." A sob caught in her throat.

"Not your fault," he muttered. He jerked open the car door and paced beside the car. When he stopped pacing, he placed his hands on the hood, obviously fighting for control. After a long minute, he swiped a hand across his face, and got back inside without glancing at Rose. "Let's go, Irish."

Oliver pulled out onto the highway after casting Rose a sympathetic half-smile. "I'll get you a 7-Up. Everything will work out when we get to St. Louis. You'll see."

Rose took a bite of cracker and a sip of water, then leaned her head back after rolling down her window.

Pirate curled up on Jack's lap and whimpered. Jack absentmindedly rubbed the little dog's head.

Rose sniffled and laid the wet cloth on her forehead.

"I know that was hard, Rose, but now it's out in the open and you don't have to hide it anymore." Oliver shifted gears and sped up. "You're not alone."

Jack mumbled, "Wish the bastard wasn't dead so I could kill him."

Oliver nodded. "Same thing I said when she told me last night. It would be satisfying."

"You're a good friend, Irish." Jack glanced at Oliver, then turned to Rose. "I'll take care of you, Rose. You can count on me."

"I know, and thank you. But you've got your life to live. This is my burden to bear." Rose let out a long sigh and stared out the window.

A few miles down the road, Oliver broke the silence. "If you want to turn around right now and go back to Crossett, me and my family will help take care of you both."

"No. I want to go to St. Louis." Rose met Oliver's gaze in the rearview mirror. "We have a better chance there. Can't go back."

"I'm with Rose." Jack chewed his bottom lip. "We have a better chance with Aunt Katherine. At least I think so."

"Then on we go."

Oliver stopped in the first town and he and Jack went into the small roadside mom and pop grocery.

Armed with more 7-Up, they continued north.

He only had to stop once more for Rose after getting the drink and crackers.

When he reached the Buffalo River, he pulled off so they could stretch their legs and eat.

With the Missouri state line ahead, Oliver was sure they would make it to St. Louis by dark.

While he couldn't predict what lay ahead for Jack and Rose, he wouldn't leave them until he was sure they were safe and would be well cared for with kindness.

The aunt and uncle better not say one judgmental thing to Rose or cast blame on her, or he'd load her up and take her back home with no hesitation.

His conscience wouldn't allow anything less.

She deserved a chance, and so did Jack.

And he was going to see that they got it, if at all possible.

# CHAPTER 17

Black clouds and thunder rolled across the sky, darkening the early afternoon. Large rain drops pelted the Woody Wagon, and the windshield wipers swished back and forth. They'd crossed the Missouri state line a while back.

An animal darted across the road, and Oliver swerved to miss it. The front tire hit something solid, and the car jolted as a scraping sound grated along the undercarriage.

Oliver gripped the steering wheel and slowed. Jack bolted upright, and Rose let out a gasp.

"What was that?" Her voice trembled.

"Not exactly sure." Oliver leaned forward, attempting to see through the deluge. "We better find a place to pull over."

Jack pointed ahead. "Up there. A grove of trees. Maybe we can take shelter underneath." He craned his neck to view the sky. "Looks like a heck of a storm."

Rose grabbed a blanket. "Feels like the temperature's dropping."

Oliver slowed even more. This was not a good time for a flat tire. He wrestled with the steering wheel, bringing the car to rest beneath the stand of trees. "Hope we don't get stuck when we try to get back out of here. We've got a flat."

"Want me to see?" Jack pulled his hat lower.

"No need. Whatever we hit must've knocked a hole in the tire." Oliver turned off the motor.

Jack swiveled toward Oliver. "Got a spare?"

"Yeah, but we'll have to wait out this storm. Maybe it'll let up." He glanced over the seat at Rose. "Sorry for another delay."

"Nothing to be sorry for. You didn't create the weather." She reached for her mother's journal and leaned back. "I've been wanting to read more in Ma's journal, but I can't while we're traveling. It makes me more nauseated."

Jack put Pirate on his lap and turned sideways. "Read something to us. Maybe it will help us remember our mother and pass the time."

While rain and small pellets of hail pounded the roof of the car, Rose opened the journal. "This entry is July 12th, 1931. She says, *Today I found out I am in the family way again. While I welcome another baby, times are so hard for us, I don't know how we'll feed one more mouth. Ezra promises to find work. Said he heard rumors of the government helping poor folks, but I don't hold out much hope.*"

Jack let out a whistle. "Guess we didn't know how hard our folks had it."

"The whole country suffered in The Great Depression. My mum has told stories of how they'd pick strawberries or dig potatoes or anything else they could find. And my father fought in the boxing rings to make money." Oliver tapped the steering wheel. "Hope we never see times that hard again."

"Go on, Rose." Jack scratched Pirate's head. "She would have been pregnant with me. What else does she say?"

Rose turned the page. "She skips days and a lot of it is things like the sun came out today, or it's raining again. Here's the next interesting one. *Ezra came home today with a new plan. Says he can get wealthy making moonshine. Lord knows we need something to bring in money, but my gut tells this won't be the solution. Ezra is not a strong man. He gives in to temptation much too easily. I fear what might happen to our family. But on a more positive note, I gave birth to a healthy baby boy. We named him Jack.*"

She looked up, with tears glistening in her violet eyes. "Guess we know how the moonshine story ended. I still find myself thinking we better get home before Pa knows we're gone. When I have that thought, the fear is so real it chokes me." Her voice trembled, and lightning flashed across the sky.

Jack nodded. "I feel the same. And I can't keep from thinking about Harlan and wondering what really happened and where he went."

A clap of thunder shook the car, causing all of them to jump.

"That was a little too close for comfort." Oliver jerked his cap off and ran a hand through his hair. "Second guessing parking under these trees, but at least they offer some shelter."

For the next hour, Rose read different passages from Florence Blaine's journal. About halfway through, she paused, glanced up, and sucked in a breath.

"What is it?" Jack leaned over the seat.

"It seems to be the first entry about our father's violence. This one is dated February 1934. *For two cents, I'd pack up the kids and leave. I never thought my husband would raise a hand to me, but the bruise on my cheek tells a different story. I will not tolerate abuse, regardless of whether he was drunk or sober. He said he was under a lot of stress. Well, isn't the whole country? No excuse. If it happens again, I will leave him.*"

Rose looked up, tears trickling down her cheeks. "That was the beginning of the violence. And it never stopped."

"Yet, your mother never left him?" Oliver asked.

"I'm sure she had nowhere to go."

"Keep reading." Jack stared straight ahead.

"Here's another one. *Ezra hit me again today, then laid into Harlan. I fought him and swore I would leave. Then he fell to his knees and begged for forgiveness. Hitting me is one thing, but not the children.*"

Jack sighed. "If only she knew. Is there anything at all positive, or is it all doom and gloom?"

"Let me skip to the last entry. I really don't want to read all of it. It hurts too much." Rose flipped the pages, landing on the last one. "Oh my. It gets worse. She says, *I am sick. I don't know what's wrong, but I know it's serious. The pain is almost unbearable and even with medication the doctor provides, it never leaves. I don't know how much time I have left, but my biggest fear is leaving my children in the hands of their father, who has grown increasingly more violent. This is not the man I married. Whatever happens, I want my children to know I will watch over them forever and always."* Rose closed the journal and sobbed into her hands. "Our poor mama."

Jack swiped angrily at tears. "Damn the man. I wish she would've found the courage to leave him."

Besides the rain pounding on the roof, silence filled the car. There was nothing else to say.

Finally, the rain let up to a drizzle.

"Reckon it's now or never." Oliver opened the car door and stepped out into ankle deep water.

Jack passed Pirate over the seat to Rose and joined him. "I'll help."

"Thank goodness we don't have to unload the wagon to get to the spare. Gonna need the jack and some tools, though."

"What do you want me to do?" Jack shifted from one foot to the other, the soft ground beneath squishing with each movement.

"Help me move things around back here so we can get what we need." He pulled out the food basket. "Set this up with Rose."

Jack took the basket and sloshed to Rose's door. "Oliver says we need to put this up here while we get the tools we need."

Rose scooted over and took the basket. "If I can do anything besides hold Pirate, let me know." Pirate wagged his tail and barked. She held him tighter.

"I think we've got it."

Oliver pulled out the jack and lug wrench. "It's going to be tricky to keep this from sinking down into the mud when we jack up the car. Let's look for something to set the jack on. A flat rock maybe?"

"I'll look over on that side." He pointed across the road.

Oliver observed him trudging down the side of the road, his shoulders hunched, and head lowered. Jack was putting on a brave face, but Rose's news was a gut punch. A boy trying to be a man. His heart went out to them both. He headed down the opposite side of the road.

Jack soon returned with a piece of discarded wood. "Think this might work?"

Oliver had found a semi-flat rock. "Maybe both together will do the trick."

By the time Oliver finished changing the flat and putting the tools away, he and Jack were both covered in mud and soaked to the bone.

He slid back behind the wheel and cranked the engine. "We're stopping at the first gas station we come to. Gotta get out of these wet clothes."

Jack shook the water off his hat and laid it on the seat, then opened the glove box. "I'll look at the map."

"We should be pretty close to Springfield, I think. That's a good sized town. We can get dry clothes and maybe eat in a cafe before we go on." Oliver glanced at Rose. "Feel like eating anything?"

She nodded. "Maybe."

Jack pointed to a spot on the map. "Looks like we are only about twenty miles away."

"Good." Oliver gripped the wheel and put the car in reverse. The wheels spun and he let off the clutch. After a couple of tries, he made contact with the blacktop and shifted into second gear.

"Look." Rose pointed. "There's a double rainbow."

"That can only mean good luck." Jack turned. "Remember what Ma used to say?"

"That a double rainbow was a sign of hope and a new beginning." Rose sighed. "Sure hope that's right for all of us."

"The Irish believe there is a pot of gold at the end of a rainbow guarded by a leprechaun." Oliver chuckled. "Not sure I believe in little leprechauns, but I'd like to find a pot of gold."

"I always wanted to pan for gold, like I read about in books. Wonder if there's any gold in Missouri?" Jack studied the map. "Looks like we'll be getting onto Highway 66 at Springfield, then maybe four hours more to St. Louis."

"Sounds good." Oliver turned the heater on full blast, but it only blew cold air. He shivered. "You okay, Jack? You have to be as cold as I am."

"Yeah, I'm cold. But I'm okay."

Rose offered a blanket to her brother. "Want this?"

"Nah. I'd just get it muddy. Thanks anyway."

Oliver thought about the small bundle of clothing Jack and Rose had. "Do you have a coat, Jack? What about you, Rose? It's going to be much colder in St. Louis than it was in Arkansas."

"Had a coat but Harlan didn't bring it." Rose pulled Pirate onto her lap and the little dog whimpered. "Pirate's helping keep me warm."

"Wish I'd thought about that before we left home. I'm sure the twins had an extra coat you could've had. And I know I had one that would've fit you, Jack." He scrubbed his two-day growth of stubble, longing for a shave.

"We'll be okay. Not used to having much."

Oliver mentally counted the money in his pocket, wondering if he could spare enough to buy coats for them.

Maybe once they got to St. Louis.

For now, he only wanted to get dry and get them all something hot to eat. A bowl of his mum's Irish stew would be welcomed about now.

He was proud of Jack and the way he stood with his sister.

The boy was wise beyond his years.

Maybe that's what hard living had done for him.

When they reached the outskirts of Springfield, Oliver pulled into a gas station. A sign in the window of a cafe across the road advertised a hot meal for only a dollar fifty and coffee for a nickel.

That would be money well-spent.

# CHAPTER 18

They'd no sooner left the cafe than the sky opened up again, dumping buckets of rain. Rose scooted to the edge of the seat as Oliver strained to see through the windshield. She'd traded with Jack, and now sat in the front with Oliver.

The warm meal had done wonders for her. She unconsciously laid a hand on her flat stomach. "How can you even see where you're going?" She wiped moisture off the inside of the glass with her hand.

"Not easy for sure. Taking it slow. I know I turn up here somewhere soon." He hunched over the steering wheel, gripping it with both hands.

Jack leaned forward. "Route 66. That's the highway that runs all the way from St. Louis to California. I remember reading about it in a history book."

"I don't know anything about California, but I'll be happy to see St. Louis." Oliver slammed on the brakes and skidded sideways when a tractor pulled out in front of him. "Damn! Guess he didn't see me. And now we're stuck behind a tractor on this two-lane road."

"Maybe he'll turn off soon." Rose chewed her fingernails. She felt bad that Oliver was being put out so much for them. Yet, he'd offered—not offered, insisted. She flashed back to a time when her father had run a man off the road, then jumped out and fought him because he'd pulled in front of him. Thank goodness Oliver was nothing like her father.

She still struggled to understand and accept his brand of kindness. His offer for marriage went above and beyond simple kindness. He was willing to give up his dreams, his life to provide for her and her bastard child. Who does that? She'd never allow it. The burden of ruining his life would be more than she could bear. No, this was something she would have to do alone.

Sure enough, a few miles down the road, the tractor turned off and Oliver sped up.

While the rain continued beating on the roof of the car, the fresh scent of rain-washed air filtered in. The road ahead was now virtually empty.

"This doesn't look much like a major highway. Wonder if I missed my turn?" Oliver tossed a glance at Jack. "Mind taking another look at the map. Got a feeling I'm off."

Rose handed the map to her brother. "Don't see how you can tell. I haven't seen a road sign."

"True. Of course, it's hard to see much of anything in this rain."

Jack studied the map, then peered out the window. "Agree with you. Don't look much like a highway. More like a country road."

At that moment, the engine knocked, backfired, and died. Oliver shifted back into first gear and popped the clutch.

Nothing happened, and the car coasted down the narrow road at a snail's pace.

He turned the key over and the starter ground but wouldn't connect. He then tried popping the clutch one more time with no luck. With both hands on the wheel, he steered to the side of the road. "This can't be good."

Jack leaned over the seat. "What do you reckon?"

"Don't know, but if I had to guess, I'd say it has something to do with whatever gave us the flat tire back down the road. Or maybe there was water in the gas where we filled up in Springfield. I don't recall the service station attendant checking anything because it was raining so hard."

Rose twisted her hands in her lap while Oliver got out and raised the hood. Jack joined him. She could only catch pieces of their conversation as the rain beat against the roof. They were both going to be soaked again.

After a few minutes, Oliver slammed the hood, and they got back in the car.

"It's only a guess." Oliver blew out a breath and shook water off his cap. "Most likely, we knocked a hole in the oil pan and lost all the oil, which would cause the engine to lock down. The dipstick registered nothing. I can only hope we aren't looking at a complete engine rebuild. The other thing I could see is a busted belt, which is an easy fix."

"What are we going to do now?" Rose chewed her fingernails.

"Well, the only thing I know to do is try to find the nearest house and ask for help."

"In this rain?"

"Not much choice. Besides, I'm already soaked to the bone." Oliver jerked his cap off and studied the sky. "If we wait for it to stop raining, we might be here for a long time."

"How about you and Rose stay here and I'll go try to find some help?" Jack handed Pirate to Rose. The little dog let out a short bark and burrowed into the seat.

"Thanks, Jack, but I'd feel better if you stay here with Rose and Pirate." Oliver put a hand on the car door. "I can run fast."

Rose groaned. "But it's raining so hard."

Oliver chuckled. "I won't melt. It's only water." He opened the door and slammed it behind him, then pulled his cap down low and took off at a trot down the road.

Jack laid a hand on his sister's shoulder over the seat. "Don't worry. Oliver will find help."

Tears trickled down her cheeks. "Oh, Jack. I feel like I've screwed up everything. It's all my fault."

"Bullshit. None of it is your fault. If anything, it's mine and Harlan's fault for not doing something sooner."

"Nothing you could've done." She swiped at her tears and Pirate stood on his hind legs and licked her chin, which prompted her to pick him up and cuddle him. "Maybe so. Just wish I could turn back time."

"Not possible. All we can do is go forward." Jack grinned. "That is, as soon as this wagon will go again."

When she could no longer see Oliver's back, she twisted on the seat. "We're getting so close to Aunt Katherine's. I'm a little scared. What if she don't want us?"

"Then we'll worry about that if and when it happens. We can always go back to Crossett with Oliver and his family." He grabbed a blanket off the seat and wrapped it around his shoulders.

She sighed. "Maybe. But what if the law is looking for us? What then?"

"Rose, don't borrow trouble that you don't know about. Let's just focus on helping Oliver fix the car and get on down the road."

"Hope it's nothing serious."

"I agree with Oliver that it is probably a hole in the oil pan. But we won't know until we can get under it and look."

She peered through the foggy glass. Where did Oliver go? How far would he have to run before he could find help?

Seemed like the world had turned its back on Rose Blaine.

But did she really deserve it? While her heart said no, her mind wasn't sure. Bad luck seemed to follow wherever she went.

Oliver sprinted down the road, hoping against hope to see a house or another car. Plowed fields lying fallow left no doubt they were in a rural farm area.

Thankful that he kept his body in good shape between loading train cars and playing ball, he picked up speed as the rain slowed, wiping the water off his face as it dripped down the bill of his cap.

Some distance ahead, he spotted a driveway. That had to mean there was a house.

He turned into it, splattering his pant legs with mud as he ran. Trees with brilliant hues of fall leaves lined one side of the driveway, while a field full of green, low-growing plants stretched as far as he could see on the other side.

A black and white spaniel dog, followed by a smaller dog, darted toward him, barking.

He slowed to a walk and leaned down, letting the dogs sniff his hand, then scratched behind their ears.

"Hello," a deep voice called out. "Sadie, come here." The dog trotted over while the smaller dog jumped up on Oliver, demanding attention.

"Hello." Taking care not to step on the pup, Oliver strode toward a tall, lean man who wore overalls and a fedora hat.

"Can I help you?"

"Yes, sir. My car broke down a ways back and I'm hoping to find someone who can help us."

"Us?"

"I have two friends with me. Trying to get to St. Louis, but the car just stopped in the middle of the road."

"Come on up to the house," the stranger offered his hand. "I'm Layken Martin."

"Oliver Quinn. Much obliged. Don't want to put anybody out."

"It's no trouble. This rain has kept me out of the fields today, but I'm damned glad to see it. Good for the land. What do you reckon is wrong with your car?"

Oliver matched the man's long strides as they approached a wood frame farmhouse. The sweet fragrance of rain-washed air filled his lungs. A new addition jutted from one side of the modest home, raw wood waiting for paint, while a sizeable tent sat next to the other side of the house. "Not sure. Hit something in the road on the other side of Springfield that gave me a flat tire. Thinking it might've knocked a hole in the oil pan. The engine started knocking, then locked down. And I have a busted belt."

"I'm a pretty good shade-tree mechanic. Happy to go with you and take a look. Just need to tell my wife first."

They went up steps leading to a wide screened-in porch that stretched across the front of the house. Layken held open the front door to the house. "Come on in."

Oliver glanced down at his boots. "Wouldn't want to track mud into the house."

A slight woman with long brown hair braided down her back and a protruding belly stepped into the doorway. "Problem, Layken?"

"This man's car broke down. Gonna go see if I can help him out." Layken turned to Oliver. "This is my wife, Sara Beth."

Sara Beth stuck out her hand. "Pleased to meet you."

Her warm smile lit up dark brown eyes and her small hand got lost in Oliver's large one, yet she had a firm grip. "Likewise, ma'am. Oliver Quinn's the name."

"You're soaked to the bone. Looks like you might be close to Layken's size. Let me get you a change of clothes."

"That's not necessary. Got a feeling I'll be a lot wetter before we get the wagon running again."

"Still. Wouldn't want you to take cold."

Layken grinned at Oliver. "Sara Beth likes to take care of everyone."

"I can see that, and I'm deeply grateful." A pang of homesickness hit Oliver in the gut. His mum always wanted to take care of everyone.

A slender young boy with a mop of dark curls, who looked to be around twelve or thirteen, strode out onto the porch carrying a rabbit under one arm. "What's happening?"

"This man's having some car trouble and Layken's going to see if he can help him." Sara Beth reached for the bunny, and Oliver couldn't help but grin. The bunny was obviously a pet.

"I want to come."

"Not this time, Tab. Need you to stay with Sara Beth." Layken pulled the keys out of his pocket.

"Yes, sir."

What a polite young man.

A tall, white-haired black man with stooped shoulders shuffled into the living room. "Heard the commotion." He pulled up short when he saw Oliver. "Company?"

Layken explained again about the car trouble, then introduced Oliver. "Mr. Quinn, this is Seymour King. He lives here with us."

Oliver offered his hand. "Nice to meet you, Mr. King." He couldn't help wondering about this odd mixture of people. The boy could be Layken's but Seymour King couldn't be any kin. It was none of his business. Yet, he wondered how many more people lived in the small farmhouse.

"Call me Seymour. Mr. King was my father." He shook Oliver's hand. "Want I should come with you'uns?"

"I'd rather you stay with Sara Beth, Uncle Seymour." The old man nodded and laid a hand on Tab's shoulder. "Let's me and you go finish putting away the jars from Sara Beth's canning."

Another glance at Sara Beth left no doubt she was in the family way. Oliver thought about Rose and her condition. Maybe the car breaking down here would be a godsend.

At the least, these people were friendly and willing to help.

And Rose would have another woman to talk to.

She needed that.

Layken kissed Sara Beth on the cheek and pointed to the rusty Dodge pickup parked near the house. "Oliver, let's go see what we can figure out."

Oliver followed him and got inside. "You're obviously a farmer. What kind of crops do you grow?"

Layken started the pickup and nosed it toward the blacktop. "You won't believe it, but when I came back home from the Army last year, I decided to plant peanuts. Folks around here thought I was crazy, but they grow fast, and I easily make two full harvests a year. Plus, they bring in a lot more than wheat or sorghum." He swept a hand toward a field on his right. "I'm getting ready to harvest my second crop this year before the first frost, soon as this rain moves on."

"You were in the Army?"

Layken nodded. "Fought in the war overseas. My folks passed away while I was serving and I came home to a ton of problems, but things are working out."

"I wanted to join the military when the war broke out, but I was too young. Besides, my mum needed me at home. Looks like you're going to be a father soon."

"Never imagined that one. I tell you, son, you never know what life is going to throw at you and if I've learned anything at all, it's to roll with the punches." Layken shot him a glance. "You Irish?"

Oliver grinned. "My folks were from Ireland, but I was born in the United States. Grew up hearing the accent and never lost it. The older boy. Is he your son?"

"Tab? No. Long story behind that one." Layken pointed ahead. "That your wagon?"

"That's her. Sure hope I can get her back on the road soon."

The urgency to get Rose and Jack to St. Louis sat heavy on Oliver's shoulders. They were depending on him and he couldn't let them down.

Lord knows they'd been let down enough in their short lives.

# CHAPTER 19

Oliver exited the pickup when it came to a stop, and Layken followed. Thankful the rain had slowed to a slight mist, the two men hurried toward the Woody Wagon as Jack got out and joined them.

"Jack, this is Layken Martin. He's offered to help us get back on the road."

Jack stuck his hand out. "Much obliged, Mr. Martin."

"Layken, son. You can call me Layken." He turned to Oliver. "Raise the hood and let's take a look."

Oliver released the hood latch and propped it open. He pointed. "There's the busted belt."

Layken pulled the oil stick out. "Not a drop of oil in it. If you've got a hole in the oil pan, it might take a bit to repair it or to get a new one in. I don't suggest trying to crank it. Wouldn't want to throw a rod."

"That's what I thought when it started knocking." Oliver jerked off his cap and ran a hand through his hair, shaking out droplets of water. "Sure hate to delay our trip."

"Looks like you don't have much of a choice." Layken wiped his hands on his overalls. "Let's hook onto her and get it up to the house." He motioned to Jack. "There's a chain in the back of the pickup."

Jack trotted over and returned with a heavy chain. He kneeled and secured it to the Woody Wagon bumper.

Layken turned his pickup around and backed up, then killed the engine. Within a few minutes, he had the other end of the chain attached to his bumper. "We'll take it slow and easy. Put her in neutral and steer. Lucy will do the rest."

"Lucy?" Oliver slammed the hood.

"That's what my dad named this old pickup, and it stuck." Layken chuckled. "Ready?"

Jack hopped into the back of Layken's pickup where he could keep an eye on the chain.

Oliver got inside the Woody Wagon and waved to Layken. After he put it in neutral, he let off the clutch and steered, the tightening of the chain jerking hard, clinking against itself. He glanced at Rose. "These are good folks. Layken's wife wanted to give me dry clothes."

"That was nice of her." Rose clutched Pirate.

"Her name is Sara Beth, and she's in the family way. Might be someone you can talk to that will understand your situation more than me or Jack."

Rose murmured, "It would be nice to talk to another woman." She jolted when the car went over a bump. "But I'm embarrassed."

"You have nothing to be ashamed of, Rose. We have to make the best of what life throws our way." Oliver steered to keep the wagon between the lines while Lucy jerked the wagon forward. "At least that's what Mum always says."

"Your mum is a wonderful woman. I almost wish we'd stayed in Crossett."

"It's not too late. That is, once we get the car fixed." He fought to keep worry from his voice. "Sure hoping this isn't going to be an expensive repair."

"Jack still has his pay. We can pitch in. Maybe you should've taken the money Harlan offered."

Oliver shook his head. "Harlan needed it worse than we did. No way I'd take it. First thing is to find exactly what's wrong." He shot Rose a glance. "We may be stuck on this farm for a few days."

"They say everything happens for a reason, but I swear I can't see the reason for any of this. At least the rain is taking a break." She peered out the window.

"See. Things are already looking up and we've found someone who will help us out." He reached over and scratched the little dog's head. "Pirate's being awful quiet. He's going to have two dogs to play with here."

"He's such a good boy. Hardly needs anything at all." Rose petted him. "Hope my baby is that good."

"I'm glad to hear you talking like the baby is a person, because it is, or will be." Oliver made a hard left as Layken turned into his driveway.

"You're right." She peered ahead. "Looks like an inviting place."

"Pretty sure you'll find that it is. I hate to put people out, but Layken and his wife are welcoming. See, there are the dogs." Both dogs ran to meet them, tongues lolling out and tails wagging. Pirate's ears perked up at their barking and he whined.

Rose pointed toward the tent. "How many people live here?"

"Not exactly sure. I met Layken, his wife, a boy, and an old man. Don't know yet if there are more." He guided the wagon behind the pickup as Layken circled the house, coming to a stop near a barn that appeared to be newer than the house. Oliver opened the car door. "It's okay to get out."

Rose stepped out of the car with Pirate in her arms. The little dog wiggled loose and joined the other dogs, yipping and sniffing while a tabby cat dashed inside the open barn door.

Jack hopped out of the back of the pickup and petted the dogs before disconnecting the chain.

Layken disconnected his end and tossed it into the pickup bed. Then he approached Rose with an outstretched hand. "I'm Layken. Welcome to our home."

She glanced at Oliver, then spoke barely above a whisper. "I'm Rose. Thank you so much."

"No trouble." He pointed toward the house. "Go on up to the house and meet Sara Beth. She's expecting you."

She hesitated. Oliver put a hand on her shoulder. "Want me to go with you?"

She nodded and looked down.

"Rose is shy." He looped an arm through hers.

"Go ahead. Me and Jack will push the car inside the barn. Be easier to work on it out of the weather." Layken turned to Jack. "Son, mind helping me?"

"Happy to." Jack positioned himself at the back of the wagon while Layken took the job of steering and helping push.

"I'll be right back." Oliver noted chickens blissfully clucking and pecking the ground inside their pen and a small herd of goats munching on grain in another pen. The sounds and smells of life in the country brought a certain sense of peace. He knocked on the back door.

Sara Beth opened it and ushered them inside. "Come on in. I've been waiting for you." She wrapped Rose in a quick hug. "I'm Sara Beth. Sure sorry for the troubles you're having, but I have to tell you I'm excited to have another female around to talk to. You have the most beautiful eyes I've ever seen," she gushed. Then she pointed to the old man and boy and began introducing them.

Oliver stayed by the door, mindful of the mud on his shoes, and laid a hand on Rose's shoulder. "You'll be okay with Sara Beth. Gotta go help Layken and Jack."

"Of course." Rose gave a half-smile.

"Thank you, Sara Beth." Oliver turned to go.

Seymour and Tab fell into step with Oliver. "We're coming with you," the old man said.

Oliver nodded. "Happy to have the help."

They left, closing the door behind them while the dogs scampered ahead.

Rose took in the immaculate, though well-used kitchen with flowered curtains hanging limp in the window and worn linoleum covering the floor. Delectable smells came from a pot boiling on the stove and a blue speckled enamel coffeepot sat on a back burner with a low flame.

"Something smells good." Rose turned to Sara Beth. "Is there anything I can help with?"

Sara Beth waved her away. "Goodness no. I've got soup cooking for supper. We've been canning vegetables from the garden all day, but we're done." She put her hands on her back and stretched. "I swear this baby is making it harder to do my chores every day."

Her dark eyes sparkled and Rose had to wonder what it would feel like to have that kind of joy for a new life growing inside her. While she'd managed to make some semblance of peace with her condition, she felt no joy. Maybe that would change when she held the babe in her arms. "I'm a good worker. Happy to help you with anything I can while we're here." A bunny hopped across the floor, startling Rose.

Sara Beth scooped him up, then laughed. "He didn't mean to scare you. This is my pet bunny, Cuddles." She buried her nose in his fur. "We've been through a lot together."

Rose covered her mouth. "Never knew anyone who had a pet rabbit."

"He's the best." She held the bunny out to Rose. "Want to hold him? I'm going to make us some tea and we can talk."

"Sure." Rose took the soft rabbit and held him close, thankful Sara Beth chose not to question the bruises on her face and around her neck, or bandage on her arm. The bunny's nose twitched as he sniffed her.

Sara Beth chatted while she put a teakettle on the stove. "Where are you from, Rose? Oliver said you were on your way to St. Louis."

"We are. Came from Arkansas. Going to an aunt's house. Was hoping to be there by nightfall, but then the car stopped."

"I'm glad Oliver came to us for help. We've got plenty of room for everybody, and like I said, I'm thrilled to have another girl in the house." Sara Beth grabbed two cups from the shelf. "These men are fine company, but don't have a clue about girl stuff."

Rose petted Cuddles and glanced through the doorway into the tidy living room. Something about the home reminded her of Oliver's. Perhaps it was simply the love that made it similar. "Who all lives here with you?"

"Right now, just me, Layken, Tab, and Uncle Seymour. Tab's mother and his brother and sister are gone to visit family in Louisiana and looking to move there."

Rose raised an eyebrow. "Tab isn't your son?"

"It's a long story, but no. Found him living in a tree house in the woods last year, then circumstances forced him to move in with us. He's a great kid."

"A boy living in a tree house?" Rose thought of Jack and his desire for freedom. He'd love living in a tree house in the woods.

"Sad tale. But everything turned out okay, and it got better when we moved his mother and the other kids here. That's why we have the tent. They were staying in it." The teakettle whistled and Sara Beth poured hot water over the tea leaves, then pointed to the table. "Let's sit. I need to rest. Layken is forever getting onto me for being on my feet too much and they swell. Our neighbor, Mrs. Grover, says it's all part of being pregnant."

"I can only imagine." She wondered if Sara Beth had experienced the morning sickness, but couldn't bring herself to ask. "How is the old man your uncle?" Rose put the bunny back onto the floor and dropped into a chair.

"He's not a real uncle. Been with me since I was born. Came here to the farm last year after Layken and I married. We love him like family."

"When's your baby due?"

"According to the doctor, sometime soon. But you never know, especially with the first one." She strained the tea into cups and joined Rose at the table, resting one hand on her stomach. "I cannot wait to hold this baby in my arms, and Layken is almost more excited than me."

Rose wanted more than anything to tell Sara Beth her story, but pride and shame stopped her. How could she admit to this beautiful, happy woman that she'd been raped? She'd bet nothing that ugly had ever touched Sara Beth's world. She blew on the hot tea.

Sara Beth's easy, gentle way had Rose relaxing and enjoying the conversation.

She told about her mother dying, and it shocked her to learn that Sara Beth had lost her mother six years earlier. Rose skirted around the reason for her father's death, but couldn't deny the pity in Sara Beth's eyes when she learned that she and Jack were now orphans.

"What about your father?" Rose lifted her eyes to meet Sara Beth's.

"I have no father." Did Sara Beth's tone harden, or did Rose imagine it? What did that mean? Yet, not wanting to pry, she simply nodded.

Tears sprang into her eyes when Sara Beth reached across the table and laid her hand on top of Rose's. Would she ever get used to kindness? At least she'd managed not to jerk away. That was progress.

While the knowledge that no one would ever hit her again sank in little bits at a time, Rose carried the fresh scars.

Eventually, they would scab over and begin to heal, but it wouldn't happen overnight. It would take some time.

For now, she'd take each small win.

Gratitude washed over her for the unexpected gift of meeting Sara Beth. Something told Rose she'd found a friend who wouldn't judge her.

If only she could find the strength and courage to confide in her.

It would ease her mind to talk about it if the opportunity arose.

Perhaps if they stayed long enough.

# CHAPTER 20

Oliver stepped outside with Seymour at his side, in time to see Layken and Jack struggling to push the Woody Wagon inside the barn. With all the wood panels, the wagon weighed over two-thousand pounds. "Hold up," he called out. "Let us help."

Layken raised up and Jack stood back. "This wagon's heavier than it looks." He motioned to Seymour. "Mind steering while we push?"

"Happy to." Seymour got behind the wheel while the others pushed from behind.

With everyone putting muscle behind it, the wagon easily rolled inside the barn.

Jack let out a low whistle. "Nice barn."

Tab laughed. "Shoulda' seen what was left of it last year after Earl burned it down."

"Really? Who is Earl?" Jack glanced around, as if half expecting someone to jump out. The only movement came from the cat, who prowled through a stack of wood looking for a meal.

Layken interrupted. "Tab, how about you and Jack go grab those blocks we saved in the back."

"Is Tab serious?" Oliver pulled his cap lower. "Your barn burned?"

"Another long story, but it's true. Then all the neighbors came together to help us tear it down and rebuild. That's how we do things around here."

Seymour joined them. "Beat anything I ever seen."

"This must be a great community of people. Back home, my mum is always taking food or clothes to someone in need," Oliver said.

Layken nodded. "Exactly the way it's supposed to be. Neighbors helping neighbors is what makes this country great." He ran a hand through his hair. "With this cloud cover, it'll get dark early this evening. Won't be able to see much in here, but we can start tearing into it tomorrow. With any luck, we'll know by the end of the day what it's going to take to fix it."

Oliver leaned against the side of the car. "I'm sure you've got your own stuff to tend to, Layken. Me and Jack can work on the car, or we can help you with whatever you have going on."

Layken scrubbed the back of his neck. "Peanuts are ready to harvest once this rain moves on. I could sure use another set of hands, but I know you're anxious to get back on the road."

"We are. But still, we'd be happy to help with the harvest."

The two boys returned with arms full of wooden blocks, which they dropped next to the car.

"Thanks, guys. Let's go ahead and get it jacked up before we call it quits. Sara Beth will be expecting us at the house soon. But you do know we are going to have to lift the engine to get to the oil pan, don't you?"

Oliver rubbed his chin. "Hadn't thought that far ahead."

Layken lifted the hood and peered inside. "Going to have to remove the hoses and the radiator, then unbolt the engine, if it is indeed a hole in the oil pan, as you suspect. Still, we need to jack it up to get to the motor mounts."

Oliver nodded and opened the back of the wagon to get the jack. "Once we finish, I'll need to clean up some before I go to the house. Reckon I could change into clean clothes here in the barn?"

"Sure. You'll find a sink with running water in the back next to Uncle Seymour's bedroom. But you're more than welcome to use the bathroom in the house." Layken pointed toward a section of the barn partitioned off. "Tab, you and Jack go on to the house and let Sara Beth know we'll be along shortly."

Seymour scratched at the wiry stubble on his chin. "I'll stay and help you two."

"Much appreciated, Mr. King." Oliver dropped the jack next to the car.

"Son, call me Seymour. We're not formal around here."

"Thanks, Seymour. Appreciate it." He'd forgotten the old man had asked him to call him by his given name when he'd met him earlier.

Between the three men, they made quick work of jacking up the wagon and setting it on the blocks. Tomorrow, they'd find out what was wrong.

Layken and Seymour moseyed toward the house while Oliver stripped off the wet muddy clothes and cleaned up. He hung the discards over the wooden partition, ran a hand through his hair, and jammed his paddy cap on his head.

He entered the house in time to see Layken embrace Sara Beth, then order her to sit while he took over in the kitchen. The concern the man showed his wife touched Oliver. That's exactly the kind of man he wanted to be, just as his father had been. He glanced at Rose as he hung his cap on a peg next to Layken's, happy to see her relaxed and smiling for a change. Good. Although the dark circles under her eyes betrayed the weariness.

Tab had taken Jack on a tour through the house and could be heard bragging about how he'd helped Layken build the new addition that was now his bedroom. Pride reflected in the young boy's tone. Despite the boy having a mother and siblings, it appeared he was at the farm to stay.

Seymour busied himself stacking logs in the living room fireplace and lighting a fire to chase away the damp chill in the fall evening air.

The only thing that could make the scene more complete would be if Oliver's mum and sisters were there. He liked the feel of this farm and these people, but he missed his family, and now, with a delay, he'd have to find a telephone and call her.

Sara Beth motioned to an empty chair next to Rose. "Have a seat, Oliver. I apologize that I can't properly serve you supper, but my husband has banished me from the kitchen." She raised a hand to fan her face. "Yet, I have to admit, he looks mighty fine in an apron."

Layken stirred the soup and bent over to pull a pan out of the oven. "Flattery will get you everywhere, dear wife. But we all know I can't begin to compete with your kitchen skills."

"Whatever it is sure smells good." Oliver's stomach growled. Had it been that long since they'd eaten? Indeed, hours had passed since leaving the cafe in Springfield. "There's a basket of food my mum packed for us in the wagon. I'm happy to contribute."

"Tonight's on us." Layken jerked his hand away from a hot cast-iron skillet of cornbread, then reached for a towel. "We want you to feel at home."

Sara Beth pointed to the cabinet. "Don't forget the butter, honey."

Layken reached for the butter dish and called out, "Boys, Seymour, come and get it. Supper's ready. Oliver, mind helping me grab some extra chairs?"

"Sure thing." Oliver followed Layken to the front porch. They returned with a chair under each arm.

Layken set the soup and cornbread in the middle of the table. "Dig in. Don't be bashful."

Once everyone had food, Tab stared hard at Rose with his mouth full. "What happened to you, lady?"

Rose choked on a reply, and Jack jumped in. "She had an accident, Tab. But she'll be fine."

"Tab, first of all, her name is Rose, not lady, and second of all, it's rude to ask things like that," Sara Beth gently admonished the boy.

He ducked his head. "Sorry."

"It's okay, Tab." Rose blushed. "It's what Jack said."

"Oliver, if you don't mind me asking, are you and Rose a couple?" Layken spread butter on the hot cornbread.

"We're friends. I offered to bring Rose and Jack to St. Louis." Oliver ladled soup into his bowl. "Wasn't anticipating car trouble. The Woody has been great. Guessing I shoulda kept a closer eye on that oil stick."

Jack swallowed a mouthful. "It was raining so hard in Springfield, the man at the gas station didn't bother to check anything."

"We'll get it figured out." Layken turned to Sara Beth. "Oliver said they could stay long enough for him and Jack to help me get the peanuts in."

Sara Beth beamed. "That's so generous. The way Layken works, it goes quick."

"It's the least we can do to show our gratitude for your hospitality." Oliver nodded at Jack. "Right, Jack?"

"Right. Happy to help. Never worked on a farm before. But me and Oliver worked in the sawmill back home. Not afraid of hard work." Jack reached for a second piece of cornbread.

Layken laid a hand on Sara Beth's arm. "I know you all must be exhausted. About sleeping arrangements for the night, what do you think, sweetheart?"

"Let's give Rose your old room. I'll just need to move my sewing off the bed. If the boys don't mind, they can sleep in the tent."

"We have cots, so camping out is not a problem." Oliver couldn't help but be grateful Rose would have a real bed. She needed rest. The way she barely nibbled her food told him she wasn't feeling well.

"That will work out perfectly." Sara Beth flashed a smile.

"Can I camp out in the tent with Jack and Oliver?" Tab leaned across the table.

"Okay by me, if they don't mind."

"Sure, Tab. That'd be just fine." Oliver grinned at the boy. "Say, you ever play baseball?"

The boy's eyes lit up. "Sometimes me and Layken toss around a ball when he's not too tired."

Layken chuckled. "The downside of getting older and working hard. I used to love to play with the local boys in town."

"My dream is to play in the big leagues." Oliver took a sip of water. "That's part of why I'm on the way to St. Louis. Rose and Jack have an uncle that used to play for the Browns. I want a shot at trying out for the team."

Tab bounced his knee and squinted one eye. "Man, that'd be super great, Oliver. We listen to all the ball games on the radio."

"It's just a dream, but you never know if you don't try."

"That's good advice, son. Dreams are what built America." Layken dipped a spoon into his soup bowl.

"Exactly what my father used to say. My folks immigrated from Ireland with dreams of a better life." Oliver pointed his spoon at Tab. "You've got a great opportunity here, Tab. Do you go to school?"

Tab sat up straighter. "Sure do. The bus comes and takes me into Everton. I love school. They serve great food."

Layken laughed. "Hope that's not the only reason you like school, Tab. You're there to learn and have a chance at a better life."

Jack's voice took on deep longing. "I'd love the chance to go back to school. Think they'd take me in Everton? I'm already sixteen, really too old for school."

"Never too old for school, Jack." Layken pushed back from the table. "Stick around here and we'll make sure you get a good education."

Rose glanced up. "You can go to school in St. Louis, Jack."

Jack looked down. "It's a big town. What if kids make fun of me?"

"Then we'll deal with that if and when it happens, but you're going to school and that's final." Rose doubled over and wrapped her arms around her stomach. Fear filled her eyes. "I'm not feeling well."

Oliver and Jack both jumped to their feet at the same time

Sara Beth pushed away from the table. "Come with me, Rose. You've had a long day. Let's get you settled in your room."

Layken joined his wife, and they led Rose down the hallway to the bedroom, with Oliver, Jack, and Tab trailing behind.

Sara Beth turned around. "Go back to your supper, boys. I'll take care of Rose."

"We need to change the bandage on her arm." Oliver ran a hand through his hair. "The doctor said to clean the wound and apply fresh dressing every couple of days."

Jack turned. "I'll go get the clean bandages, and Rose's clothes."

Oliver fought against worry as it claimed a big spot in his gut. Rose was just tired. It had been a long day for everyone.

At least, he hoped that was all.

She'd been through so much.

Was it catching up to her?

Was her body trying to reject the horrible man's baby inside her?

Hopefully, she'd feel better tomorrow.

# CHAPTER 21

After Layken left the room, Rose sat on the side of the bed, while Sara Beth gently removed the bandage from her arm, then fetched supplies to clean it. She avoided looking into the woman's eyes, afraid of what Sara Beth would see. The clink of silverware against bowls and rumble of male conversation let her know the men had continued with their meal.

Thank goodness.

She hoped they wouldn't consider it bad manners, the abrupt way she'd left the table, but the sharp pain had frightened her.

No doubt Oliver and Jack would be worried. A knock on the door made her jump.

"Yes?" Sara Beth opened the door.

Oliver handed her a fresh bandage and the bundle of Rose's clothes. He peeked around Sara Beth. "Rose? You okay?"

"Just tired, Oliver. Thanks." Debilitating fatigue washed over her, leaving her weak and helpless.

Sara Beth shooed him away, applied the fresh bandage, and straightened. She laid a gentle hand on Rose's cheek. "Get some rest, dear. Tomorrow will be better."

Rose grabbed her hand. "Could you sit with me for a minute?"

Sara Beth dropped beside her onto the bed. "Of course, dear. Is there anything I can get for you?"

Music from the radio filtered through the closed door, only interrupted by the low timbre of male voices.

"No. Nothing. But I would like to tell you something."

"You can tell me anything, Rose. I know your bruises aren't from an accident. Only fingers leave those kinds of marks. You're carrying a big burden and it's going to take a toll on your health. Let me help." She smoothed back Rose's hair.

Tears sprang unbidden in Rose's eyes. "It's hard to talk about."

"Most big things are. I'm a good listener. Would another cup of tea help?"

Rose nodded, not trusting her voice.

"Then wait right here and I'll be back in no time."

As soon as Sara Beth closed the door behind her, Rose lay back and buried her face in the feather pillow, inhaling the crisp clean covering. The coil springs beneath the mattress creaked.

What was she thinking? Could she really confide in Sara Beth? She had to admit the woman's kindness made it seem easy.

She regretted causing a scene and more worry for Oliver and Jack, but the pain had been severe and scared her more than she'd willingly admit.

Thank goodness it passed almost as quickly as it came. She closed her eyes and waited for Sara Beth to return.

When the door opened again, Layken accompanied Sara Beth, setting a tray on the nightstand. He laid a hand on Rose's shoulder. "I hope you'll feel better by morning."

"Thank you," Rose managed.

Layken kissed his wife on the cheek and closed the door behind him.

Rose pushed up to a sitting position, her back resting against the iron bedstead. "I truly don't know how to thank you enough."

Sara Beth waved her hand in dismissal. "Don't even think about it." She passed Rose a cup of steaming tea, took one for herself, and settled onto the side of the bed. "Now, what was it you wanted to talk about?"

Rose blew on the hot tea, relishing the way warm moisture caressed her face and how the soothing fragrance of chamomile danced around her nostrils. Cradling the cup between her hands, she let out a long sigh. "I'll start at the beginning."

Over the next half hour, through bouts of sobbing, Rose recounted her mother's death, her father's disappearance into alcohol, and the escalation of violence.

Sara Beth only interrupted once. "Why didn't you go to the authorities?"

"Pa always made sure we lived out away from everything and everyone. He kept a tight rein on where we went and when. Never had a chance. Tried running away once, and it took a month to recover from that beating. Besides, who'd believe me?" Rose sipped the tea and continued her story, eventually ending with the rape. "So, now I'm going to have a baby, and Pa and the man who raped me are dead. It was Pa who gave me these bruises. He intended to kill me. He said horrible things and called me unspeakable names."

Sara Beth drew in a sharp breath and took the teacup from Rose. She drew Rose into her arms. "Oh, sweet girl, I am so sorry." She rocked her back and forth.

"I don't know what to do or how I'm going to get through this," Rose sobbed.

"I'll tell you what you're going to do." Sara Beth let go and leaned back, handing Rose a handkerchief. "You're going to take the best care of yourself that you can and hope for a healthy baby."

"But what about the rest of my life? All I want is a chance to live without fear of being hit, to get an education and experience things like a normal teenager. And now what?" She blew her nose and twisted the handkerchief in her hands.

"I understand, but the good Lord obviously has other plans for you. I hate to say it, but I'm glad your car broke down here."

Rose blew her nose and wiped away her tears. "Jack and Oliver know. I had to tell them everything, because Oliver had to keep stopping for me to throw up with the morning sickness. He offered to take us to our aunt in St. Louis out of the kindness of his heart. He also offered to marry me and give the baby a name." She glanced up. "Of course, I couldn't let him do that. If and when I ever marry, it will have to be because of love, not pity or desperation. Will you tell Layken? I'll be so embarrassed."

"I can assure you Layken will not judge. In fact, he will be fit to be tied and want justice for you."

Rose managed a weak smile. "Same as Oliver and Jack."

"See. You're surrounded by people who care about you, and we'll make sure you get everything you need, including a thorough exam by the doctor."

Rose closed her eyes, letting Sara Beth's words sink in. Truthfully, she did feel the love and concern from everyone, even if she didn't deserve it.

Sara Beth stood. "I'm going to let you get some rest. Please, if you need anything at all or if the pain comes back, we're in the room right next door. Promise me you'll make yourself at home."

"I promise. Thank you." Before Sara Beth had completely closed the door, balancing the tray in one hand, Rose had snuggled beneath the covers and gave into exhaustion.

---

Oliver jumped to his feet when Sara Beth entered the living room. "Is she okay?"

Layken took the tray from his wife and pointed to the couch without a word as he strode toward the kitchen.

Sara Beth sat, cradling her unborn baby with both hands. "She's exhausted and after the trauma she's been through, it's a wonder she's still standing."

Oliver glanced at Jack, who raised one eyebrow. "She told you?"

Sara Beth nodded.

"Told you what?" Tab turned away from the radio in obvious curiosity.

"None of your business, young man." Sara Beth shook her finger at him. "Besides, you need to be getting ready for bed if you're going to camp out. Uncle Seymour already go to bed?"

Layken returned from the kitchen and joined Sara Beth. He put a protective arm around her shoulders and scooted the coffee table closer. Then he picked up Sara Beth's feet and propped them on the table. "Turned in earlier. The old man is moving slower these days. Says the cooler weather makes his bones ache."

Sara Beth frowned. "Let's try to make sure he takes it a little easier, especially now that Jack and Oliver are here to help with the harvest."

Oliver loved the unspoken concern and affection that passed between the couple. "Me and Jack are more than happy to help. We were at a loss about what to do for Rose. I stopped along the way and bought her 7-Up and crackers. Thought that might make her feel better." A log shifted in the fireplace, sending a spray of sparks.

Sara Beth waited until Tab left the room before continuing. "She needs to see a doctor and let him give her a thorough examination."

Oliver nodded. "I agree. And I have to find a telephone to call my mum."

"We'll tear into the car first thing in the morning. Then at least we'll know what we're dealing with." Layken rubbed Sara Beth's shoulders. "Everton's a small town, but it has a good doctor."

Jack stood and stretched. "I'm going to fetch our cots from the Woody. Anything else?"

Sara Beth leaned over to pick up Cuddles, then slipped off her shoes and adjusted her feet on the table. "You don't have to do that unless you just want to. There are beds and covers in the tent." She pointed down the hall. "The bathroom is the second door on the left."

Oliver turned to Jack. "Can you check on Pirate for me and bring in the food basket?"

Tab hurried back through with a pillow and blanket under one arm. "Sara Beth, can Sadie, Pearl, and Pirate camp out in the tent with us? I'll make sure they're not muddy."

"Okay by me if it's okay with Jack and Oliver."

"We don't mind." Oliver grinned at the boy.

Jack motioned to him. "Want to come with me, Tab?"

Once they left the room, Oliver turned to Sara Beth and Layken. "I'm plenty worried about Rose. She's been through so much. She's plagued with nightmares and flashbacks."

Layken's eyebrows shot up. "What are you talking about?"

"I'll let Sara Beth fill you in, but I'm glad she confided in someone." Oliver got to his feet when the boys came back inside.

Layken pointed to the kitchen cabinet. "Just set the basket there so Sara Beth and Rose can go through it tomorrow. You younguns have lots of troubles. We're happy to help you out."

Oliver motioned to Tab and Jack. "You guys go ahead. I'll be there in a minute. Pirate okay?"

"Pirate's having the time of his life with Sadie and Pearl." Jack motioned to Tab. "Lead the way."

As the two younger boys left, Oliver faced Layken and Sara Beth. "Thank you both for everything. I sincerely mean that from all three of us."

"Our pleasure." Layken switched off the radio. "Make yourselves at home and tomorrow we'll figure out what to do next."

Sara Beth pushed up from the couch and hugged Oliver with one arm. "What Layken said."

Oliver went through the front door as Sara Beth and Layken turned out lights.

He glanced up at the clear sky, sparkling with bright stars.

The storms had passed, leaving the smell of wet dirt and cool fall air behind. The tall trees rustled in the wind.

Was that the scent of hope for better days ahead?

Oliver had to believe that maybe it was.

A shooting star caught his eye as he neared the tent. He took a second to make a wish—a wish for Rose to feel better, for Jack to find a happy life, and a chance for Oliver to live his dream.

Not too much to ask for.

He opened the tent flap and stepped inside. Tab had lit a lantern and the three dogs settled comfortably on a blanket in the corner, with Pirate between the two girls.

Jack, with his arms behind his head, lay stretched out on a single mattress with Tab next to him on a smaller cot.

"Figured to give you the bigger bed." Jack pointed to the other side of the tent.

"Tired as I am, the ground would feel just as good." Oliver rubbed the dogs' heads, slipped off his boots, and dropped onto the mattress.

"We're lucky, Oliver." Jack turned his head toward him.

"Lucky indeed, Jack." While worry niggled the back of his mind, Oliver had to agree. They couldn't have known this farm would provide what they all needed, especially Rose.

He considered for a minute that the doctor might advise against Rose traveling. Then what? They couldn't stay here indefinitely.

Oliver released a heavy sigh as Tab blew out the lantern. Soft snores soon filled the tent.

Tomorrow would hopefully bring answers.

Remembering his mother's often shared advice not to worry about unknowns, Oliver turned onto his side.

Once he knew what it would take to repair the car, he could make some decisions.

But what about Rose? Would a doctor be able to give her the relief she needed?

He fell into an exhausted slumber, his mind filled with questions and likely scenarios.

# CHAPTER 22

The next day dawned clear and crisp with the lingering scent of rain-washed earth. Oliver left the two younger boys sleeping and made his way toward the smell of coffee. The three dogs followed him, tails wagging, their breath fogging in the cool air.

He prayed that Rose had slept well and would feel better. Once again, he was thankful for Sara Beth and Layken and their generous hospitality.

As he rounded the corner of the house, Uncle Seymour came from the barn, hitching up his suspenders. The old man waved a greeting.

Oliver paused to wait for him. "Mornin'."

"Looks like it's going to be a good day." Seymour motioned toward the awakening sky. "Not a cloud in sight so far."

"A welcome relief after the storms." Oliver held the back door open while Seymour lumbered inside. Then he followed, mindful of the older man's slower steps.

The blue speckled enamel coffeepot simmered on the stove. Cuddles munched on a bowl of lettuce in the corner and Layken sat at the table sipping on a cup. A row of empty cups occupied a space on the kitchen counter. "Hope you slept okay, Oliver."

"Yes sir. The tent was comfortable."

Sara Beth tied an apron around her plump middle and placed a kiss on the old man's cheek. "You went to bed early last night, Uncle Seymour. You feelin' okay?"

"Fit enough. Arthritis acting up a bit."

She filled two cups and handed them to Seymour and Oliver. "You're not getting any younger. You need to take it easy. Once I gather eggs, I'll fix breakfast."

Layken pushed up from the table. "I'll get the eggs, sweetheart."

She smiled. "And wake up Tab. Don't want him to miss the bus."

Oliver took a welcome sip of the black coffee and set his cup down. "Please allow me to get the eggs. It's the least I can do."

Sara Beth handed him a basket. "Rose is already up. She's in the bathroom."

Oliver took the basket. "Sick?"

Sara Beth nodded. "But I'm making her some ginger tea Mrs. Grover told me about when I first had the morning sickness."

"You're a lifesaver, Sara Beth." He headed outside toward the chicken coop. While Oliver had never gathered eggs, he figured it couldn't be that hard.

Sara Beth called out the door. "Grab a scoop of feed and scatter it on the ground. They'll all get off their nests."

Oliver nodded, thankful for the tip.

Layken fell in step next to him. "I'll wake up Tab. One of his chores is to milk the goats. I take it you've never done farm work?"

"No. But I'm a fast learner."

Layken pointed to a metal bucket. "Chicken feed's in there. It makes the old gals forget all about their eggs."

Oliver pushed his cap back and flipped the lid off the bucket. Armed with a scoop of feed, he bent over and stepped into the chicken coop. The hens clucked softly and eyed him warily as the scent of wet hay tickled his nostrils. "Here you go, girls." He scattered the feed on the ground and one by one, the hens abandoned their nests, making gathering the eggs easy.

Tab and Jack rounded the corner of the house, followed by Layken and all three dogs. Oliver waved to them, and Jack sauntered up to the coop. "You look like a natural-born farmer, Irish. Tab's gonna show me how to milk the goats."

Oliver chuckled. "Looks like we're both getting a crash course." He stepped out of the pen with a full basket.

Layken took the basket from Oliver. "Soon as we eat a bite, we'll get started on the car."

"The sooner the better, so at least I'll know what I'm dealing with."

The two men headed back inside the house, while Tab and Jack went into the goat pen.

Rose sat at the table next to Seymour, cradling a steaming cup. A slight tinge of pink on her cheeks contrasted with the circles under her eyes.

Oliver jerked his cap off. "Morning, Rose. Did you sleep well?"

"Best sleep I've had in weeks. Even the nightmares left me alone for a change."

Oliver reached for his coffee and pulled out a chair. "Glad to hear that." He laid a hand on her thin arm. "And today we're going to take you to see a doctor."

She ducked her head. "Never seen no doctor before. It's kinda scary."

Sara Beth cracked eggs while Layken set a skillet on the stove for her. "Nothing scary about Doctor Jennings. He's very kind. He's been taking care of me through this pregnancy." She shooed her husband away. "Drink your coffee. I've got this."

Layken grinned. "Just trying to help."

"And I love you for it, but you're in my way."

Oliver chuckled. "Nothing like brutal honesty."

Tab and Jack came inside, a wide grin covering Jack's face. "I milked a goat."

Rose gasped. "You did what?"

"Tab showed me how to milk a goat." He held up the bucket. "And it worked."

Sara Beth took the bucket, then pointed toward the hallway. "Tab, get ready for school. I'll have breakfast on the table in a few minutes. The bus will be here soon."

Oliver didn't miss the longing that crossed Jack's face. "Once we get to St. Louis, you can enroll in school."

Jack shuffled his feet. "What if I don't go on to St. Louis?"

"What are you talking about, Jack?" Rose set her cup down. "We're in this together, remember?"

"I know, sis, but Tab's been telling me all about the school in Everton and how there's all different ages of kids and some are farm kids that have to miss school to help with the harvest and still the teachers make sure they don't fall behind. I just think I'd stand a better chance in a small school."

"Nothing that you have to decide today." Oliver said. "Besides, it would ultimately be up to Layken and Sara Beth if they want to take on another mouth to feed."

Jack drew himself up to full height. "I can carry my own weight. Wouldn't be a burden."

Sara Beth stirred the eggs. "Jack, you'd be more than welcome to stay here with us. But as Oliver said, it's nothing you have to decide today."

Tab joined them at the table, his face washed and hair combed. "I'd love it if Jack would stay. I'd have an older brother."

Oliver reflected on his own thoughts a few days ago about having Jack as a brother. The younger boy's carefree personality and quick smile made it easy.

Sara Beth placed a platter mounded with scrambled eggs and biscuits in the middle of the table. "Don't put pressure on Jack, Tab. Let's see how this all plays out. Now, eat up."

Silence fell around the table, each lost in their thoughts, as they ate.

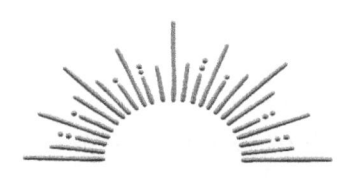

All except for Rose. She slowly sipped the ginger tea and pondered the idea of Jack staying behind on the farm. While she'd hate to go on alone, she couldn't begrudge Jack for wanting to go to school.

She wanted the same thing, only that wasn't in the cards for her. Amos Parker had seen to that. The very thought of his name brought shudders.

Thankful no one noticed, she continued to sip the tea, longing for a biscuit and a bite of eggs. But she didn't dare for fear it would send her back to the bathroom.

Tab finished eating first, dropped his empty plate in the kitchen sink, and made a beeline for the front door. "Going to wait for the bus."

"Have a good day, Tab." Sara Beth buttered another biscuit.

"See you later, son." Layken pushed back from the table and stood. "Oliver, you and Jack about ready to get started?"

Jack swiped another biscuit and finished off his coffee. "Thanks for breakfast, Sara Beth."

Oliver gathered his empty plate and stood. "Ready. And yes, thank you for breakfast. I'm sure you have work to do, Layken. Me and Jack can handle it."

"I don't doubt that you can, but you're stuck with me helping. It's too wet to start harvesting anyway." Layken kissed Sara Beth on the cheek. "Promise me you won't overdo it today, sweetheart."

Sara Beth flashed a wide smile. "I promise. I'm going to do some sewing. Nothing heavy."

Seymour pushed his chair back. "Great breakfast, as always, little girl." He wobbled as he stood, and Sara Beth jumped up and grabbed his arm. "Uncle Seymour. What's wrong?"

The old man ran a hand across his wiry stubble. "Nothin' but old age and arthritic knees."

Layken stepped forward. "Why don't you take it easy today, Seymour? There's nothing that needs tending to that can't wait."

"Believe I will, son. If you need me, I'll be in my room." Seymour lumbered out the door toward the barn.

Rose didn't miss the glance that passed between Sara Beth and Layken. Worry clouded Sara Beth's eyes. "Please keep an eye on him, honey."

"I will. Try not to worry."

Layken, Oliver, and Jack followed Seymour out, while Sara Beth gathered up the remaining dishes.

"Let me clean up the kitchen, Sara Beth." Rose stood. "I need to do something that makes me feel normal."

"If you're sure." Sara Beth blew out a sigh. "I really do want to get some sewing done today. Been making blankets and things for the baby. And I keep having to expand my wardrobe to match my growing belly."

"I'm good with a needle and thread if you need any help." Rose filled the sink with hot water and added soap.

"That'd be great. Sewing relaxes me." Sara Beth untied her apron and hung it on a nail. "Come on to the living room when you're done in here."

Rose considered what it might feel like to prepare for a joyous birth instead of a dreaded one. She laid a hand on her flat stomach and tried to imagine the tiny life forming, but couldn't fathom it. While apprehension about seeing a doctor lingered, another part of her hoped he might be able to help.

A flashback of her father punching her hard in the stomach brought unbidden tears and a hard gasp. It was almost as if she could feel it all over again and a sharp pain shot through her abdomen.

She gripped the edge of the counter and drew in slow breaths until the cramp subsided. Picking up each dish, she dropped them into the soapy water and stared out the kitchen window at the three dogs running and playing. Pirate fit right in here. And Jack did as well. How would she be able to force herself to go on to St. Louis by herself? Yet she couldn't make Jack go with her.

When they went into town, she would call Aunt Katherine. If she didn't want Rose to come, there would be no choice but to return to Arkansas. If she wasn't wanted, it would be better to know that now rather than later.

She methodically washed and dried each dish, putting them away on the shelves, then dried her hands on a dishtowel and joined Sara

Beth in the living room where she hunched over an electric sewing machine.

Rose peered over her shoulder. "You have an electric machine? I've only seen them in stores."

Sara Beth glanced up. "It belonged to Layken's mother."

"Oh, do they still live around here?"

"No. Both of them passed away while Layken was in the Army. He was the sole heir to this farm."

Rose pulled up a chair and Sara Beth handed her a tiny nightgown. "This needs a hem, if you want to help."

She took the soft cotton garment from Sara Beth and reached for a needle sticking out of a pincushion. "If you don't mind me asking, how did you and Layken meet? You seem so well suited for each other."

Sara Beth let out a chuckle. "You won't believe this, but the man who called himself my father forced me to marry Layken. It was nothing more than a business arrangement at first."

"How awful. Why did he force you to marry?" Rose threaded the needle.

"Long story, so I'll give you the short version." Sara Beth leaned down and picked up Cuddles, settling him on her lap. "Homer Williams is the banker in Everton. Layken's father had taken out a bank loan and when he died, the loan went unpaid. So that meant Layken inherited the debt along with the farm. Homer wanted to remarry and needed me out of the house. So, he made a bargain with Layken that if he'd marry me, he'd give him two years to pay off the note. Otherwise, he'd foreclose on the farm and Layken would lose everything."

Rose gasped. "So, you and Layken didn't know each other before?"

"No. We first saw each other at the courthouse when we got married." Sara Beth stroked the bunny's ears. "Believe me, it was awkward as all get-out."

"I can imagine." Rose deftly wove the needle in and out of the fabric.

"But as we worked together to save the farm, we fell in love. Now I can't imagine any other kind of a life. And we are so close to paying off the debt. Layken figures when he brings in the crop that's in the field now, we'll be able to take care of it and be free from Homer Williams for good."

Rose contemplated what Sara Beth shared. It proved that other people had struggles, too. Somehow, that thought made her feel less alone, less different.

As far as she could tell, no one skated through life without problems.

It helped somewhat to see what others had faced and how they'd overcome.

Perhaps she could do the same. She squared her shoulders and lifted her chin.

She'd for sure give it her best shot.

# CHAPTER 23

Several hours later, inside the musty barn, Oliver leaned the dirty oil pan against the side of the wagon. And while the hole in the pan wasn't huge, the car wasn't going anywhere until it was either repaired or replaced. He hadn't counted on all the work involved in disconnecting all the hoses and removing the radiator to lift the engine high enough to clear the cross-member. It was the only way to get to the damaged oil pan. Layken rigged a pulley with a chain thrown over a barn rafter and together, the men pulled until the engine swung above the Woody. Layken wrapped the end of the chain around a post and secured it.

"You're lucky the hole wasn't any bigger, or you wouldn't have made it as far as you did." Layken wiped dirt off his overalls and shooed the cat away that wound around his legs.

"Are there any garages in Everton?" Oliver pulled a rag out of his back pocket and wiped the grime off his hands.

"A couple. Main thing you'll have to decide is if you want to order in a new pan or have this one welded." Layken lifted the broken fan belt. "This part will be easy enough to replace and you can probably get it today, but the oil pan is a different story."

Jack crawled from under the car with a wrench in his hand, only to be met with Pirate's wet kisses. He ruffled the scruffy little dog's fur. "A good weld can hold for years, and I'm sure it costs less than a replacement."

Oliver nodded. "I 'spect you're right, Jack. Guess we'll find out soon enough." He couldn't help hoping for a quick solution so they could get back on the road, although he'd already committed to helping Layken harvest the crop. Either way, they'd be there a few more days.

And maybe that was a good thing, as Rose seemed to be more relaxed than he'd seen her, even though the morning sickness continued.

"I reckon we can head on into town if Rose is up to it." Layken paused. "But first I need to check on Seymour. He doesn't seem to be himself lately and Sara Beth is plenty worried. Maybe I can talk him into coming with us and seeing the doctor."

Oliver picked up the oil pan. "I'll put this in the back of your truck and go check on Rose."

Jack fell into step next to him. "I sure do like it here, Oliver. I know Rose is dead-set on going to Aunt Katherine's, but she's in a different situation than me."

Oliver clapped him on the shoulder. "Let's just see how it all plays out. Say, since it's too muddy to work in the field this afternoon, how about we get a baseball game going when Tab gets home from school?"

"He's a nice kid. If I had ever had a little brother, I would've wanted him to be like Tab."

Oliver glanced at Jack. "Did Tab tell you how he came to be here?"

"A little. Seems like he got beat up pretty bad by a man living with his mother, so he ran away and built a tree house in the forest. You gotta admire that kind of spunk."

"He couldn't have been very old. That took a lot of courage."

Jack kicked at the soft dirt. "I shoulda' took Rose and ran away." The muscle in his jaw tensed. "If only I'd paid more attention."

"Don't beat yourself up, Jack. You couldn't have known."

"I didn't know she was getting raped, but I knew about all the beatings she took. Wasn't right. Nothing about it was right. It's like we were all stuck in a nightmare with no way out. I can see that so clearly now."

Oliver stopped walking and faced Jack. "The past is over. All we can do is make the future better. We're taking Rose to the doctor in Everton and thinking positive that he can help her feel better."

"Sure hope so."

"I know both you and Rose worry about Harlan, but I think he's capable of taking care of himself. He certainly stepped up to protect you both at the end." Oliver laid a hand on the boy's shoulder. "I'm proud of you for sticking with Rose."

Jack glanced away. "But if I decide to stay here, I'll feel like I'm letting her down."

"I have a feeling she'll understand. And I know she wants what's best for you, just like you do her."

Layken caught up with them before they reached the house. "The old man is certainly under the weather. I've never seen him take to the bed during the day. But he refuses to go see the doctor. Says an aspirin will cure his ailments."

"Sure sorry to hear that. Maybe it's just the change in the weather."

"Could be. Don't really know how old he is. He's never said, but he's certainly gone downhill in the past year." Layken pointed toward his pickup. "Drop the pan in there and let's see if Rose is ready to go."

Oliver nodded. "Jack, you going with us or staying here?"

"If there's room, I'd like to go. I'm curious about the town. Besides, I can ride in the back. Maybe we could drive by the school?"

"Sure thing." Layken shot him a grin.

While Layken and Jack went inside, Oliver placed the damaged oil pan in the back of the pickup, then hurried to join the rest.

When he stepped inside, Rose was finishing the last stitch in a hem on a tiny garment. He swallowed hard. Being around Sara Beth and seeing her so joyful about her baby had to be bittersweet for Rose.

Yet, she offered to help sew baby clothes. Perhaps it was therapeutic.

She glanced up. "I'll be ready to go in a few minutes." Uncertainty reflected in her violet-blue eyes. "You sure you want me to see a doctor? Won't it cost money?"

"We're sure." Oliver, Layken, and Sara Beth answered in unison, which brought a tiny hint of a smile to Rose's face.

Oliver added, "And don't worry about money. The main thing is that you get to feeling better."

She placed the sewing on a table and stood. "I guess so."

Sara Beth put Cuddles down and stretched. "It's not a guess so, it's a know so. Go on and don't be afraid. I promise you, Doctor Jennings will be gentle."

"Fine." Rose turned to Jack. "You going?"

"Yep. I want to see the town and Layken said he'd drive past the school."

She smoothed back her hair. "I'm happy you're interested in school."

"Rose, it's chilly outside. Do you have a sweater or coat?" Sara Beth leaned into Layken as he stood behind her and kissed the top of her head.

"No. We left in a big hurry, didn't have time to grab much."

"Well, then, lucky for you, I'm too fat to fit into any of my clothes right now and I have a sweater you can have. Same for you, Jack. Layken has an extra jacket you can borrow."

"Thanks." Jack glanced at Rose and grinned.

Sara Beth waddled down the hallway and returned with a sweater and jacket. "Here you go. Now get on into town and hurry back."

Layken kissed her on the cheek and turned to go. "I checked on Seymour. He's taken to the bed. If you feel like it, you might see if he'd like some tea or maybe an aspirin."

Worry marred her pretty face. "I'll see to him. Now, go on so you can get back. And ask Doctor Jennings to stop by next time he's out this way." She shooed them out the door.

Oliver took the time to examine the countryside on the way into town. It was truly beautiful here with all the trees turning colors and fields lying fallow. It seemed everyone but Layken had finished with the crops for the year. Maybe there was really something to be said for raising peanuts.

Rose sat in the middle between him and Layken, and Jack had settled in the back, with his cap pulled low.

Layken first stopped at Vandegrift's gas station. A big man who looked to be in his fifties, wearing overalls and a straw hat, lumbered out. "Need a fill-up?"

"Yes sir, and some information." Layken got out of the pickup and Oliver followed suit.

"What can I help you with?" Mr. Vandegrift unscrewed the gas cap.

"We've got a busted oil pan that we either need to get welded or buy new. What do you suggest?"

Once the gas nozzle was secured and the tank filling, Mr. Vandegrift peered in the back of the pickup as Jack held up the oil pan. "Not a big hole. I'd suggest welding it. If'n you want to buy a new one, you'll have to either order it or drive to Greenfield or Springfield."

"Who around here does welding?" Oliver asked.

"Check with old man Travis. That is, if you can catch him. He's gone a lot."

Layken prodded. "Where's his shop?"

"Two blocks over from the general store to the west, next to the mill."

Layken nodded. "Much obliged. Say, you wouldn't happen to have a replacement for this?" Oliver held up the broken fan belt.

"Sure do. It'll cost you $1.50."

"I'll take it." Oliver pulled bills out of his pocket. "And I'm paying for the gas, too."

The big man nodded and disappeared into the station, only to return with a new fan belt.

"You don't have to pay for my gas." Layken leaned against the side of the pickup.

"I sorta do, Layken. You and Sara Beth are doing so much for us."

"It's what folks do around here. We help each other. Makes life lots better for everyone."

"I couldn't agree more, but still I have to do my part." Oliver climbed back into the pickup and dropped the new fan belt onto the floorboard.

Before Layken got inside, he leaned over the truck bed. "Once we see if Travis is around, I'll drive by the school on the way to the doctor, Jack."

"Appreciate that." Jack rested against the back of the cab.

It took less than five minutes to drive to the welding shop. The small town of Everton spanned only a handful of blocks in total.

Layken stopped, but the padlock on the door left little doubt old man Travis wasn't there. "We'll circle back by before we leave town. Maybe he'll show up." He rolled down the window. "We're heading to the school, Jack."

Jack perched on the side of the truck bed.

Layken drove slowly by the rock building with a sign in front that read *Everton School*.

Oliver noted the large empty field behind the school. Perhaps the school had a baseball team. That would be a great opportunity, not only for Jack to get an education, but to be around other kids his age and play a sport. Oliver could easily see how it appealed.

Rose leaned forward as Oliver rolled down his window. "Looks nice. Small, but nice. Maybe this is what Jack needs."

"I'm glad to hear you say that, Rose." Oliver propped his arm on the window seal. "He seems pretty set on it."

"I want what's best for him. He's never had a chance at a normal life." Rose folded her hands in her lap.

"And neither have you." Oliver hated seeing the frown lines appear. "But don't you give up on yourself, Rose. Promise me."

She raised her violet-blue eyes with a slight hint of a smile. "I promise. Sara Beth said the same thing."

Layken circled the block. "Sara Beth knows. She's been through a lot. Don't know all she's shared with you, but she had a really tough time after her mother died and left her with an abusive father."

Rose murmured, "I certainly know what that's like."

Oliver rolled up his window when Rose shivered. "Layken, how did you and Sara Beth meet?"

Layken chuckled. "Long story. I made a bargain with the banker for more time to pay off a loan against the farm. His part of the bargain was that I marry Sara Beth. Best thing that ever happened to me."

"Sara Beth told me about it," Rose said. "It seems almost made up the way you two seem now."

"We began as partners. I'd get to save my farm. Sara Beth would get her freedom. Didn't count on falling in love along the way, but that's what happened."

"Life's full of surprises, isn't it?" Oliver pondered that thought.

It had certainly been full of surprises for him since the night he met Rose and her brothers at the dance, which now seemed ages ago.

He'd been drawn to Rose from the first time he laid eyes on her.

Never in a million years had he imagined what would happen after that first meeting.

And now, here they were, on a journey toward a better life.

A life filled with possibilities. Even with an unwanted baby in the mix, Rose had options.

Jack had options.

And Oliver had a chance at a possible connection leading him to living out his dream of playing major league baseball.

Yes, life was full of surprises—some good and some not so good.

Still, miracles all the same.

# CHAPTER 24

Rose fought to calm the butterflies in her stomach as Layken pulled to a stop in front of Dr. Jennings's office a few short minutes later. It resembled a small cottage more than it did a professional office. Oliver got out, then offered his arm to Rose.

"Want me to come with you?" Oliver gripped her elbow.

"Would you mind terribly? I have to admit, I'm frightened." Her legs trembled beneath her.

Jack jumped over the side of the pickup. "I'll come with you."

Oliver nodded and stepped back.

Rose took Jack's arm and together they marched up the steps to the front door. A part of her wanted to turn and bolt back to the safety of Layken's truck. She put a trembling hand on her stomach and sucked in a deep breath. As soon as she knocked, a white-haired woman answered the door. "I'm here to see the doctor," her voice cracked.

"Come on in." The older lady hurried them inside and closed the door. "Just have a seat in the parlor and he'll be right with you."

Rose took in the inviting warmth of the fireplace, green velvet chairs, and the dark mahogany coffee table with lion's heads for feet. She perched on the edge of one chair as Jack dropped into another one. She whispered, "This is fancy."

Jack grinned. "Doctoring must pay good."

A balding man of slight build stepped into the room. "Martha said someone is here to see me." He stuck out his hand, first to Jack, then to Rose. "I'm Doctor Jennings. Who is the patient?"

Rose stood. "I am, sir."

"Then come on back with me to the examination room." He peered over spectacles at Jack. "I'd prefer it if you'd wait here, young man."

Jack nodded, relief showing in his face. "I'd prefer that too, Doc."

Rose followed the doctor down a hallway into a room that looked more like a bedroom than an examination room, except for the narrow hard table and medical supplies on shelves. She trembled when the doctor closed the door.

"Now, what seems to be ailing you, Miss?"

"Rose," she said, barely above a whisper. "Rose Blaine."

"All right, Rose Blaine. What can I do for you?"

She couldn't help but flinch as his eyes went first to the bruising around her neck, to the bandage around her arm, and then back to her face.

"Well, sir. I'm going to have a baby and I've been awful sick."

"Looks like you've been in an accident as well."

"No accident." She blinked hard to hold back tears that filled her eyes.

The doctor raised his bushy eyebrows. "I want to do a complete examination and that will require you to remove all of your clothing, including your unmentionables, and slip into one of our gowns. Martha will be in to help you, if you want."

"I don't need any help." Rose's hand shook as she took the gown he offered.

"Very well, then. Just open the door when you're ready."

As soon as he closed the door, Rose sucked in a deep breath. This was going to be humiliating at best. Yet, she owed it to everyone to go through with the exam. Maybe, just maybe, the doctor could give her something to make her feel better. She hated being nauseous and having no energy. Yet Sara Beth had assured her those feelings would pass.

For a brief second, as she removed her clothing, a memory of the violent punch her father had delivered to her abdomen flashed across her mind, and it brought a hard shudder. Had he done internal damage not only to her but to the life growing inside?

She carefully hung her borrowed clothes on a hall tree in the corner and slipped into a white hospital gown with no sleeves and barely anything to hold it on her frail body.

She clutched it close around her and opened the door.

Doctor Jennings returned to the room within seconds, followed by Martha, who gave her a wan smile. The kindness in both their eyes touched her, and she struggled again to hold back tears.

Martha patted her on the shoulder. "There, there. If crying helps, let it out."

Doctor Jennings pointed to the narrow bed. "Let's get started."

Rose sniffled as she lay back on the hard surface. "I was attacked."

"I can see that." The doctor gently felt around her neck area. "I'd say you were lucky to escape."

"You don't know the half of it." Rose avoided looking into his eyes as he moved his hands around her face and head.

"And is this pregnancy the result of the attack?"

"No. It happened before, but it was forced." She couldn't believe she was so easily saying these words to strangers. Yet, she didn't see judgment in their eyes.

Martha clucked her tongue. "You poor dear."

"And this cut on your arm?" The doctor gently removed the bandage.

"Got that when my pa took the knife from me, but a doctor in Crossett, Arkansas stitched it up."

"And he did a fine job, too. I do want to clean it and re-bandage it after I finish the exam." He pressed gently on her stomach, eliciting a slight groan when he touched a tender spot. He then pulled two metal stirrups out of a drawer and inserted them into the end of the hard bed. "I'll need you to scoot down and put your feet in these stirrups."

Nausea washed over Rose. She'd never willingly spread her legs for anyone. How could she do this? It was as if she had to relive Amos Parker's sneer, nasty breath, and rough hands tearing at her clothing. The memory battled against her resolve.

Martha stepped forward. "There's nothing to be afraid of, dear. I promise the doctor will not hurt you." She touched Rose's shoulder. "I'm right here, if you want to hold my hand."

Rose turned toward her and gripped the woman's wrinkled hand, then scooted down, placing each foot into a stirrup. "Thank you, ma'am," she whispered.

She closed her eyes as the doctor pressed lightly on her stomach again, then turned on a bright light and pulled a stool up to the end of the table. "You're going to feel a little bit of pressure."

When something cold and hard entered her, she sprang forward, gripping Martha's hand as if her life depended on it.

"Just relax." Martha gently pressed her back against the table. "The doctor needs to be able to look at everything."

Doctor Jennings added, "It will only take a minute. Sorry I didn't warn you about what a speculum would feel like. But Martha is right. It allows me to see inside you. It's the only way."

Rose blew out a long breath and squeezed her eyes tight, tears running down the sides of her face, as she fell back against the hard surface.

True to his word, in less than a minute, he removed the speculum and pulled her gown down. "All done. Now that wasn't so bad, was it?"

Rose's cheeks burned hot. "It hurt."

Doctor Jennings stood and patted her shoulder. "Sorry. Wish there was an easier way."

"Is everything okay?" Rose took the tissue Martha handed to her.

"There is no doubt you are pregnant. And there appears to be a small tear in the cervix wall."

"What does that mean?" Rose held her breath.

"It means you are at risk of losing this baby if you don't take it easy. Have you had any abdominal pain or any bleeding?"

"No bleeding, but I've had some sharp pains in my stomach the last couple of days."

The doctor nodded. "I'm going to suggest complete bed rest for a few days, then I'd like to examine you again." He paused. "Your body has been through a severe trauma."

"Is there anything you can give me to help with the sickness?" Rose put a hand to her forehead, releasing her grip on Martha.

"There's a new medicine that I could prescribe for you, but the studies show it doesn't help all that much and could be a risk to the baby. Honestly, I'd recommend ginger or peppermint tea. That should bring a bit of relief."

Doctor Jennings pulled up a chair and poured a carbolic acid compound onto her arm before wrapping it in a clean bandage. "Is that young man in the parlor the father of this baby?"

The scent of the antiseptic tickled her nostrils, and a flush went up Rose's neck. "No. That's my brother. My attacker is dead."

The doctor raised his eyebrows. "Young lady, I can tell you've been through a lot. Will you please tell me more so I can decide the best way to treat all of your injuries, including the ones in your mind?"

"Can I get dressed please?" Rose held her arm still as he finished applying the new bandage.

"Of course." He motioned to his wife. "Martha, my dear, can you assist Rose?"

"Happy to." Martha reached for the discarded clothes as Doctor Jennings closed the door.

Rose shyly dropped the gown and took the garments the older woman handed to her.

"Oh, honey, you've got bruises all over you. Whoever did this to you needs to be reported to the authorities." She helped slip Rose's dress over her head.

"No need. He's dead, too."

A gasp escaped the woman as she took a step back. "Let me get the doctor back in, and I hope you'll confide in him. We are here to help."

Nodding, Rose finished dressing and sat back on the exam table while Martha opened the door.

Over the next several minutes, Rose twisted her hands and quietly recounted the events that led up to the death of Amos Parker and Ezra Blaine. When she stopped talking, the doctor rubbed his chin.

"First and foremost, you need to understand none of these events were your fault. You were a victim. Do not waste one minute blaming yourself. You need to focus on happy thoughts for your future and the future of this baby. A positive attitude will go a long way in helping you feel better both inside and out."

Martha laid a hand on Rose's shoulder. "Sweetheart, where are you staying?"

"With Layken Martin and his wife. Our car broke down at their farm. We were on the way to my aunt's house in St. Louis."

"Your car couldn't have chosen a better place to stop. Fine people, the Martins." The doctor adjusted his glasses. "Again, I recommend complete bed rest for the next few days. Then I'll do another exam."

Rose folded her hands in her lap. "Thank you both. I appreciate your kindness." For the first time since she left the poor excuse of a home in Arkansas, she could say she felt some semblance of peace. They were right. None of this was her fault. Now if only she could convince the nightmares that kept coming. Perhaps in time those would go away.

The doctor stood and escorted her back to the parlor, with Martha close behind.

Jack jumped to his feet. "Is she okay, Doc?"

"I've ordered complete bed rest for the next few days. It's critical that she get some proper nutrition and no exertion."

"I'll make sure of it." Jack folded his hat in his hands, then reached into his pocket. "How much do we owe you?"

The doctor waved him away. "First visit is free. Keep your money."

Rose stood next to Jack, and an idea hit her. "Doctor Jennings, you wouldn't have a telephone we could use, do you?" She glanced at Jack. "We should try to call Aunt Katherine."

The doctor nodded. "There's a phone in my office. You're welcome to use it."

Jack shifted from foot to foot. "I'll get Layken and Oliver. I know Oliver wanted to call his mother, too."

Grateful for Jack's suggestion, Rose hated to admit she had no idea how to use a telephone, but Oliver would. She nodded at her brother.

"Martha will show you to my office. Use the phone however long you need to."

"Does it cost money?" Again, Rose hated to show her ignorance.

The doctor chuckled. "You can leave fifty cents on my desk to cover the expense, if it makes you feel better." He turned to his wife. "Martha, please make sure these folks get what they need. I've got to head over to the Harvey place."

Before he could leave, Oliver, Layken, and Jack came inside.

Layken shook the doctor's hand. "Glad to see you, Doc. Say, Seymour is a bit under the weather. Sara Beth is hoping you might stop in and take a look at him if you're out our way."

"Tell Sara Beth I'd be glad to. I need to check on her as well. How's she feeling?"

"Feisty, but she gets tired easy and says her back hurts all the time."

"Hmm. That baby is getting ready. Back aches are common in the last few days. I'll be out tomorrow or the next day." The doctor pointed at Rose. "Now, you mind what I told you, young lady." Doctor Jennings grabbed his medical bag and left, while Martha escorted the group to the office.

"Here you go." She pointed to the phone. "Just pick it up and tell Gloria who you want to call and she'll put it through."

Rose stared at the black instrument sitting on the desk, as Martha left the room. How could it even work? She glanced at Oliver. "Will you do it?"

"Sure." Oliver picked up the receiver. "Yes, ma'am. Can you connect a call to Rube Livingston in St. Louis, Missouri?"

He waited several minutes before speaking again. "Hello. Is this Mr. Livingston?"

Rose could only hear Oliver's part of the conversation, but she held her breath. At least Uncle Rube had picked up. That meant he was still alive.

"Sir, this is Oliver Quinn, and I'm here with your niece and nephew, Rose and Jack. Rose would like to speak with you." He handed the receiver to Rose, and she put it up to her ear.

"Uncle Rube, it's Rose."

"Rose, honey, I've been so worried about you. Harlan showed up here yesterday and told me everything that happened to you kids. I'm so sorry."

"Harlan is there? Is he okay?"

"He was. Didn't stay. Said he needed to find you and Jack. Said you were supposed to be here."

"Yes sir, we would've been, but our car broke down." She shifted the piece to her other ear. "Can I talk to Aunt Katherine?"

Uncle Rube's voice broke. "My dear, your Aunt Katherine passed away three months ago."

Rose's knees buckled. "Aunt Katherine's dead?"

# CHAPTER 25

Oliver gripped Rose's elbow to steady her as her face turned pasty white. While he could only hear Rose's side of the conversation, the news of her aunt's death dealt a hard blow. Would it change her mind about going on?

He tried not to let disappointment creep in, as the opportunity to meet the baseball veteran slipped away.

Rose choked on a sob. "Oh, no! I'm so sorry. She was a kind and wonderful person." She gripped the edge of the desk with her free hand. "I feel just awful to burden you even more with our troubles. We didn't have anywhere else to turn, and we couldn't stay there."

With tears streaming down her cheeks, she nodded as if her uncle could see her. "Okay, I will. I'm going to give the telephone back to Oliver. He needs to talk to you." She passed the receiver to Oliver, and collapsed into the nearest chair, silently sobbing. Jack laid a hand on her shoulder.

"Hello, again, sir. I'm so sorry to hear that your wife has passed away. As Rose told you, I was bringing them to St. Louis when my car broke down. I was sure looking forward to meeting you. You see, I've been playing baseball since I could walk and have always dreamed of playing with the St. Louis Browns."

Rube cleared his throat. "Thank you for your generous offering to bring Jack and Rose up here. From what little Harlan told me, they've had more than a rough go. Between you and me, I never cared for Ezra Blaine. But if you're really serious about playing ball, I'd be happy to introduce you to Bill DeWitt. Do you know who he is?"

"Yes sir. He manages the team. It'd be an honor to meet him. I really want a chance to try out. All I need is one shot."

"He's only in town for another week, so the window is pretty tight for an introduction. Think you can get the car running and be here before next Friday?"

Oliver swallowed hard. "Sure going to try, sir, and thank you."

"My pleasure. Take care of my niece and nephew."

"I will, sir."

"See you when you get here."

"Goodbye." Oliver hung up and turned to Rose and Jack. "I know that was tough news, but your uncle wants us to come on anyway."

Rose sniffled and swiped at tears. "He said Aunt Katherine left something important for me. Something that belonged to my grandmother, who died before I was born. This is all really bad. The doctor told me he wants me to have complete bedrest for a few days." She raised red puffy eyes to Oliver. "You and Jack should go on without me. I don't want you to miss this opportunity. It was my promise to you…our bargain."

Jack stood stock still as if frozen in place, a multitude of expressions flashing across his face.

Oliver fought rising anxiety. Rose's health was more important than playing ball, yet she'd be in good hands with Sara Beth. Still, his conscience wouldn't let him go off and leave her. "We'll talk about it. First, I have to get the car running."

He turned to Layken. "I have a chance to meet the manager of the ball team, but he's only in town a few more days."

Layken clapped him on the shoulder. "Then we'll have to make sure that happens. Don't worry about Rose. We'll take good care of her. Soon as we're done here, we can go back by the welding shop."

"Just need to put in a quick call to my mum." Oliver picked up the receiver.

"Operator. How can I help you?" The woman's singsong voice came across the wire.

"Can you connect me with Millie's Pastry Shop in Crossett, Arkansas?"

"Hold please."

Oliver tapped his finger on the desk while he waited, his mind whirling with a million thoughts. Also, he wanted to know exactly what the doctor told Rose and wished he'd heard the instructions firsthand. Knowing Rose, she'd put herself last to give him an opportunity to realize his dream.

"Millie's Pastry Shop. How can I help you?" He immediately recognized his mother's voice.

"Mum, it's me Oliver."

"Oh, son, I've been so worried about you. Been having a bad feeling. Are you all right?"

"Everyone is okay, but the Woody broke down, so we're stuck for a few days until I can get it fixed. Hit something in the road and it knocked a hole in the oil pan."

"Oh dear. I knew something was wrong. Where are you? How are Jack and Rose?"

"We're near a small town in Missouri, staying with some nice folks on a farm. Jack and Rose are fine."

"Rose is feeling better?" Genuine concern reflected in her voice.

While Oliver wanted to tell her everything, now wasn't the time. "Yes, and she saw a doctor today. How are the twins?"

"Being their usual selves, but they sure miss you, and so do I. I'm glad Rose saw a doctor. Lord knows she's been through the wringer. Son, please let me know when you make it to St. Louis."

"I will, Mum. Can't talk long. Borrowing a phone at the doctor's office. I love you. Give my love to Margaret and Elizabeth and I promise I'll call you again soon."

"I'm praying for you all."

"Thanks, Mum. Try not to worry. We're in good hands. Love you."

"Love you, too."

The click on the other end told him she'd hung up. He placed the receiver back on the cradle.

Jack fished a fifty-cent piece out of his pocket and laid it on the doctor's desk. "Doc said to leave this to cover the calls."

Oliver nodded as Martha peeked around the door. "We're all done, ma'am. Please tell the doctor thank you for us."

She smiled. "You kids take care now. Layken, give my love to Sara Beth."

"Will do, Mrs. Jennings." Layken tipped his fedora and turned to the others. "Let's go see if Travis is back at his shop."

At the door, Rose turned around and ran back to Mrs. Jennings, throwing her arms around her. "Thank you for everything."

The older woman patted her back. "Follow the doctor's orders. Okay? Everything is going to be fine. You're a strong girl."

Rose sniffled. "I don't feel very strong, but yes, I will follow his instructions." She hurried back to the waiting men.

Once they were in the pickup, Oliver turned to Rose. "Tell me exactly what the doctor said. Was he able to give you anything to help you feel better?"

"He told me I am to go on strict bedrest for a few days…that there is a risk of losing the baby if I don't."

"Then we'll make sure you follow his orders." Again, waves of disappointment washed over him at the thought of not making it to St. Louis in time. He was so close to his dream, yet an enormous gap stood in the way. No matter what, Rose's health was more important than anything else. And that was that.

"He also treated my arm and put on a fresh bandage." She grew quiet. "I told him and his wife everything. Had to explain the bruises."

"Glad you did."

"It felt good to say it all out loud and not get condemned for any of it. He made me believe none of it's my fault."

"Because it isn't." Oliver stared out the window as they passed by a gristmill. The rhythmic motion of the water wheel reminded him of the constant movement of life. Everything was always in a state of change.

"Oliver," Rose mumbled. "I know how important getting to St. Louis is to you, and I will do everything in my power to help you get there. I haven't forgotten my bargain."

Oliver patted her arm. "Don't worry. The main thing is to take care of yourself. Everything else will work itself out."

"Still, I promised. And I never go back on a promise."

"Let's take one day at a time. If I don't make it in time, there will be other opportunities." If only he could convince himself of that.

Layken pulled to a stop in front of the welding shop. "Looks like he might be here. Don't see the padlock." He opened his door, as did Oliver.

Jack hopped out of the back of the pickup, carrying the oil pan. "We might be in luck."

Oliver hoped so, as he pushed through the door.

Inside the shop, a single lightbulb hung from the ceiling and pieces of metal, all different shapes and sizes, lined one wall, while a long metal table held bins of welding rods. Toward the back, a Lincoln welder rested on what appeared to be a car frame with wheels.

A tall thin man leaned over the rig, wiping it down. A welding hood hung on a nail next to welding gloves and a myriad of long hoses.

"Hello," Oliver called out. "You Mister Travis?"

The man scratched his head. "That'd be me. What can I do for you?"

"Got an oil pan that needs to be welded. Reckon you could take care of that for me?" He took the oil pan from Jack and held it out.

"I could, but my rig's busted right now. Waiting on a part from Joplin."

"When do you think it'll get here?"

"Supposed to be here in a couple of days. Hope you're not in a hurry."

"I sort of am. Needing to get to St. Louis."

"If you need it faster, you'll have to take it into Springfield or over to Greenfield. That's the best I can offer."

Oliver pulled off his cap and blew out a frustrated breath. Delays cropped up at every turn.

Layken stepped forward. "Could carry you over to Greenfield, but it'd be at least a few days. Gotta get the peanuts in before it's too late."

"Thanks, Layken, but I couldn't put you out like that." Oliver turned back to Mr. Travis. "You pretty sure you'll be up and running again soon?"

"Unless the train derails."

Oliver didn't know what that meant other than maybe the part needed to repair the welder was coming by train. He'd seen the train tracks and depot when they'd left the doctor's office. "Then I'll check back with you in a couple of days. Can I leave this here with you?" He held up the oil pan.

"Fine by me." Mr. Travis pointed toward the cluttered metal table. "Put it over there."

Jack stepped forward. "Never seen anybody weld before. Mind if I come watch you sometime?"

"If'n you want. Got no objections. I like it when youngsters get interested. There's always going to be a need for welders in this world. I hear tell welders up in Detroit City are bringing in fifty dollars a week making automobiles."

The grin that spread across Jack's face lit up his eyes. "That'd be sweet."

Mr. Travis lit a cigarette and blew a smoke ring. "You in school?"

"Not yet, but thinking I'm going to."

"You get in school and if you're looking for some work on the weekends, come see me."

Jack slapped his thigh. "I will. Yes sir, I will."

Oliver dropped the oil pan on the table. "Do you need my name or anything?"

"Son, I won't forget you or that the oil pan belongs to you. Don't worry. This is a small shop. Things don't get lost or misplaced."

"That's good. But just for the record, my name's Oliver." He turned to leave, then whirled back around. "Forgot to ask what you'll charge."

"Shouldn't be more than five or six dollars at the most, maybe less, depending on how long it takes. I'll do you a good job."

Oliver mentally counted the money in his pocket, thankful he'd drawn his pay before they'd left. "That I believe, sir. Thank you."

They bid their farewells, and as soon as they were back in the pickup, Layken headed for the farm.

Oliver filled Rose in while they rode.

"That's good, Oliver. It sounds like the car will be fixed in time to get to St. Louis."

"But what about you? The doctor said bedrest."

"Been thinking. We can make a bed in the backseat of the Woody. Slept there on the way up."

"I suppose that would work. Still, I'd feel better if he clears you to travel."

Layken shifted gears. "You are welcome to stay with us. Sara Beth will take good care of you, Rose. It's what she does best."

"She is a special person." Rose laid a hand on her stomach and winced.

"You okay?" Oliver felt her stiffen next to him.

"Just a sharp pain again. But it's already passing."

"We'll be home shortly and you're going straight to bed." Layken increased his speed. "Oliver, think you and Jack might be up to helping me service the tractor and get it ready to start working early in the morning? With Seymour under the weather, I could use your help."

"We'd be happy to." Oliver tried again to ignore the worry that crept in. Rose was not well. "And after Tab gets home, I'd like to get up a baseball game. Would you play?"

"Sure. Been a while, but I've tossed the ball around with Tab a few times. He's interested in learning."

Just that bit of information gave Oliver the happy feeling he got every time he picked up a bat and ball. He could easily see where Jack would fit in at the farm with Tab, but hoped he'd at least go with Rose to their uncle's house. Then he'd bring him back should he decide he didn't want to stay in St. Louis.

His mind awhirl, he watched the passing scenery. The leaves painted a striking picture with all different shades of yellows, browns, and oranges. Human hands couldn't match nature's handiwork.

When they arrived back at the farm, Sara Beth had dinner waiting for them. While they ate, Rose filled Sara Beth in on the doctor visit and the phone call.

As soon as they finished eating, Jack and Oliver washed and dried the dishes, despite Sara Beth's protests.

Then, leaving Rose in Sara Beth's capable hands, they followed Layken out to the tractor.

Oliver walked around the modern tractor and let out a whistle. "Nice piece of machinery, Layken."

"As with everything around here, there's a story behind it." He pulled out the oil stick. "My tractor burnt up in the barn last year."

Jack kicked at a tire. "That's terrible."

Layken continued. "A neighboring farmer is having some health problems. He offered to lend me his tractor if I'd get his crop in for him. We got it harvested last month."

"Neighbors helping neighbors." Oliver took off his cap, shook it out, and put it back on his head. "That's the way it should be."

"It's the way it is around here and even in town. The folks in Everton are good to help each other, although they gave Sara Beth a lot of grief after her mother died."

"That seems odd."

Layken chuckled. "Seems they thought she was a witch because she reads tarot cards and because her mother was a gypsy. That was why Homer Williams wanted her married off. The Widow Jones wouldn't marry him until she was out of his house. Worked out well for me."

"I'd say it did. You two seem suited for each other. I have no clue what tarot cards are, but they sound harmless enough." Some part of

Oliver longed to have a solid relationship with someone the way Layken and Sara Beth did.

Maybe eventually with Rose, if things worked out? His offer to marry her and give the baby a name still stood. And who knows? As it had with Sara Beth and Layken, maybe it could grow into something lasting.

He brought his thoughts back to the present. No need in contemplating an unsure future.

Rose would always be free to make her own choices, if he had anything to say about it.

Same with Jack.

For all they'd endured, the freedom to choose had been hard-earned.

He had a strong feeling their uncle would feel the same way.

# CHAPTER 26

Rose allowed Sara Beth to help her put on a soft worn nightgown and get into the bed. She hated the thought of being confined, but the pains that shot through her belly kept her from complaining about it. While she'd once thought she wanted the baby to die, now faced with the possibility, shame filled her. After all, even though it resulted from violent rape, the child carried her blood. It was a part of her and that she'd tried to wish it away brought tears to her eyes. The baby was the innocent one.

"How on earth am I supposed to pass the hours confined to the bed?" Rose asked. "I'm not accustomed to laying around."

"Believe me, I understand." Sara Beth smoothed the covers. "What were your days like before?"

"I did all the cooking, cleaning, laundry, and mending for my father and brothers. There was always work to be done." Rose sighed. "Then I met Oliver one night at a dance. He insisted that I dance with him, even though I don't know how. I got a glimpse of what it might be like to live in a normal, loving household. It changed something in me. Made me even more determined to escape from the hell I was stuck in."

"I wondered where you met Oliver. He seems to care very much for you."

"He's a kind and generous person, and so are his mother and sisters. I am forever grateful."

Sara Beth patted her shoulder. "Don't underestimate or discount his feelings for you. What I see when he looks at you goes beyond kindness."

Rose ran a hand across her forehead. "There's no hope for anything more. Look at me, pregnant with a horrible man's baby. He deserves better."

"Maybe, but one thing I've learned is the heart has a mind of its own. I never intended to fall in love with Layken, but as we worked side by side to save this farm, the heart took over." Sara Beth smiled. "Do you like to read?"

"I used to love reading but haven't held a book in a long time."

"Well, then, lucky for you, I have quite an assortment of books and magazines that you are welcome to. Do you have a favorite book?"

Rose searched her memory for anything familiar. "I have a feeling I'd enjoy anything you recommend, Sara Beth. You can surprise me." She tugged the covers over her.

"I'll start with some magazines. Mind if I bring my sewing in here and keep you company?"

"I'd like that. And I don't see any reason I can't sit up in bed and sew with you."

"While I appreciate the offer, I think the doctor wants you laying flat, not sitting up. Otherwise, he wouldn't have said bedrest. He would've said chair rest."

Rose sighed. "Guess you've got a point. It would be a bit hard to sew laying down."

Sara Beth patted her shoulder. "Just relax, and I'll be back in a minute or two. And how about a cup of my special pregnancy tea?"

"That would be nice." Tears sprang unbidden. The way Layken and Sara Beth opened their home to them without batting an eye or expecting payment in return spoke volumes. It's the way things should be with folks. In her wildest fantasies, she couldn't fathom her father lifting a finger to help anyone in need.

Her thoughts turned to Oliver and the time crunch. The order for bedrest couldn't have come at a worse time. She'd meant what she said about making a bed in the back of the wagon. Still, the thought of being on the road and getting sicker didn't sit well. It would put an even bigger burden on Oliver and on Jack…that is, if Jack decided to go on with them. And if he didn't, she'd miss her brother, but there was no doubt Layken and Sara Beth would give him the best opportunities possible. And she understood the fear of going to a big city. It would be different for sure. Maybe staying on the farm and going to school in Everton would be what he needed. She'd seen the look of anticipation on his face when they'd driven past the school.

Sara Beth returned with a stack of magazines under one arm and a cup of tea in her free hand. She set the cup on a nightstand, reached behind Rose, and fluffed the pillows. "Can't drink tea laying down, but as soon as you're finished, I want to see you laying flat. No questions asked."

"Yes, ma'am." Rose had to admit it was a foreign feeling to have someone fuss over her. She shrunk into herself as she remembered her father's cruelty, and how he'd forced her to get up and tend to household chores when she was sick with influenza. He'd called her lazy and worthless. That was a lie.

"Here you go." Sara Beth passed a cup with steaming tea before easing down into a chair she'd scooted close to the bed. "Now, tell me everything that happened at the doctor. I know it's big."

Over the next few minutes, through bouts of tears and sips of tea, Rose shared everything the doctor had said and ended with devastating news of her aunt's death. "So, now I don't know what to do. Uncle Rube said to come on and he'd take care of us, but he doesn't know I'm pregnant. And Oliver is refusing to continue without me. Even though I offered to make a bed in the back of the wagon, he's still saying no." She ran a finger around the rim of the teacup.

"Oliver is wise, honey. What if you were to get sicker along the way? What then? At least here, we have a good doctor close by."

"I know. I just don't want to ruin his chance to meet my uncle and possibly the manager of the ball team. Not sure I could live with that." She couldn't stand the thought of being responsible for crushing his dreams, as she knew firsthand what that did to a person.

Circumstances had ripped away her dream of getting an education and living like a normal teenager, leaving an open gaping wound deep inside.

Sara Beth patted her arm. "Don't worry about Oliver. He strikes me as being a solid and resourceful person. If he misses this chance, there will be others."

"That's what he said."

"Of course he did. The main thing is for you to get past this hump and have a healthy pregnancy."

"You might hate me for this, but early on, when I first knew I was pregnant, I prayed for the baby to die. Now, with that possibility, I'm ashamed of my selfishness."

"Nothing to be ashamed of. You're human and so young. You were violated. It's a normal reaction. So, don't beat yourself up. You're doing your best now and that's what counts. Today is really all anyone has."

When Rose finished her tea, she passed her cup to Sara Beth and snuggled under the covers. "Thank you for everything, Sara Beth. You and Layken are so kind."

Sara Beth waved her away. "We're just doing what any decent person would do. We had a lot of help from neighbors when we were in dire straits. Just passing that along." She pushed to her feet and reached for the empty cup. "If you still want company, I'll get my sewing. But if you'd rather take a nap, I'll leave you alone and check back in after a while."

Rose yawned. "I am feeling a bit tired. Maybe I'll take a nap, then read some. I've been so isolated from the world." She pointed to the stack of magazines on the bed. "I'll enjoy seeing what's happening in other places."

"If you need anything, just call out." Sara Beth flashed a smile. "I'll leave your door open so I can hear you." She laid a hand on Rose's forehead. "Just rest."

"Thank you."

Rose adjusted the pillows and snuggled under the soft worn sheets and colorful quilt.

How would she ever get used to this level of kindness and acceptance? Her father had made her believe she was unworthy of anything but hard work and a heavy hand.

He was wrong, and she'd prove it. Martha Jennings had said she was a strong girl. Now to convince herself.

Someday she'd have the chance to help someone else in need. She smiled at that thought.

Once Sara Beth had left the room, Rose laid a hand across her stomach and closed her eyes.

She whispered, "I'm sorry, little one. I never really wanted you to die. None of this is your fault, and I know that now. I was being selfish and only thinking of myself."

Did she imagine a tiny twinge of movement? It was way too early for that.

Continuing, she said, "Even though you were conceived in violence, I promise on my mother's grave you will never know it. I will protect you with my life."

Choking back a sob, she wished with all her heart that her mother was still alive. Sara Beth's kindness went a long way to soothe her frayed spirit, but only a mother could truly kiss away the hurt and pain.

At that thought, she gasped. She would be this child's mother, the one to comfort it when storms raged outside, the one who'd bandage a skinned knee, the one who'd hold it and rock it when it was sick.

She would be a mother.

As that sunk in, she made a vow. "I will be the best mother I know how to be, just like my mother was."

Rose closed her eyes, long last at peace with the new life growing inside. A dream soon swept her away, and she was standing in a field of brilliantly hued flowers, the sun lying softly on her shoulders.

"Mommy. Mommy. Look. I can fly." A tiny version of herself, with a golden halo of hair streaming behind her, ran in circles, her arms extended.

Rose smiled, and warmth flooded through her being. "Yes, you can." She held out her hand. "Let's fly together."

The child ran toward her. Just before she touched the small hand that reached for her, she jerked awake, tears streaming down her cheeks.

She turned into the pillow and sobbed.

Her child, a beautiful little girl.

She hugged herself and prayed for herself and for the baby.

If only Rose could've seen the beautiful, glowing angel hovering over her bed.

# CHAPTER 27

A couple of hours later, Oliver wiped his hands on a rag and stepped back. Pirate, Sadie, and Pearl raced around the yard, chasing each other and terrorizing the cat if he dared to stick his head out of the barn.

The tractor was ready to go and Layken had explained how they'd harvest the crop. Normally, they'd leave the peanuts in the field to dry for a few days, then they'd separate them from the plant, but Layken said his buyer wanted them straight out of the ground. That would make it all go faster.

Jack climbed onto the tractor with Layken for a demonstration on how to raise and lower the pair of plow points.

Layken explained, "One of us will drive the tractor. I'm hoping Seymour will feel up to it. When I checked on him earlier, he said he was feeling better. But if not, Jack, you'll drive, and Oliver and I will gather the peanuts when the plow turns them over."

Jack worked the lever, making the plow go up and down. "I'll do whatever you need. Never drove a tractor, but it can't be that hard."

Oliver stepped onto the side of the tractor and observed while Jack got a crash course on the operation of the tractor. He clapped Jack on the shoulder. "Another adventure."

Layken grinned. "Never thought of farming as an adventure, but I suppose it could be."

Excitement shone in Jack's eyes. "I think I'd like farming."

"It's a lot of backbreaking work, long hours, and a meager living, but I wouldn't want to be doing anything else. It's in my blood."

"Mind if I drive it, you know, practice?" Jack pushed in on the clutch.

"Sure. Fire it up and take it for a spin."

Oliver jumped down and turned at the sound of the screen door slamming. Tab trotted toward them.

"Hi, fellas." Tab waved.

Oliver waved back, as Jack drove away on the tractor. "How was school?"

"Good. We had a substitute teacher, and he taught us all about the solar system. Who knew there were so many planets and stars up in the sky?"

"I can tell you love learning."

Tab grinned. "Well, mostly. Don't care much for English or writing, but I like math and science." He pointed toward the disappearing tractor. "What's going on?"

"Jack's getting a tractor lesson. Layken says we start harvesting tomorrow." Oliver found the thirteen-year-old's enthusiasm refreshing.

"Dang it. I want to stay home and help."

"Reckon that'd be up to Layken and Sara Beth."

"I wouldn't be the first kid that missed school to harvest. I'll ask Sara Beth."

"Hey, are you up for a baseball game?"

Tab let out a loud whoop and sprinted toward the house. "Yes, sir, Mister Oliver. I'll change out of my school clothes."

Oliver couldn't help but grin at the boy's enthusiasm.

As soon as Jack rounded the house and parked, he and Layken joined Oliver.

"Tab's home, and we're going to play a game of baseball. Want to play?" Oliver asked.

"You know I'll play." Jack took off his cap and hit it against his leg.

Layken pointed to the outside water spigot. "Let's rinse off. I'll play."

Sara Beth accompanied Tab when he bounded out of the house. She put an arm around Layken's waist. "I need to check on Uncle Seymour." She turned to Oliver. "Rose is resting."

"I'm glad to hear that. Thank you for looking out for her." Oliver wished he could convey in words how deep his gratitude went.

"She means a lot to you, doesn't she?" Sara Beth raised an eyebrow.

"I feel responsible for both her and Jack. But yes, she is very special to me." He hoped the bedrest would help Rose get past the danger of losing the baby.

Layken looped his arm through Sara Beth's. "I'll come with you to check on Seymour." He pointed toward a pile of discarded pieces of wood planks, various shapes and sizes. "Maybe you can find what you need to set up bases."

"Sure thing." Oliver motioned to Jack and Tab. "Grab four about the same size. We need home, first, second, and third." He headed toward the Woody parked inside the barn. "Getting the ball, bat, and glove."

When he returned, Jack was setting home plate with a square piece of plank, while Tab held three more similar pieces. "Looks great, Jack." He dropped the ball and bat beside it.

"How do we measure to first?" Tab scrunched up his face.

"On a real field, it's ninety feet from home to first, but we're going to keep it smaller. Let's set them about thirty feet apart. Just pace it off. Second base should line up with the home plate." Oliver glanced around, searching for something to serve as a pitcher's mound while Jack and Tab set the bases. Not seeing anything, he went back into the barn.

A torn piece of a rubber tire caught his eye and he grabbed it as Sara Beth and Layken walked back through with Seymour. The old man rubbed his left shoulder. "Hear tell there's about to be a baseball game. Need a catcher?"

Oliver grinned. "Sure thing. But only if you're up to it."

"Think I can handle it. Feeling much better."

Sara Beth laid a hand on his arm. "Don't overdo it, Uncle Seymour. I'd be pleased if you'd sit with me and watch."

"I promise I'll sit down if I get tired." He patted her hand. "I'm not too old to have a little fun."

Oliver easily read the relief on Sara Beth's face, her love for the old man apparent. He hurried to set the pitcher's mound.

Tab brought a chair from the kitchen for Sara Beth. She propped her feet up on a wooden box, nestled Cuddles in her lap, and yelled, "Play ball." All three dogs parked themselves next to her.

Layken started out pitching, with Oliver in the batter's box and Jack and Tab in the outfield.

While Oliver tried to hold back, the sound of the ball swooshing toward him spiked his heartrate, and he hit it hard, loving the crack of the bat as it connected with the ball. Jack and Tab both raced to catch it, as did all three dogs, while he easily rounded all the bases. He stretched his legs, loving the run. This was his game. But more than that, it was his dream for an easier life for his mum and sisters. That is, if he could get signed to a team. His father had always told him to never give up on a dream, and he wouldn't. Even when Patrick Quinn knew he wasn't going to survive the accident, he spoke of bigger and better things for his family. Now, it was Oliver's turn to carry that forward.

And he never forgot a quote from his biggest baseball hero, Babe Ruth, who passed away a few months earlier in August 1948. *You just can't beat the person who never gives up.*

It was true. And Oliver was no quitter—never had been, never would be.

He traded with Layken and pitched while he stepped up to bat. This time, Jack leaped high in the air and caught it, throwing it to Tab, who missed it and scrambled to recover as Layken rounded third base.

Sara Beth cheered from the sideline, while the chickens clucked, and the goats bleated. The dogs barked and itched to join in. Sara Beth called them back. "Sadie, Pearl, Pirate, sit. Don't want you to get stepped on." They reluctantly obeyed, tails beating furiously against the ground.

One by one, they took turns at the bat while Oliver and Layken took turns pitching. Oliver loved everything about the game, but especially the way it made him feel when he played well.

He was good at it and he knew it. Not in an egotistical sort of way, but in a confident way that came from years of practice.

Seymour caught the ball when Tab missed and easily tossed it to Oliver for another pitch.

Oliver tucked the ball under his arm and walked over to Tab. "Let me help you." He pointed to the piece of wood that was the home plate. "Your legs need to be a little more than hip width apart. Bend your knees a little. Don't lock them. Hold your elbows out and the bat behind your head. Lean into the pitch. Keep your eye on the ball." After adjusting the position of the bat in Tab's hands, he returned to the pitcher's mound.

"Ready?"

Tab grinned. "Ready."

Oliver pitched, and Tab swung. The tip of the bat connected with the ball, sending it to the right, away from the makeshift field. Pirate took the opportunity to dart out and grab the ball in his mouth. He trotted over to Oliver and dropped it.

Seymour chuckled. "Looks like Pirate's a better catcher than I am."

Oliver patted Pirate's head. "He's had a lot of practice. Often, it's just me and him."

Sara Beth called Pirate back to her and the little dog trotted over to join the others.

Layken called out, "Concentrate, Tab. You can do this."

The game continued and Tab jumped, letting out a big whoop when he hit the ball, sending it flying on the third try.

While Jack got him out at first base, nothing could wipe the grin off Tab's face.

They played a few more rounds, each taking turns batting and playing the field. Even Seymour took a turn at the bat.

Oliver stood on the pitcher's mound and shaded his eyes against the sun.

As he pulled back his arm to throw the ball, a blood-curdling scream came from inside the house.

The hair stood up on the back of his neck. He dropped the ball and raced to the back door.

# CHAPTER 28

Oliver took the back steps in one leap. A shiver raced up his spine. That scream was one of pure pain and terror. He raced through the house toward the bedroom. Rose lay in a crumpled heap on the floor, a puddle of blood forming under her.

He knelt beside her. "Rose, can you hear me? It's Oliver. Can you open your eyes?"

She moaned and gripped her stomach with both hands. "Oh, God, it hurts so bad, Oliver." Tears streamed down her face.

Oliver scooped her up and laid her back on the bed as Sara Beth hurried in, her face drained of color.

"Oh, dear. Poor Rose. Oliver, go send Layken for the doctor."

"Yes, ma'am." He stood rooted in place. Surely he could do more.

"Go!"

He turned on his heel and sprinted down the hallway, almost colliding with Layken. "Sara Beth says to go fetch the doctor. Rose is bleeding real bad."

Layken grabbed his keys and darted out the door.

Jack, Tab, and Seymour stood rooted in place. Tab clutched Cuddles against his chest.

Sara Beth yelled, "Someone put water on the stove."

Seymour answered, "I will."

"Jack, you and Tab hang out with Seymour. We may need your help." Oliver hurried back to the bedroom. His heart squeezed as if in a vise. He hated to see anyone suffer and there was no doubt Rose had suffered more than anyone he knew. When would she get a break?

Sara Beth struggled to place a towel under Rose. Oliver stepped around the puddle of blood. "Let me help." He easily lifted Rose and Sara Beth slid a folded towel under her.

Rose moaned, and her eyelids fluttered. Her face was devoid of all color except for dark circles under her eyes.

"Can you hear me, Rose?" Sara Beth put a hand on her forehead. Rose didn't answer.

"Get a washrag from the bathroom and wet it, Oliver."

He hurried to do her bidding, hands shaking as he held the rag under the faucet. His thoughts in a jumble, he fought against guilt. He should have been in here with Rose instead of playing. But Sara Beth had said she was sleeping.

"Here." He passed the wet rag to Sara Beth. "Is she going to be okay?"

"I don't know. I'm not a doctor, but from all this blood, I'm afraid she might've lost the baby. Can you get a bucket with some soap from the kitchen and help me clean up the floor?"

"Sure." He jerked off his cap and raked a hand through his hair. "I shoulda been in here with her."

"No," Sara Beth replied. "It wouldn't have made any difference. If anyone stayed with her, it should have been me."

"I'll get a bucket. Anything else?" Oliver jammed his cap back on his head.

"I don't think so. Hope the doctor hurries."

Oliver couldn't agree more. While he was sure Layken would go as fast as he could, would the doctor even be there? In the kitchen, he searched for a bucket.

"What are you looking for, son?" Seymour stood next to the stove.

"A bucket and some soap. There's a lot of blood on the floor."

Seymour pointed to a cabinet under the sink. "In there."

Jack and Tab sat at the table. Worry showed in Jack's face and Tab registered confusion.

"Is Rose going to die, Oliver?" Jack sniffled and swiped a hand across his eyes. "I won't be able to stand it if something happens to her."

"She's not going to die. We'll know more when the doctor gets here."

"Wish he'd hurry."

"That makes two of us, Jack."

"Let me know if I can do anything."

"Why don't you and Tab go gather up all the bases and put the bat, ball, and glove back in the Woody?" At least that would give them something to do.

Both boys pushed to their feet.

Tab put Cuddles on the couch and hurried to catch up to Jack.

"Sure. But you have to promise you'll let me know if things turn worse." Jack put on his cap.

"I promise."

Oliver located the bucket and soap, then filled it with water. He glanced around for a towel and grabbed one off a nail next to the sink.

"Tell Sara Beth the water's hot if she needs it." Seymour turned off the burner.

"Thank you, Seymour."

He hurried back down the hallway, careful not to slosh out any of the water. Rose lay flat on her back. Sara Beth had pulled the quilt up over her and the wet rag lay on her forehead.

"Seymour said the water's hot if you need it." Setting the bucket down, he rolled up his sleeves, dropped to his knees, and began scrubbing. His heart broke for Rose.

"I had thought to make some tea for her, but she's out of it." Sara Beth leaned over Rose and flipped the wet rag over. "At least the pain seems to have subsided, so that's good. Let me help you with that."

"I've got it. You don't need to try to get up and down from the floor."

Sara Beth pulled a chair next to the bed and sat. "You've got a point."

Rose stirred and moaned. Her eyes fluttered open. "Sara Beth?"

"Yes, dear. I'm right here and so's Oliver."

"It hurt so bad and blood went everywhere. I'm sorry for making a mess."

"Do not even start with the apologies, sweetheart. Are you hurting now?"

"Not as bad as it was."

Oliver raised up. "Rose, the doctor is on the way. Layken went to get him."

She put her hands on her stomach. "I feel different."

"Honey, don't think about anything right now. Wait until Doctor Jennings gets here and he'll answer all your questions."

"The baby?"

Sara Beth took her hand. "We don't know, honey."

Rose turned her face toward the wall. "I had a dream. It was a little girl."

"You don't know yet if you've lost the baby, Rose. Don't jump to conclusions."

"I feel…empty and weak."

"You lost a lot of blood." Oliver wiped his hands on the towel, rounded the bed, and leaned down to meet her gaze. "I'm so sorry, Rose. I shoulda' stayed with you." He reached for her hand.

"Nothing you could've done. I could hear you playing baseball and it made me smile. Especially when Tab got so excited. Was going to come out and watch when the pain hit and I guess I passed out."

Sara Beth stood. "I'm going to fix you some tea, Rose."

Oliver sat in the chair Sara Beth vacated. "Tell me about your dream."

Rose raised a shaky hand to her forehead and slid the rag off. "I was outside in a beautiful field of flowers and this little girl with golden hair and an angelic face was twirling around. She called me mommy and said she could fly. When I reached out for her, I woke up."

Oliver rubbed her arm and cleared his throat as his eyes misted. "What a wonderful dream."

Rose let out a choking sob. "It was a little girl, Oliver. A beautiful little girl."

"Shh. You don't know that she's gone."

"I can feel it." She turned away. "I wished her away and now she's gone."

"Rose, please stop. Don't think those kinds of thoughts. It doesn't help any."

"How can I not? I was responsible for her well-being."

"You did the best you could under the circumstances." Oliver reached for the rag and wiped her tears away. "Just rest. The doctor will be here soon."

Rose closed her eyes and sank into the pillow.

Sara Beth returned with a cup of tea and Oliver finished cleaning up the blood, then took the bucket back to the kitchen.

He dumped the bloody water out the back door and rinsed the bucket. He flashed to a time when he had to help his mother tend to a wounded baby deer who was bleeding from where a hunter had grazed it with a bullet. But that was an animal. This was Rose.

His thoughts ran amuck.

---

Rose let Sara Beth prop her up and took the cup of tea. No matter what they said, she knew. The baby was gone.

While she wanted to scream and cry, instead, she sipped the tea and held the tears at bay. If nothing else in life, she'd learned to mask her emotions. At least until she was alone.

Sara Beth groaned and clutched her stomach. "Oh, my. This little one is getting anxious to make an appearance."

The stark contrast between them hit Rose. Sara Beth was about to give birth to a healthy baby while she'd just lost hers.

It changed things. Her heart silently broke into tiny pieces.

She prayed the doctor would hurry. She took a couple of sips of tea and handed it back to Sara Beth. "I can't drink anymore."

"Are you in pain?"

"Cramping." She swung her legs over the side of the bed. "Need to go to the bathroom."

"I don't think that's a good idea, but if you insist, I'll go with you." Sara Beth stood. "Just let me get you a clean gown and some of my menstrual rags."

Rose offered a weak smile. "Okay. How can I ever thank you for everything?"

Sara Beth patted her shoulder. "By getting well. That's enough. I'll be right back."

Rose fought against nausea and dizziness. Maybe Sara Beth was right. Maybe it was a bad idea to go to the bathroom. But the need to clean up was strong. She stared at the bloody towel beneath her, wishing the doctor would hurry.

When Sara Beth returned, Oliver came with her. "Hope you don't mind, but I thought it was a good idea to have Oliver with us in case you faint again."

Oliver moved to her side. "Lean on me, Rose."

"I hate for you to see me like this." Rose ducked her head.

"You forget I grew up in a house full of women. Don't give it a thought."

She got up on shaky legs and leaned heavily on Oliver. Once she was in the bathroom, he backed out and Sara Beth went in.

"I'll be right outside the door," Oliver assured her.

With Sara Beth's help, she washed the blood off her legs, leaning against the sink. "I'm dizzy."

"Then let's hurry and get you back to bed." Sara Beth handed her clean underwear and rags. "We're almost ready, Oliver."

"I'm here."

Sara Beth opened the door after she slipped a clean gown over Rose's head, and Oliver stepped in. Instead of helping her walk, he scooped her up and carried her back to the bedroom, where Sara Beth hurriedly jerked off the bloody towel and turned back the covers.

Rose sank into the strength of Oliver's arms. "I think I can walk."

"Not taking any chances. Besides, you're as light as a feather." He deposited her on the bed. "I hear a car outside. Maybe the doctor's here. I'll go see."

"I hope so." Rose laid a hand across her eyes, as Oliver hurried out.

Voices drifted through the house, and she took a deep breath, fighting nausea.

Doctor Jennings stepped into the room. "What's going on, young lady?"

"I had some horrible pains and so much blood went everywhere. I think I have lost the baby."

The kind doctor peered over his glasses. "Let's not jump to conclusions. I need to do an exam."

After a few minutes, he stood and tucked his stethoscope away. "Well, you're right about one thing. You've had a miscarriage. Now, you are going to have to give your body time to heal, so you have to promise me you'll take it easy for at least a couple of days."

He turned to Sara Beth. "Do you have Red Raspberry Leaf tea?"

She nodded.

"I'd suggest several cups a day to help stop the blood flow. But other than that, there's not much to be done. It will take time."

Rose gripped his hand. "I feel just awful, doctor. I wished this baby away."

"No, dear. It doesn't work like that. Your body suffered a trauma, and that's what caused it. I was so afraid that would be the case."

Tears flowed down her cheeks. "I dreamed it was a little girl."

"There, now. Don't torture yourself. You'll heal up just fine and when the time is right, you'll make a terrific mother." He turned to

Sara Beth. "Since I'm here, let's take a look at you. Been having any contractions?"

Sara Beth smiled. "Maybe. Not sure what that feels like, but I've had some tightening sensations. And I'd be obliged if you'd take a look at Uncle Seymour while you're here. He's been a little under the weather."

"Happy to." The doctor adjusted his glasses. "I'd say your time to give birth is getting close."

When the doctor and Sara Beth left the room, Rose turned on her side and let the tears fall.

Oliver peeked in. "Can I get you anything, Rose?"

She motioned for him to come in. "Just time."

He dropped into the chair next to the bed. "Been thinking. Not going to push it to get to St. Louis. We'll go on when you're ready and not before."

"I've been thinking, too." She worried with the hem of the quilt over her. "Not sure I want to stay with Uncle Rube by myself. Don't know what to do."

"Nothing to do today. Just rest and get your strength back. Then we'll figure it out."

"Thank you, Oliver." She reached for his hand.

"No thanks necessary."

She closed her eyes, leaving her hand nestled in his. Just that small act brought a huge amount of comfort.

"If something like this had happened in my father's house, he wouldn't have lifted a finger to help. In fact, he would have told me I deserved it."

"Rose, your father is gone. He can't hurt you anymore. Let go of that thought and focus on the good."

She sighed. "Of course."

She'd get through this just like she'd gotten through every other difficult time.

And maybe she'd come out stronger and wiser.

At least she hoped so.

One thing she knew. She had people who cared about her and would help any way possible. For that, she was extremely grateful.

She tightened her grip on Oliver's hand, as if it were a lifeline.

# CHAPTER 29

Over the next three days, Oliver, Jack, and Tab worked from sunup to sundown in the field, alongside Layken and Seymour harvesting the peanut crop.

Tab had been ecstatic when Layken and Sara Beth agreed to let him stay home from school.

As it approached evening, after helping Sara Beth start supper, Rose sat on the porch swing holding Cuddles and watching Seymour drive the tractor slowly down the rows, while the others followed behind, tossing the peanuts into wagons. They were so close to being finished.

The dogs chased each other around the yard. Pirate stopped long enough to grab a stick with his mouth, and Rose laughed at his attempt to throw it for the other two.

A stunningly brilliant sunset formed over the tops of the trees and the breeze carried a fresh, clean scent. It was beautiful and peaceful here. Just what she needed to begin to heal from everything awful that had happened to her over the past five years.

She had a lot to think about. While a part of her was relieved to no longer be pregnant, another part of her grieved for the unborn child. She'd never forget the dream and how beautiful the little girl was. Maybe someday she'd see her again.

Sara Beth joined her and the swing creaked as she dropped onto it. "Thank you for helping me get supper going. You're starting to get some color back in your face. Feeling better?"

"I don't ever mind helping. My hands need something to do. My body feels better, but my heart hurts and my mind is in a jumble." She stroked the bunny's soft fur.

"Understandable. Everything has changed for you. What do you want to do now?"

"Been trying to figure it out. I don't think I want to live in St. Louis with Uncle Rube by myself." She twisted her hands in her lap. "Jack seems pretty determined to stay here and go to school."

"He's more than welcome to stay here with us. He's a good kid and has a big heart. I like the way he's kind to Tab and patient with all the questions that boy can toss out."

"You and Layken are like Oliver's mother…good, caring people." She tugged a light shawl around her shoulders against the cool fall air.

"We just do what we feel is right. We had lots of help from our neighbors last year, as we worked to save this farm." She pointed to the tractor. "That's a good example. When Layken's tractor burned inside the barn last year, we had no idea how he would be able to keep farming. But then a neighboring farmer needed help with his crops and offered to loan the tractor in exchange for Layken's help."

"What a generous offer." Rose pushed the swing with her toe. "I'm not afraid of hard work and guess I'll be needing to get a job, but more than anything, like Jack, I want to go to school and finish getting my education."

Sara Beth laid a hand on Rose's. "I want you to know that you are also welcome to stay here with Jack, if you want."

"I appreciate that. But I don't know. Lots to think about. First, I need to go see Uncle Rube. Then, I'll make some decisions."

"Oliver cares for you, Rose."

"And I do him, too. You should have seen me the night we met. I was so clumsy trying to dance with him and scared to death my father would see us and hurt him." She chuckled. "He told me I had the prettiest eyes he'd ever seen."

"I agree with Oliver. Don't think I've ever met anyone with violet eyes."

"He's a good man, and I feel lucky to have met him that night."

"Life is full of surprises."

"Anyway, I don't know what lies ahead for me. I only know I won't allow myself to be abused by anyone ever again."

"I'm happy to hear you say that. No one deserves to be hit and demeaned." She stared off into the distance. "My used-to-be father would hit me. Always on the face. Layken has never even raised his voice to me, much less a hand."

"Why do you call him your used-to-be father?" Rose glanced at her friend.

"I was raised by him, but Uncle Seymour finally told me the truth. My mother was raped, and I was a product of that. When Homer Williams married her, he gave me his name, but never his love. I didn't understand any of it until I knew the whole story."

Rose gasped. "Your mother was raped, just like me."

"Yes. I always wondered why I never looked anything like Homer Williams."

"I wish she was here so I could talk to her. She'd understand."

Sara Beth reached for her hand and squeezed it. "She would. I wish she was here too, so she could help me birth this baby."

The two sat in silence, gently swinging back and forth.

Suddenly, Sara Beth clutched her belly. "Oh, God. That really hurt. I wonder if it's time."

When she stood, water streamed down her legs into a puddle on the porch.

Rose jumped up and set the rabbit down. "Your water broke. You're going to have this baby." Her voice shook along with her hands. "What can I do?"

"Please go get Layken." Sara Beth cradled her stomach, scooped up Cuddles, and waddled into the house.

Sprinting from the porch, Rose ran all the way to the field, waving her arms. Seymour stopped the tractor and Oliver strode toward her.

"What's wrong, Rose?"

Out of breath, she bent over. "Sara Beth."

"What about Sara Beth?" Layken joined them.

"The baby's coming. Her water broke."

With Oliver close behind, Layken raced to the house. He called over his shoulder as he tossed his pickup keys to Oliver. "Go get the doctor. Hurry."

Oliver caught the keys and jumped into the pickup.

Rose took a minute to catch her breath, then Jack, Tab, and Seymour hurried back to the house with her.

Tab frowned. "Is Sara Beth going to be okay, Rose?"

"She'll be fine, but this baby is coming."

Jack steadied her when she stumbled over a clod of dirt. "You don't look so good, sister."

"I'm okay. Out of breath and feeling a little weak from running, but I had to get help. Let's hurry and see what we can do."

She hoped the doctor would come quickly.

Once inside the house, she called out. "Sara Beth, Layken, what can we do?"

Layken's baritone voice came from the bedroom. "Rose, Sara Beth wants you to come in."

Her heart pounding, she dashed down the hallway to the bedroom. She paused in the doorway. Sara Beth lay propped up on pillows, sweating and breathing hard, clutching Layken's hand as he smoothed back her hair. "What can I do?"

Sara Beth sucked in a breath and winced as another contraction hit. "The doctor told me warm compresses would help ease the pains when they started." She pointed toward the hall closet. "You'll find a stack of towels in there I saved just for that purpose."

"Got it. Anything else?" Rose stood at the foot of the bed feeling more helpless than she had in her entire life, except for when her mother had died.

"Feed the boys and make sure Tab takes care of Cuddles." She turned to Layken. "You need to eat, too. It may be a long night."

"I'm not going anywhere, sweetheart. Right now I couldn't force down a bite." He grinned. "Our baby's coming."

Sara Beth glowed. "That it is." She groaned as another pain hit. "They're coming closer together."

Rose stepped away. "I'll make the warm compresses first, then feed the boys. Hope the doctor gets here soon."

"Thanks, Rose."

"Happy to help. Just let me know if you need anything else." She glanced at Layken. "How about a cup of coffee for you?"

"That'd be great." He never let go of Sara Beth's hand.

The love the couple shared warmed her heart. Someday she'd have that. Her heart knew it. She'd been given a second chance at life and she wouldn't waste it.

She hurried to gather the towels, make compresses, and boil coffee.

---

Oliver pushed the old pickup as fast as it would go, praying he'd remember the way to the doctor's office. Thank goodness Everton was a small place. He could always stop and ask if he couldn't find it right off.

Urgency pressed him forward.

He pulled to a stop in front of Dr. Jennings' place and jumped out of the truck, hardly bothering to turn off the engine.

Taking the steps two at a time, he knocked on the door. Mrs. Jennings opened the door and the scent of roast beef drifted through the doorway.

"What is it, young man?"

"It's Sara Beth Martin. She's gone into labor, and we need the doctor to come."

"Oh, my." She stepped aside. "Come in and I'll get him. He's just finishing his supper."

"Sorry to intrude, but I guess babies don't care."

She chuckled. "You would be right about that." She called out. "Harold, Sara Beth's gone into labor. They need you."

The doctor appeared in the doorway, wiping his mouth. "Tell me what's happening."

"Don't know much, other than her water broke and Layken sent me to fetch you."

"Well, I'll get my things together and be on out. You had supper yet?"

"No sir, but that's okay. I want to get back as quick as I can."

The doctor nodded. "I understand." He turned to his wife. "Don't wait up for me, honey. You never know with the first one how long it might take."

She patted her husband's arm. "Tell Sara Beth I'm praying for her."

He reached for his hat. "I'll be right behind you."

Oliver sprinted back to the pickup and nosed it toward the farm.

He hoped Sara Beth wouldn't have a hard time and be able to deliver a healthy baby. She and Layken deserved that.

They were salt-of-the-earth people.

If only his mum was there. She always knew what to do.

A pang of homesickness washed over him.

At least they lacked very little to finish gathering the crop.

Then he could focus on getting the Woody on the road again.

"Patience, Oliver," he muttered. "Everything in its time."

Was that his father's booming voice he heard in his head?

# CHAPTER 30

Sara Beth's labor continued throughout the night. Tab and Jack turned in a little before midnight, and Seymour followed soon afterward. Oliver and Rose sat on the couch in the living room, waiting, while the only sounds in the house came from Sara Beth as she groaned and panted, occasionally letting out a low growl or muffled scream.

Oliver twisted around on the couch to face Rose. He tucked a stray hair behind her ear. "We haven't had a chance to talk since…" He lowered his gaze to his hands.

"It's okay to say it, Oliver. I miscarried."

He gazed into her violet-blue eyes, seeing a deep tiredness. "Okay. Since you lost the baby. How are you feeling?"

"Tired all the time, but the doctor said that's normal. I'll get my strength back."

"I know this changes everything for you. Do you still want to go on to St. Louis?"

"I've been thinking a lot about it." She leaned against the back of the couch and blew out a soft sigh. "Yes. Uncle Rube said Aunt Katherine left something for me. It seems important. And I need to see if his place is where I want to be. I've got my doubts about living by myself with him."

Oliver arched an eyebrow. "Why is that?"

"Just that I really don't know him and without Jack or Harlan, I'd be a little lost. Jack's determined to stay here and going to school, and I am fine with that."

"I think it's a great option for Jack, but he hates to disappoint you."

"I know, but I've told him he has to do what's best for him, just like I do." She stared down at her hands. "We've both been given a chance at making a good life. Harlan, too. At least I hope so. I wonder every day where he is and what he's doing. I think I'll be able to make some concrete decisions after I see Uncle Rube."

"That's wise. Haven't really found a way to show you how I feel, but I'm truly sorry you lost the baby."

"It's a mixed blessing. At least I can get an education now and find out what it's like to be somewhat normal."

"My father had a saying that seems to be true. He said, one dream must die to let another live."

A tear trickled down her cheek. "That is very true. And how does that apply to you? What do you have to give up to live your dream of playing baseball?"

Oliver wiped away the stray tear with the pad of his thumb and hesitated. That was a hard question. "I guess I have to give up my family and my job at the sawmill, to some extent. I keep telling myself I can juggle it all and be home when it's off season. But that may be a pipe dream."

"I remember Uncle Rube was gone a lot. That's why Aunt Katherine lived near us for a while. She and my mom were close."

"I wish I had all the answers for everyone. Life has sure taken some twists for all of us. Jack is the only one that seems one-hundred percent sure about what he wants to do."

"Right before she went into labor, Sara Beth told me I'm welcome to stay here with Jack, but I don't think that's what's best for me. I need a chance to experience life, not to be isolated on a farm."

"I agree. This is going to sound selfish, but I'm hoping you'll come back to Crossett with me and live with us. My mum and sisters would be happy about that."

She raised her eyes. "And you?"

Oliver rubbed the back of his neck. "I'd be more than happy about that. Rose, I've had the desire to make things better for you since the night we met. Maybe it's not what you want to hear, but I have to be honest. I've come to care deeply for you."

"How is that possible? I've been nothing but a burden."

"Not the way I see it." He pushed to his feet, feeling the need to change the subject. "Want more coffee?"

She nodded. "Looks like it's going to be a long night."

Oliver grinned. "Babies take their own sweet time coming into this world. I'll be right back. How about another piece of that chocolate cake you baked?"

"I'll come with you." She stood and slipped her small hand into Oliver's.

He liked that. He liked that a lot. Every protective instinct he had arose. He wanted to make sure Rose had nothing but good things ahead. She'd already suffered enough for one lifetime.

And maybe she would decide to go back to Crossett with him. The thought of seeing her every day and watching her blossom into a happy and confident young woman made his chest swell.

Whatever she decided, he'd support her.

---

Around four the next morning, squalls from the bedroom announced the baby's arrival. Oliver stirred from where he'd fallen asleep on the couch, Rose nestled against his side. He eased off the couch, careful not to awaken her, and meandered down the hallway, stopping at the bedroom door.

The sight of Layken holding the newborn in his arms left him misty-eyed. When he spotted him, Layken choked out, "It's a boy. We have a baby boy."

Dr. Jennings packed his black bag and patted Sara Beth on her shoulder. "You did good, little mama. I insist you take it easy for a few days. There are plenty of people here to tend to things."

Sara Beth managed a tired smile. "I will, sir. Thank you."

Layken placed the baby in her arms. "I'll walk you out, doctor." He motioned to Oliver. "Stay with Sara Beth?"

"Sure." He took a few hesitant steps inside the room.

"Come here, Oliver." She patted the side of the bed. "Want to see Henry Jacob Martin?"

Once he settled onto the bed, she passed the swaddled bundle to him.

His heart ratcheted. "He's so tiny." He stared down at the red face with eyes squinched shut and a fist in his mouth.

"Tiny, but got some mighty big lungs. The doctor says he's perfect." Her face glowed.

"I think I have to agree with Doctor Jennings. He looks perfect to me and I love the name."

"Jacob was Layken's father and Henry was his grandfather, so this little man will carry on the Martin name."

Oliver passed the baby back to her. "Can I get you anything?"

"I'd love a cool drink of water. Thank you."

"Be right back." He hurried to the kitchen as Rose stirred and sat up on the couch.

"Everything all right?"

"The baby's here. It's a boy. Go see." He pointed to the bedroom. "Sara Beth wants a drink of water and Layken walked the doctor out."

When he returned with a glass of water, Rose sat on the end of the bed with Henry in her arms. Tears streamed down her face and it broke his heart to see how strongly holding the little one affected her. It was understandable, though.

She glanced up when he handed Sara Beth the water. "Isn't he beautiful, Oliver?"

"That he is." He placed a hand on her shoulder and peered down at the infant. "As I told Sara Beth, he's perfect."

"Don't worry about anything, Sara Beth." Rose swiped at her tears. "I'll take care of the house for you. You're going to do nothing but rest and take care of this little one."

Sara Beth shifted on the bed and swung her legs over. "Will you hold Henry while I go to the bathroom?"

"My pleasure." Rose ran a finger across the baby's cheek. "I think I'm in love."

Oliver placed a hand on Sara Beth's elbow, steadying her. "You sure you're okay?"

She cradled her stomach with one hand and leaned on Oliver. "Think so. Will you wait outside the door?"

"Of course." He flashed a smile at Rose, who cuddled the baby close and swayed back and forth, an angelic look on her face.

Yes, she'd make a wonderful mother someday.

Oliver gasped at the next thought.

What if one day he was standing in Layken's shoes and holding his and Rose's baby?

A big part of him hoped that was in the cards.

But she was young and needed an opportunity to explore whatever life had to offer. If that included him, it would be wonderful.

And if it didn't?

Well, he'd cross that bridge when it got built.

He'd always root for her and whatever her dreams were. Fate had thrown them together. He'd never forget the first time he saw Rose, how her beautiful eyes mesmerized him. She'd come so far in finding herself, her strength, and her dreams since that night.

He was proud of the way she was taking charge of her life with caution and a bit of hard-earned wisdom.

There was a reason he'd been drawn to her at the dance.

His mum always said, there was a purpose for everything and everyone throughout life.

Sara Beth flushed the toilet and opened the door, gripping the door frame with white knuckles. "I'm dizzy. Can you help me back to bed, Oliver?"

Oliver didn't hesitate. He put an arm around her waist and all but carried her back to the bedroom as Layken returned. "She got dizzy going to the bathroom."

Layken turned down the covers. "You, my love, are confined to this bed." He helped her in and pulled up the covers, then turned to Rose with outstretched arms. "Here, I'll take him."

Rose kissed the baby on his cheek and handed him to Layken. "I'll go get breakfast started." She patted Sara Beth's leg. "If you need anything, just yell."

Oliver followed Rose to the kitchen. "I'm proud of you."

"For what?"

"I saw how holding the baby affected you, but you handled it. Just know I saw and I know."

She smiled at him. "Want to help me with breakfast?"

"It'd be my pleasure. Then me and the boys are going to finish harvesting the peanuts for Layken today."

Seymour lumbered in through the back door, adjusting his suspenders and a big question in his eyes.

Oliver nodded. "Henry Jacob Martin is here."

A wide grin split Seymour's face, and his eyes lit up. "That's just dandy. Just dandy."

# CHAPTER 31

After breakfast, the men headed to the field, minus Layken. With Seymour driving the tractor, and Oliver, Jack, and Tab helping, they finished gathering the peanuts. Once they had them all piled in the barn and covered with a tarp, everyone suffered from lack of sleep and fatigue. By midafternoon, Oliver grew restless.

Now that Rose was healing and growing stronger, the need to get the Woody fixed and going on to St. Louis was forefront in his mind. He still had the key to Layken's pickup in his pocket from yesterday's dash to town to get the doctor.

He wandered down the hallway to the bedroom. The door was open and Layken lay stretched out on the bed beside Sara Beth, both asleep with the new baby nestled between them. At the foot of the bed, Cuddles had his head tucked under his front legs, snoozing.

For a brief moment, he took in the scene. It warmed his heart and brought a smile. This was life at its best, something for every decent man to aspire to.

Backing out quietly, he scrubbed the back of his neck and wrestled with the thought of taking the pickup back to town without first asking permission. It went against his nature.

Rose had asked Jack and Tab to set up the wash tubs outside and she busied herself with the mound of laundry generated from the birthing process.

He joined them, happy to see both boys helping.

Jack pinned a sheet on the clothesline, with Tab holding one end of it. He glanced at Oliver. "Getting restless?"

Oliver grinned. "How can you tell? Wanting to go check on the oil pan, but Layken's asleep and I certainly don't want to wake him. They had a long night."

Seymour ambled up, rubbing his eyes from a nap. "Problem?"

"No problem. I want to go check on the welding, but don't want to take the pickup without asking Layken and he's asleep."

"You know he's going to say yes, so go ahead." The old man gave a toothy grin. "I'll tell him if he gets up."

"You sure? Don't want to step on any toes."

Seymour waved him away. "Never seen Layken turn down helping anyone yet. It's okay."

Oliver jerked off his paddy cap and ran a hand through his hair. "Then I'll head out and be back as quick as I can." He turned to Rose. "Need anything from town?"

"Yes, actually, I do. Could you pick up a roast at the store if we have the money for it? I'd like to cook it for supper to celebrate Henry's arrival. Oh, and I noticed this morning when I made biscuits, we're low on flour." She ran a towel through the wringer and let it drop into the rinse water, as all three dogs rounded the corner of the house in pursuit of the barn cat, who easily outmaneuvered them and shimmied up a tree.

Oliver whistled for Pirate. He'd take him to town with him and give Sadie and Pearl a break, although the three got along as if they'd always been together.

He picked up the little dog. "Roast and flour. Anything else?"

Rose shook her head. "Can't think of it."

"Then I'll be on my way." He strode around the house to the pickup, whistling while he walked. Something about the day felt different.

Maybe it was the new life that had entered earlier, or maybe it was the satisfaction of finishing the harvest.

All he knew was that his step was lighter and heart hopeful. If he could pick up the oil pan and get it put back on, they could continue their journey in the next day or so. He could still make the deadline for the meeting with Mr. DeWitt.

The thought of talking with the manager of the team brought butterflies to his stomach. This was his chance, the one he'd dreamed of since he could remember.

He gazed up at the clear sky, a contrast with the brown, orange, and gold leaves on the trees. "For you, Dad. The dream you never got to live."

While he drove, he thought about the good times when his father took the time to teach him to pitch, catch, and swing the bat. *Swing for the fence,* he'd tell him. Then there were the ball games he'd attend when his father played for the Crossett Millers. The desire had been strong in Patrick Quinn to make a better life for his family in whatever way he could. He was good at fighting in the boxing rings, but the sawmill provided security and a regular paycheck. He sacrificed his dream for the family. That was until the fateful day when a saw blade ripped through his leg, severing the main artery.

Now it was Oliver's turn to provide a better life for them all, and perhaps that included Rose. He couldn't think of anything more rewarding.

He pulled to a stop in front of the welding shop, relieved to see the door open.

"Stay," he commanded Pirate as he opened the pickup door.

The little dog whimpered, but obeyed, plastering his face against the window.

"Hello," he called out as he hurried inside.

"Back here."

Oliver strode to the back side of the shop. "Mr. Travis, I'm here to check on my oil pan. You had a chance to weld it yet?"

The welder pushed up his face shield. "Sure did. Finished it about ten minutes ago."

"Must've felt it." Oliver chuckled.

The man pointed toward the metal table. "Over there."

Oliver picked it up and examined it. "You did a great job. Can't hardly tell where the hole was. What do I owe you?"

"How about three dollars? That fair? Didn't take but a few minutes and one rod."

"Fair enough." He pulled the worn money pouch out of his pocket and counted out the bills, noting what he had left.

He shook the man's hand, thanking him for it, and made a beeline for the store, then started back toward the farm when he remembered he'd need oil to put back in the car.

Swinging by the gas station, he filled up Layken's pickup, then picked up five quarts, turning loose of another two dollars.

With any luck, he'd have the oil pan back on and the Woody ready by nightfall.

But would Rose be up to traveling yet? Although she put on a brave face, the circles under her eyes said she hadn't fully recovered.

He mulled over their conversation, especially Rose's reaction to his declaration that he'd come to care deeply for her.

No doubt she appreciated all he did, but she might not share his growing feelings. One thing was for sure, he'd never push her.

She deserved the opportunity to make her own decisions. Should she decide to go back to Crossett with him, Elizabeth and Margaret would be ecstatic.

Truthfully, so would he.

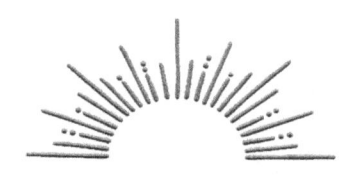

---

Rose stopped working on the laundry and brushed back a stray hair, blowing out a sigh. All she wanted to do was lie down, but she had to keep going. After all Sara Beth had done for her, she relished the chance to repay her.

Jack frowned. "Rose, would you please go inside and rest? Let us finish this."

"I'm okay. Just had to breathe for a minute."

"You look like you're about to fall over. I'm telling you, we can finish up what's left, right, Tab?"

"Sure, Jack. I help Sara Beth with laundry all the time. I know how." The thirteen-year-old puffed out his chest.

Rose grinned at the display. "You boys are something else. Guess I could go rest for a bit. When Oliver gets back, I want to start supper."

Jack pointed to the back door. "Go. That's an order."

She dried her hands and stepped into the cool interior of the house. She poured a glass of tea and took it to her favorite spot—the porch swing. After a sip, she closed her eyes, and with her toe, put the swing into motion.

The dogs barking jarred her a few minutes later, and she jumped up. "Shh," she called to them. The last thing she wanted was for them to wake Sara Beth, Layken, or the baby. "Here, girls." She opened the screen door and stood on the top step.

Coming up the long driveway, a man wearing a worn hat pulled low ambled along carrying a bedroll and knapsack. There was something oddly familiar in his gait. For a moment, her breath caught in her throat. Whoever he was looked uncannily like her dead pa.

The dogs sat at the bottom of the steps, their tails wagging, but at least they stopped barking.

As the man drew closer, she sucked in a breath and bounded off the steps, with Sadie and Pearl on her heels. "Harlan!" She ran toward him as tears sprang into her eyes.

He shifted a bedroll to his back. "Rose."

When she reached him, he embraced her. "Harlan. How did you find us?"

He hugged her tight and cleared his throat, then held her at arm's length, looking her up and down. "I called Uncle Rube yesterday, sure you'd be there, and he told me where you were. I was worried about you and Jack. Had to come and see what was happening and why you weren't in St. Louis."

He looked thinner and older than she remembered. She took in the scruffy beard and dusty clothes. It was obvious he'd been on the road for a while. He looked so much like their father. Yet there was something different about her brother. He'd lost the hard look in his eyes. "Come on up to the house. I'll tell you everything. Jack's going to be so happy to see you." While they walked, she caught him up on the car issue, then avoided telling him about the miscarriage. What good would it do?

When they reached the house, he deposited his bedroll and knapsack on the front porch. Then she led him through the kitchen and out the back door.

"Jack, look who's here."

With soap up to his elbows, Jack glanced up, then did a double-take. "Harlan?"

"Hey, little brother. I see you've resorted to doing women's work." He grinned widely.

"Hot damn!" Jack wiped his hands on his pants and bolted toward his brother, giving him a man hug while Harlan tousled his hair. "How did you find us?"

After Harlan explained, Rose took hold of his arm and pointed toward Seymour and Tab, making introductions all around. Then, she explained about Sara Beth, Layken, and the new baby.

"What a surprise." Rose couldn't believe he was there. "I want to hear everything. Where have you been? What have you been doing?"

Jack nodded. "Share, big brother."

"Got anything to drink? Been walking a long way."

Rose rushed into the house and poured another glass of tea, then went back out.

Harlan took a big gulp and wiped his mouth. "Been traveling around mostly. The jalopy took out on me the second day and I sold it for a little money in Hot Springs. Hopped a few freights and got rides with some truckers." He shrugged. "That's about it. Just been trying to figure out what to do next." He glanced around. "Where's Irish?"

"Gone into Everton. A man was patching the hole in the oil pan, so he wanted to check on it. He should be back soon." Rose took his hand, still having a hard time believing he'd found them. "Let's all go to the front porch so we can talk without disturbing Sara Beth and Layken."

Tab and Seymour hung up the last of the laundry and motioned to them to go on. Seymour said, "We'll finish up here. You kids go visit."

Jack stopped in the kitchen long enough to snag a leftover biscuit from breakfast and a glass of tea for himself.

On the front porch, Harlan settled into a straight-back chair and rolled a cigarette, while Jack sat cross-legged on the porch floor. Rose took her place on the swing. They'd no sooner settled in when Oliver drove the pickup up the driveway and parked it.

He got out and lifted Pirate down. The little dog immediately dashed to join Sadie and Pearl, while they sniffed him all over. Oliver grabbed the oil pan from the back, holding it up. "Got it."

Jack got to his feet and let out a whoop, followed by, "You'll never believe who wandered up, Oliver."

Oliver approached the porch, then stopped in his tracks. "Harlan?"

Harlan stood and blew out a stream of smoke. "It's me, Irish."

"Well, I'll be damned. Good to see you, man." He opened the screen door and stepped onto the porch, hand extended.

"Good to see you, too. Sounds like you've all had a bit of trouble."

"A bit, but things are looking up."

When Oliver shot her a glance, Rose looked away. She knew the question in his eyes.

Jack interjected, telling Harlan all about learning to milk the goats and harvest peanuts. Harlan let out a chuckle. "Been getting a country education, little brother."

Oliver said, "Hope you guys don't mind, but I'm going to go work on the Woody while there's still daylight. Come out to the barn and keep me company, if you want."

"We'll do better than that, Irish." Harlan handed his empty tea glass to Rose. "We'll help you. Thanks for the tea, sis."

Rose smiled at her brother and laid a hand on Oliver's arm. "Did you get the roast and flour?"

Oliver slapped his forehead. "Yes. Sorry. I'll grab them."

Jack bounded down the steps. "I'll get them."

Turning back to Harlan, Oliver said, "I'm sure these two have already asked you, but fill me in on what's going on and where you've been."

When Jack returned with the groceries, he handed them to Rose, then gathered their empty glasses and followed her into the kitchen while Oliver and Harlan walked around the house toward the barn.

Jack kissed Rose's cheek. "Holler if you need anything. Gonna go to the barn." He grinned. "Can you believe it? Harlan found us."

She loved seeing her brother so happy. But then, Jack was pretty much always happy. What a contrast from the tense atmosphere they'd had at home with their father. "I'm having a hard time believing it." She pointed toward the door. "Go on, but you have to tell me everything I miss."

While she unwrapped the roast and dumped the flour into the bin, unanswered questions flooded her mind.

Would Harlan finally tell her the truth about what happened with their father back in the moonshiner shack? Would she have the courage to tell him about the miscarriage? What could he tell her about Uncle Rube's place? The big city?

So many questions.

She salted and peppered the roast and set a cast-iron skillet on the stove. Now, there was even more reason to celebrate tonight.

Remembering the jars of peaches she'd seen in the cupboard, she decided to make a cobbler, although Layken's favorite was chocolate cake.

Still, she knew how to make a delicious cobbler, just the way her mom had taught her. And tonight's celebration was as much about her brothers as it was the new baby.

Call her crazy, but she could feel her mother smiling down on them. They were all together again, regardless of how long it lasted.

Once she had browned the roast on both sides, she covered it with onions, potatoes, and carrots, and slipped it into the oven, thankful Oliver had bought a big one.

The one thing her mother had always insisted on, no matter what they had, was that there be enough for everyone.

And tonight she'd make sure of it.

She was together with her brothers.

# CHAPTER 32

Oliver carefully replaced the fragile and worn gasket around the edge of the oil pan while Harlan shared stories of living on the road and the people he'd met.

"Stumbled onto a hobo camp just outside Little Rock and stayed a couple of days. The old men gave me lots of advice about places and things to avoid. They were all nice fellas, but that's not the life I want." He paused to light another cigarette.

"What do you want, Harlan?" Jack declined when Harlan offered him a smoke.

"Want to find a place somewhere I can put down roots. The truck driver that dropped me off in Greenfield today said there are lots of jobs over in Joplin. Thinking I'll head that way."

"Jack, can you pass me the bolts? And can you and Harlan steady the motor?" Oliver leaned in to hold the oil pan in place while the motor swayed on the chain and pulley.

"Sure." Jack placed the first bolt in his hand.

Harlan crushed out his smoke and grabbed one side of the motor while Jack held the other. "Smart to rig this up on a pulley."

"Layken's idea." Oliver grunted as he struggled to thread the first bolt.

Jack pressed. "What was it like in St. Louis, Harlan?"

"Big. To be honest, I didn't care much for it. Too many people and noise. Uncle Rube's place is nice, though. You and Rose will be happy there."

Oliver tightened the bolt and glanced at Jack in time to see him look away and duck his head.

"Not going on to St. Louis, Harlan. Staying here and going to school in Everton. Tab's told me about how they have all ages and grades of kids and that the other kids don't make fun of them for being poor or behind." His voice trailed off. "I want an education."

Harlan grinned. "You were always smarter than the rest of us, Jack. If this is where you want to land, more power to you."

Oliver threaded another bolt into the oil pan. "Wait 'til you meet Layken and Sara Beth. You'll know this is a great place for Jack to finish growing up."

"Sara Beth had a baby last night," Jack said. "I haven't got to see him yet, but it's a boy."

"So I heard. Sounds like you're breaking ties with our family, little brother. Is that what you want?" Harlan braced against the fender.

"It's not like that. You and Rose will always be my family. This place just feels like where I need to be."

"Guess I can understand that."

The three continued to work together in silence until all the bolts were in place.

Layken strolled into the barn looking more rested, with Tab following behind. "Looks like you've been busy, Oliver." He glanced at Harlan and an eyebrow shot up.

Oliver straightened. "Layken, this is Jack and Rose's older brother, Harlan. He found us here today."

Layken stuck out his hand. "Nice to meet you, Harlan. Welcome to our place."

"Thank you, sir." Harlan shook his hand. "And congratulations on the new baby."

"I feel like I've been caught in a time warp. A lot has happened in the last twenty-four hours."

"Hope you don't mind, but I took your pickup into Everton while you were resting and picked up the oil pan."

"Of course I don't mind. And from the smells in the house, Rose is cooking up something delicious for supper."

Oliver grinned. "She wanted to make a roast to celebrate the new baby. That was before Harlan showed up. Now, it's a triple celebration with the peanuts gathered. How are Sara Beth and Henry doing?"

Layken's eyes lit up. "Both doing great. Never imagined what it'd feel like to be a father. My life now has a much bigger purpose." He glanced at the motor still swaying above the Woody. "Where are you with this?"

"Just finished reattaching the oil pan and about to lower the motor back down."

"Glad I showed up. Let me help. This thing is heavy." He pointed to the pulley. "Jack, if you, Tab, and Harlan will slowly lower the chain over the pulley, I can help Oliver put in place and secure the motor mounts."

By the time the men had repositioned the motor and secured it, the sun had dropped behind the horizon and they could no longer see inside the barn.

"Time to head to the house for supper." Layken clapped Oliver on the back. "Tomorrow you should get this girl running again." He glanced toward the towering, tarped pile in the back of the barn. "And thank you all for finishing the harvest."

"Our pleasure. Finished by mid-day. Wasn't that much left to gather."

"Still, know it's appreciated. My buyer will be here the day after tomorrow to pick it all up and pay me. To my estimation, it just might be enough to finish paying off the bank note." He chuckled. "Can't wait to see Homer Williams' face when I walk in the door with the money. We'll be free from him for good."

"That'll be a great day." Oliver pointed toward the brightly lit house. "Let's go get supper. I can smell it all the way out here. I think Rose has outdone herself."

Oliver had to admit Rose had shown more strength than he'd thought she had. Having a purpose in life always helped with any recovery, and she had stepped up in a big way today.

She had a big incentive.

Rose stared out the kitchen window and watched her brothers walking side-by-side. Jack was almost as tall as Harlan now. How had she not noticed that before? Jack was becoming a man. Harlan rolled a cigarette and offered it to Jack. She smiled when Jack shook his head, then bent down to pet the dogs, all three clamoring for attention.

Yes, her little brother was growing up and while she'd miss him, in her heart she knew this was the best place for him to be.

The baby set up a fuss, and she hurried down the hallway to the bedroom to see Sara Beth changing his diaper.

"Need anything, Sara Beth?" She stepped into the room.

"Everything's good. He just needed changing, and now he's hungry." Sara Beth picked up the infant and propped herself up against the headboard, then lowered her gown bodice. "He's latching on good." Her face radiated with love as she gazed down at her son.

"Does it hurt?" Rose stared.

"A little. But I'll get used to it." She adjusted the baby in her arms. "What have I missed? I feel like I've been asleep for days. That is between feedings. Something smells good and I'm suddenly ravenously hungry."

Rose smiled. "Well, let's see. The men finished harvesting the peanuts this morning. Oliver went into town and picked up the repaired oil pan. My older brother, Harlan, showed up looking for us, and I made a roast with all the trimmings and a peach cobbler for supper to celebrate it all."

Sara Beth chuckled. "What a day, huh?"

"Yes, what a day. If you don't need anything, I'll go get supper on the table."

"Thank you, Rose…for everything." She reached for Rose's hand and gave it a squeeze.

"It's the least I could do to repay you for all you and Layken have done for us."

"Still, I don't know what I'd have done without you."

"Will you feel like coming to the table? If not, I will fix you a tray."

"If Henry goes back to sleep, I'd love to get out of this bed for a few minutes." She pointed to the wooden cradle Layken had placed beside the bed. "He likes his cradle and I can rock him without having to get up."

Rose turned to leave. "Just let me know whatever you need. I am here to help."

In the kitchen, she slid the roast from the oven and placed it onto a platter, then mounded the vegetables around it. The men burst through the back door, bringing a surge of cooler air from outside.

Harlan stopped next to her, kissed her cheek, and sniffed. "I don't remember the last time I smelled anything so good, Rose. It makes me think of our mom."

"And I made a peach cobbler using her recipe."

"My mouth is watering."

"So's mine," Tab chimed in. "And I didn't even know your mom. Where's Uncle Seymour?"

Rose pointed toward the living room. "He helped me for a while in the kitchen, then picked up Cuddles and said he was going to the front porch to rest. Want to go get him?"

"Sure." Tab took off in a sprint.

"Tab, when you come back, bring another chair from the porch."

"Will do," he threw over his shoulder.

Sara Beth joined them at the table, her cheeks rosy and a permanent smile on her face.

Rose loved watching everyone enjoy the meal she'd prepared and blushed under all the praises.

It was delicious and soon there was nothing left but empty plates.

Tab and Jack offered to clean up the kitchen. Layken and Sara Beth returned to their son in the bedroom. Seymour headed out to his room, and Oliver proclaimed exhaustion and went to the tent.

Harlan laid a hand on Rose's shoulder. "Going out for a smoke. Walk with me?"

She loved this new version of her brother and had never been more happy for them all to be away from their angry and violent father. "Sure. Let me grab a sweater." Her heart ratcheted. Something in Harlan's demeanor told her he had a lot on his mind.

And so did she.

Would she have the courage to share everything?

Would Harlan?

# CHAPTER 33

Rose pulled on a sweater and grabbed a scarf before hurrying to join Harlan. The night air had turned quite cool, and she folded her arms across her chest as they walked side-by-side. The three dogs fell in step with them, stopping to sniff anything that caught their attention. Somewhere in the distance, an owl hooted. A few seconds later, another answered from far away.

She shivered at the forlorn sound. Why was it that owls always brought a feeling of foreboding? They had always affected her that way. Was she prepared for what Harlan would tell her?

Harlan rolled a cigarette and struck a match to light it. "I know you've got questions, Rose. I wasn't willing to answer them when I left you in Crossett, but I've had time to let it all settle. You deserve to know the truth."

She glanced at him and sucked in a breath. He looked so much like their father, it was almost uncanny. She fought against rising panic, reminding herself that their father was dead and Harlan wouldn't hurt her. He had inherited enough from their gentle mother to balance out the meanness of Ezra Blaine. "Whatever you have to tell me, I'm ready to hear it. All I ask is that you be honest." Her voice held more confidence than she felt.

He sucked on the cigarette and blew out a stream of smoke. A small animal scurried across the path in front of them, and the dry leaves on the trees rustled in the breeze. "When I got out to the cabin, Pa was still alive, but barely. I found him stumbling around in the kitchen, bleeding from a head wound and consumed with rage, yelling about any and everything and not making any sense."

"I guess I should feel relieved to know I didn't kill him." She trembled and grasped Harlan's arm to steady herself.

"You didn't." He took a long drag and paused. "He came after me. Had a butcher knife in his hand."

She gasped, seeing the scene unfolding in her mind as if she was a spectator. "Oh, Harlan, I'm so sorry." A sob escaped, and Harlan patted her hand.

"Don't say that, Rose. I'm the one that's sorry for not doing something sooner to put an end to the violence. He had no right to hit you or Jack."

"Or you," she whispered.

"I was the oldest. It was my responsibility. I promised Ma, and I let her down. That's something I have to live with."

Realizing the futility of arguing, she grew quiet. "What happened next?"

"When he lunged for me, I cold-cocked him but he came up fighting, the knife still in his hand. I hit him again and this time he stumbled into the table, and when he fell, the knife went through his throat." He stopped walking and crushed out his cigarette. "He bled out almost instantly, although it felt like an eternity." He grew quiet. "The truth is, neither of us killed him."

Rose wrapped her arms around her brother. "I guess I should feel relieved, but all I feel is incredibly sad. We knew he'd go completely off the rails someday. It was just a matter of time."

Harlan awkwardly patted her back. "I know. I tell myself that, but nightmares haunt me. I see him laying on the floor with the knife sticking out of his throat and so much blood."

She released him and blew out a sigh. "I have them too…the nightmares. But slowly, they are coming less often."

"Once I knew he was dead, I gathered up a few of your and Jack's clothes and brought them to you. I needed to know you both would be okay before I finished what I had to do."

"What was that?"

"I went back to the shack, dragged Amos' body inside and set fire to the place. Then I went up to the still and smashed it." He spat on the ground. "I never want to be like him, Rose."

She took his face between her hands and made him look at her. "You're not. There is good in you. I see it. You have our mother's blood, too, and she was the kindest, most gentle woman in the world."

He sighed and she let go. "I remember. Sometimes I can still smell her and feel her near."

The two were quiet for a long minute.

Rose finally broke the silence. "There's more that you don't know."

"Tell me. I've held nothing back from you."

"I was pregnant."

Harlan put both hands on her shoulders and bore a hole through her with his gaze. "Who, Rose? Tell me who." His voice shook as he obviously fought for self-control.

"Amos raped me," she barely whispered, refusing to meet his stare. "More than once. I tried to fight him off, but he was bigger and stronger, and he threatened to tell Pa I seduced him."

He dropped his hands to his side, fists clenched. "That sonofabitch. Wish I'd been the one to end his miserable life instead of Pa. Why, oh why didn't you tell me, Rose?" He scraped a hand through his shoulder-length hair. "Good Lord!"

"You weren't exactly easy to talk to, Harlan, and I was ashamed… afraid you'd blame me, just like Pa did."

"Pa knew?"

"Amos apparently bragged to him when Pa confronted him about stealing money. Pa called me all kinds of horrible names. That's when he attacked me. Only this time, I fought back. No one knew I was going to have a baby but me."

"You said, was pregnant. What happened?"

"I lost it."

"Good." A sharpness in his tone made her cringe.

"It hurt so much." Tears streamed down her face and dripped off her chin. "It was the most awful thing I've ever experienced, and if it hadn't been for Sara Beth, it would've been lots worse. I think I would have lost my mind."

Harlan put an arm around her shoulders. "I'm sorry. I didn't mean that in a hateful way, but did you really want to have Amos Parker's kid?"

"No." She swiped at her tears. "No, I didn't, but Sara Beth and Oliver helped me realize the baby was innocent and hating it wasn't right. I'd made peace with it. I even dreamed about it and I know it was a baby girl. Then, I lost it."

He pulled her into an embrace. "I'm so sorry. I can say it over and over again, but it doesn't change the fact that I should have paid more attention to what you and Jack were going through instead of focusing on myself and trying to please Pa."

"We all could've done better." She sobbed into his chest, wetting his shirt.

He let out a long sigh and tightened his embrace. "We have to let all of it go. There are new and good things ahead for us. Opportunities we can't imagine."

She raised her head and sniffled. "I know. And I don't have a clue what I'm going to do."

Harlan tucked a strand of hair under her scarf. "Go on to St. Louis. Live with Uncle Rube and be who and what you want to be."

"Do you know how scary that is?"

He chuckled. "I'm learning to not be afraid of what might be ahead. Whatever it is, has to be better than what we've left behind."

"I will go to St. Louis, but I can't promise that I'll stay. With Aunt Katherine gone, I don't like the thought of living with Uncle Rube by myself." She folded her arms.

"I can understand that. I was surprised today when Jack told me he's staying here and going to school."

"It's the best thing for him. He and Tab have really hit it off and he's excited about getting an education. Wouldn't be surprised if he doesn't find a way to go on to college."

"Let's head back. You're shivering."

She looped an arm through his. "Thank you for telling me the truth. You're right about what's ahead for all of us."

"If you don't stay in St. Louis, are you coming back here?"

"I don't want to live isolated on a farm, although I love Sara Beth and Layken. If I don't stay in St. Louis, I'll go back to Crossett with Oliver and his family."

"You falling for Irish?"

"It's not like that. He's been a good friend, going above and beyond to help us. His whole family is like Layken and Sara Beth, so kind. I simply want a chance to experience being a normal teenager. I might go back to school, and maybe his mother could get me a part-time job at the bakery where she works."

"Will you do something for me?"

"Of course. Anything."

"Wherever you end up, will you keep in touch with Uncle Rube? He will be my lifeline to you. I'll know where to find Jack, but not you."

"I promise." She glanced up at him. "Will you stay here with us for a few days?"

"No. I'm satisfied that you're both going to be okay, and like you, I want a chance to experience life, find a job, a place to live, and maybe even have a girlfriend someday."

She smiled in the darkness. "I'd like that for you."

"We've been through five years of pure hell. I'm ready to put it behind me, be the best person I can be and enjoy life."

"That sounds the same as me. And you are a good person. Don't ever think you're not. Sure, you were hard on me and Jack, but you were just trying to keep the peace with Pa."

With what sounded like gravel in his throat, Harlan ground out, "I love you, sis."

"I love you, too, Harlan."

While the details her brother had shared shook her, a part of her settled into a peaceful knowing that all would eventually work out for the three of them.

Somewhere in the back of her mind, she recalled a quote she'd read in one of Sara Beth's magazines, *To rise from the ashes, you must embrace the flame.*

And rise they would. The Blaine name would no longer be associated with the horrors their father inflicted on them.

They'd make their way through the world with heads held high.

Relief and excitement flooded through her at that thought.

Their mother would be proud of her children.

She glanced up at the clear sky in time to see a star fall.

Her lips curved upward into a contented smile.

# CHAPTER 34

Oliver awoke early the next morning filled with anticipation and excitement. He hurried to dress, slapped on his paddy cap, and slipped out of the tent without disturbing the two younger boys. The dogs trotted behind him as he made his way around the house to the kitchen door.

The welcome scent of coffee told him he wasn't the only one up early.

Rose stood at the stove, stirring gravy in a skillet. She glanced up when he stepped inside.

"Good morning." She flashed a smile.

Something was different about her. The ready smile and sparkle in her eyes spoke of a change, maybe even a degree of peace. He'd wager that Harlan's appearance had a lot to do with that improvement. "Good morning, yourself. I'm happy to see you looking so chipper."

Harlan stepped into the kitchen. "Irish."

"Harlan. Where did you sleep last night? I thought you might come into the tent with us."

"Nah. Slept on the front porch. I love the fresh air." He sniffed. "Coffee, sis?" He gave her a peck on the cheek.

She pointed to the blue-speckled pot on the stove, and cups sitting in a row on the cabinet. "Help yourselves. Breakfast is almost ready."

Oliver poured coffee into two cups and passed one to Harlan. "What are your plans today?"

"Going to head on over to Joplin." He flashed a smile in his sister's direction. "Me and Rose had a long talk last night and for now, I think we're all going to be okay. A big part of that is due to you, Irish. You've been more than a good friend."

Oliver waved him away. "Just doing what any decent fella would. Sure you don't want to stick around or go with us on to St. Louis?"

"No. Rose can fill you in on what we talked about last night, but soon as I talk to Jack this morning, I'm heading out."

Oliver sipped his coffee. "Rose, you think you might be up to traveling by tomorrow morning?"

"I can be ready today, if you want." She poured the gravy into a crock bowl. "But I'd feel bad leaving Sara Beth in a lurch with the new baby."

Layken stepped through the doorway. "You're not leaving us in a lurch. I can promise you that word has already spread about the new baby and neighbors will be pouring in with food and many offers to help." He poured a cup of coffee. "Besides, I'll be around. The man is coming tomorrow to load up the harvest."

Seymour stepped inside. "And I'll be here to do anything that needs doing."

Rose smiled, her violet eyes lighting up. "You've convinced me." She passed a coffee cup to Seymour. "I know you'll all be just fine, but I've loved helping."

Oliver dropped into a chair at the table as Rose set a platter of biscuits in the middle. "Then we just might head on out today. All that's left to do to the Woody is pour the oil in and slip the new fan belt on. Fingers crossed that she'll purr like a kitten when I crank her. Layken, would you mind if I leave Pirate here with Sadie and Pearl?"

"Don't mind at all. The little dog has fit right in with the others."

"It'll only be for a day or two. I appreciate it." His heart sped up. He could still make the deadline to meet with Bill DeWitt.

While they ate, he shared that tidbit of news with Harlan. "So, with any luck, maybe I'll get to try out for the team."

Harlan buttered a biscuit and covered it with gravy. "That's really great. Uncle Rube knows everyone in the business up there. I hope you get what you want. I'll come and watch you play once you're on the team."

Oliver stared at Harlan over the rim of his cup. Rose wasn't the only one that appeared different this morning. He'd previously only seen an angry and violent man in Harlan, not this softer, more caring version. Everyone was changing for the better.

That was good.

"Wouldn't that be something?" Oliver grinned. "Bet I could get you all free tickets."

Layken laughed. "Don't know about coming to watch, but we love listening to the games on the radio. Just think, we might know someone famous."

Now that the possibility was almost in sight, Oliver couldn't quell the intoxicating thought.

Rose poured herself a cup of coffee and joined the men. "Layken, want me to make a plate for Sara Beth?"

He took a big bite before answering. "She was still sleeping when I got up. With the baby waking her up every few hours to nurse, she has to rest when she can. Hope he didn't keep you up last night, Rose."

"Heard him a time or two, but went right back to sleep." She grinned. "His little cry is a sweet sound."

"You look different this morning." He paused with his fork midair. "It's great to see you feeling better."

She ducked her head. "Me and Harlan had a long talk last night. Cleared up a lot."

Harlan shot her a glance. "Our family is going to be okay. And we owe a ton of thanks to all of you."

The screen door squeaked as Jack and Tab came in.

"Just in time." Rose pushed back her chair.

"Don't get up. We can help ourselves." Jack grabbed plates and passed one to Tab, then reached for a cup before sitting.

Layken pointed at Tab. "Soon as you finish eating, you need to tend to chores. Monday morning, you're back in school."

"Yes, sir." Tab reached for a biscuit.

Oliver cleared his plate, downed the remainder of his coffee, and stood. "Going to go finish with the Woody."

"Mind if I come with you?" Harlan picked up his empty plate.

"No, of course not. Come on."

They deposited their dishes in the sink and headed out the back door.

Harlan rolled a cigarette while they walked.

"Wanna tell me what you and Rose talked about last night?" Oliver asked.

"She can fill you in with the details if she wants, but I told her exactly what happened back at the cabin with Pa."

"And?"

"She didn't kill Pa, and neither did I. He fell on the blade he tried to attack me with."

Oliver shuddered at the visual. He had to know if Rose had told him about the baby. "Did Rose…?"

Harlan interrupted. "Yeah, she told me. Sure do regret not being there for her and Jack."

"It was a bad situation all the way around."

"I should've paid more attention to what was happening with them. As the oldest, it was my responsibility, and I'd promised our mother I'd look out for them. We were all caught in the violent nightmare."

Oliver slapped him on the back. "No regrets. Only look forward, not backward."

"Exactly what I told Rose, and what I will tell Jack before I leave."

"Jack's a great kid. He's got a sense of humor and I don't think I've ever seen anyone so excited to learn new things. Layken will be a good role model for him."

They stepped inside the barn and Oliver raised the hood on the Woody.

"What can I do?" Harlan leaned over the fender.

"This new belt's going to be a tight fit. Maybe you can help me stretch it onto the pulley."

"Might should've put it on before we secured the motor mounts."

Oliver grabbed a long screwdriver and wound the belt around the first pulley, then with Harlan's help, slipped it over the crank pulley.

"What a great car, Oliver."

Having Harlan call him by his name surprised Oliver, but he didn't react. "I think so. Love her and she's been good. Couldn't help what happened down the road." He grabbed an oil can and punctured it while Harlan picked up another and did the same.

Within a few minutes, the engine was full of oil and ready for a test run.

"Hop in, Harlan." Oliver slid into the driver's side while Harlan got in on the passenger side. "Let's take her for a spin to feel it out."

He backed out of the barn and drove around the house, then down the driveway to the blacktop.

"She sounds solid to me." Harlan rolled down his window and stuck his elbow out.

Oliver grinned. "I think we're good to go." He glanced at Harlan. "Want I should drop you off somewhere today when we head out?"

"Nah. Joplin's the opposite direction from where you're going. I'll hitch it."

"Do you need anything? Money?"

Harlan stared at him. "You're a good man, Irish. I've got a little money. Hope to have a job come Monday morning. Thanks for the offer."

Oliver turned around and pointed the Woody back to the farm. "I'm sure glad you showed up here. Rose has been so sick and worried, but she looks good today."

Harlan clapped him on the shoulder. "Promise me you'll take care of my sister."

"You've got it." He pulled back into the driveway and parked. "Say, if you get in a bind or need anything, you can always get a message to me at Millie's Pastry Shop in Crossett where my mum works."

"Good to know, but I'm not your responsibility. I can take care of myself."

"I know. Just offering." Oliver got out of the car. "I think you'll find Jack out milking the goats or gathering eggs."

Harlan nodded and turned around. "Hey, Irish, I hope you get what you want." He strode to the back of the house.

Oliver watched him go, then took the front steps two at a time. "Rose?"

"In here." Her voice came from Sara Beth's bedroom.

He stopped in the doorway.

Rose held Henry while Sara Beth sat propped up in the bed devouring her breakfast.

"Did Rose tell you, Sara Beth?"

"Yes, and I'm thrilled for you. Don't worry about leaving. I expect a stream of folks in today with food and all kinds of things for Henry. We'll be just fine." She laughed. "Besides, I'm not an invalid. I just had a baby, something women have been doing for centuries."

Rose cuddled Henry and kissed his red cheek. "As soon as Sara Beth is done eating, I'll go get packed up."

Oliver reached Rose in three strides and peered over her shoulder. "He sure is a handsome little man."

She turned her violet-blue eyes upward and Oliver loved seeing the new sparkle. "He is that."

"Say," said Sara Beth. "Rose, would you like to be Henry's godmother?"

"Are you serious?" She rocked the baby.

"I am. You'd be a wonderful godmother."

"But I won't be living close by."

"Doesn't matter. As long as Jack is around here, you'll always be coming back."

"That is true." She curled the baby's tiny fist around her finger. "Then, yes. I'd be honored to be Henry's godmother."

Sara Beth beamed. "You have been such a blessing and godsend to us—all of you. And adding Jack to our makeshift family is an extra bonus."

Oliver took in the scene as a mixture of emotions flooded Rose's face. He hardly remembered the frail, frightened girl he first met. Her eyes brimmed with unshed happy tears, a far cry from the terror, grief, and pain he'd seen in them before.

Rose was blooming. He smiled at the visual that brought and warmth flooded his chest. A rose bud opening up to its full beauty.

His thoughts turned back to himself and what might lie ahead. Now that it was finally here, he couldn't wait to get to St. Louis. They could be there before nightfall.

Whatever Rose decided when they arrived in St. Louis, he'd stand behind her. But a big part of him hoped she would go back to Crossett with him. While she was still young and needed a chance to experience life, he'd like to be some part of that.

Perhaps tomorrow would bring answers for her.

And tomorrow, perhaps he'd finally get a shot at living his dream. Oh, how he wished his father could see him.

Tomorrow couldn't come soon enough.

## CHAPTER 35

Oliver slowed when they reached the outskirts of St. Louis later that day. The sky had clouded over, but so far no rain. The farther north they traveled, the thicker the trees had gotten, and the scenery even more breathtaking.

Jack had agreed to go with them after Rose begged. Oliver appreciated his willingness to accompany his sister to a strange place. While she'd come a long way, underneath, the shy Rose he'd first met still lived.

Harlan had drawn a rough map with directions to their uncle's house.

Rose sat in the backseat while Jack rode shotgun, the map unfolded on his lap as they passed by busy streets and more cars than Oliver had ever seen in one place.

He pointed ahead. "We're looking for Grand Avenue."

Oliver leaned forward, acutely aware of the increase in traffic. The biggest town he'd ever been in was Hot Springs, Arkansas, and that was nothing compared to this.

"There." Jack pointed. "Make a right."

Oliver turned off Route 66 onto the smaller street and slowed even more.

Rose leaned over the seat. "I've never seen so many buildings, and they're so tall."

A car honked and Oliver braked, his palms sweaty. Did he really think he could do this?

He glanced at Jack. "Where to from here?"

"Looks like we're going right through the middle of St. Louis."

"Guess that's one way to see the town." Oliver stopped at a red light.

"There's a movie theater." Rose tapped Oliver's shoulder. "And would you look at these stores?"

"It's something alright." He moved on when the light changed. "It'd take some getting used to. I have to say I prefer smaller towns. All this noise and hustle and bustle would drive me a little crazy."

"Me too." Jack studied the map. "Off Grand, you're going to make a right on Cass. Harlan said it's another big street."

Oliver gripped the steering wheel. "They all look big to me."

Rose continued gasping and pointing at the many stores, hotels, theaters, and cafes they passed.

While the driving had his nerves taut, her excitement was contagious. But at the same time, his heart sank. What if she chose to live here? This bigger town seemed to fit everything she was looking for.

Her eyes sparkled and her enthusiasm made him feel guilty for hoping she wouldn't stay.

After several turns, a few turnarounds and with lots frazzled nerves later, Oliver turned into the driveway Jack pointed toward.

He blew out a sigh of relief. "That was pretty hairy."

Jack clapped him on the shoulder. "But we made it."

Before they could get out of the car, Rube Livingston stepped out onto the porch. Tall and lanky with a shock of white hair and slightly stooped shoulders, he leaned heavily on a cane and waved to them. "You'ns come on in. I'm happy you made it."

The house was a simple two-story brick with a wide porch trimmed in bright white and green shrubbery framing it.

Jack took the lead, bounding up the steps, while Rose hung back, grasping Oliver's arm.

He patted her hand. "It's okay. Nothing to be scared of. Let's go meet your uncle."

She ducked her head and blushed. "I feel self-conscious."

"Let's go." Oliver escorted her up the steps where her uncle embraced her and shook Oliver's hand.

Rube Livingston held the door open and motioned inside. "Come on in. You kids must be hungry. Can I get you something to eat?"

"We ate back down the road a piece. But I could sure use something to drink," Jack answered.

Oliver took in the clean, modest home. His gaze landed on trophies lined up on a shelf and couldn't resist a closer look.

Rube shuffled down a short hallway. "Rose, can you help me bring refreshments?"

"Sure." They returned a few minutes later with a tray that held a pitcher of tea and glasses. Rose poured each a glass. "Thank you, Uncle Rube. I really appreciate your invitation to come here."

"Ah, Rose." The old man adjusted his glasses. "You look so much like your mother and aunt." He sniffled. "I sure do miss my Katie."

She grasped his hand. "I know you do and I hate that I didn't get here sooner."

He waved his hand. "Sit. Everyone, sit."

Oliver remained fixated in front of the shelf, taking time to read each inscription. He couldn't deny the feeling of awe that washed over him, to be in the home of one of the greatest pitchers the St. Louis Browns ever had.

"Sir, this is overwhelming." He turned around as Rube dropped into an easy chair. "What an amazing career you had."

"You remind me of myself fifty years ago. I see a fire in your eyes." Rube pointed to one wall lined with pictures. "History." His voice trailed off. "I truly loved the game."

"As do I, sir." With a glass of tea in hand, he perused each photo, naming the players he recognized. He spent a long minute staring at the plaque of Rube Jackson Livingston being inducted into the baseball hall of fame.

He read the stats, which he already knew by heart. Played five-hundred-fifty-five games, defeated the New York Yankees in two world series, and was famous for the knuckleball, which Oliver had worked hard to perfect. He turned to face the old player. "I know all of your stats, and your knuckleball made baseball history. I've worked hard to learn it, but I'm sure I'll never be as good as you."

Rube chuckled. "You know your players, son. And I'll show you a trick or two with that ball. I think Bill DeWitt will be happy to meet you tomorrow."

Oliver faced him, his heart pounding double-time. "I cannot wait, Mr. Livingston."

"Oh, for goodness sakes, call me Rube."

"I can't thank you enough for this opportunity, Rube."

"And I can't thank you enough for bringing my niece and nephew to me."

---

Rose watched the interaction with a great deal of joy. She'd been able to keep her end of the bargain to introduce Oliver to her uncle, and Oliver had gone above and beyond on his end of the bargain.

She discreetly took in the details of the living room and could easily see Aunt Katherine's touches everywhere. No doubt her uncle missed his wife terribly. They'd been married for over forty years.

All of it brought a tightness to her chest. The heavy loss of her mom and aunt twisted her gut. Could she be comfortable staying here with Uncle Rube?

A big part of her found it all fascinating, but what about when the new wore off? Uncle Rube appeared to be in fair health, but he was old. Had to be getting near to ninety. Did she really want to be responsible for his care in his declining years?

Yet, they had no children, so who would care for him? She'd seen an article in one of Sara Beth's magazines about something new called nursing homes. The article she'd read talked about the benefits of having daily nurse care, but still, it took folks out of their homes and put them in a strange place. She had a lot to think about.

"Uncle Rube, you said Aunt Katherine left something for me?" She set her tea glass on the coffee table.

"Oh, child, yes. I'll get it for you."

"If you'll tell me where it is, I'll be happy to get it."

"There is a box on the top shelf of Katie's closet. I wrote your name on the outside so it wouldn't accidentally get thrown away. I knew in my heart you'd make it here someday." He leaned forward and pointed to the stairs. "It's the first door on the right at the top of the stairs. I don't go up there much anymore. My old legs get wobbly and I can't afford to take a fall."

Jack got to his feet. "I'll go with you, sis."

She nodded, and they hurried up the stairs. She couldn't help staring at everything as she went and at the top of the stairs noted two more bedrooms and a bathroom. If she stayed, this is where she would live.

"I can't help but wonder what it'd be like to live here," she whispered to Jack.

"It's nice for sure, but I have no doubts about what I want to do. I'm going back to the farm. This big city life is not for me."

"You're doing the right thing. I just wish I had your confidence about what I want."

She stepped into the bedroom to see a fourposter bed with a colorful quilt thrown across the foot of it. She sucked in a breath. The room was so clean and nice. A part of her shrunk into herself, afraid to touch anything. Insecurities reared their ugly heads.

Jack easily reached for the rectangular box on the top shelf and handed it down to her. "Doesn't feel like it has anything in it. Want to open it up here or carry it down?"

"I think Uncle Rube would like to see me open it. I sure do wonder what's inside."

Curiosity had her wanting to peek, but she held it in check and they went back to the living room. Jack was right. The twelve-inch box weighed hardly anything at all.

She set it on the coffee table and settled on the couch, where Jack joined her.

Oliver had finally taken a seat in a chair next to Uncle Rube.

"Go ahead," Uncle Rube urged. "It's for you."

She untied the silk ribbon securing the lid and carefully removed it. When she lifted the top, her breath caught in her throat.

A note written in a beautiful flowing script lay on top of something wrapped in tissue paper.

She read it aloud. "My dear sweet Rose, if you're reading this, I am no longer here. But what is inside this box symbolizes everything the women in our family have endured for generations, and the beliefs they stood for. Your mother, my wonderful little sister, was one of the strongest women I ever knew. You have all of that strength in your blood, heart, and soul. So take this gift from your great-great grandmother and eventually pass it down to your own daughter, along with the story I'm about to share."

Tears clouded her vision as she remembered the dream and the golden-haired little girl twirling around, calling her mommy.

Folding the note, she laid it on the table and carefully pulled back the tissue paper.

An audible gasp escaped.

# CHAPTER 36

As the sun started its slow descent, Rose scooted to the edge of the couch and gingerly touched the rectangular piece of cloth lying beneath the tissue paper, along with a silver brooch. While the cloth seemed fragile, the vivid forest green, red, and blue plaid colors appeared new. She'd never been more puzzled.

Jack peered over her shoulder. "What is it, Rose?"

"I'm not sure. It feels very old, though." She turned the silver brooch over in her hand. It had four decorative thistles forming the basic shape and in the center was a crown, a cross, and some foreign words she couldn't decipher.

Uncle Rube leaned forward. "Katie said she put a full explanation in the bottom of the box. Perhaps you could read it out loud."

Rose nodded and lifted the tissue paper with the treasures and laid them on the table. A large piece of linen paper lay underneath. Her hand shook as she read, "This is a surviving piece of an ancient Scottish Tartan and the brooch that represents the McDonald clan. Your great-great grandmother, Flora McDonald, managed to save these, and pass them down to her daughter after the fall of Scotland to the English in the 1700s. A short bit of history: When England invaded Scotland, the Highlanders fought to keep their lands and way of life. A powerful group called Jacobites formed to save their country and Flora played an important role."

She glanced up. "The 1700s. Can you imagine?"

Jack whistled. "No, I can't. But I hate the idea of one country taking over another and trying to change their way of life. Is there more?"

"There is." She continued. "After the battle of Culloden, Prince Charles of Scotland was a fugitive with a price on his head. Flora, who was a widow at the time, took him into her home, disguised him in women's clothing, and introduced him as a housemaid named Betty Burke."

Jack chuckled. "How humiliating that must have been for a prince. Keep going."

She nodded. "While Prince Charles eventually managed to escape the English, Flora was arrested and imprisoned for a year. She was described as a slight, genteel woman with nerves of steel. Not long after her release from prison, she set sail for North Carolina in America with her new husband and daughter."

"Wow! What a story." Jack leaned back against the sofa. "Is that all?"

"Almost." She stopped to take a sip of tea. "So, Rose, whatever life throws at you, always remember you are a direct descendant of Flora McDonald and you have the strength to overcome anything. Cherish this treasure always, and promise to keep it in the family. Love, Your Aunt Katherine."

Tears ran down her cheeks and dripped off her chin. "This is too much."

Oliver pulled a handkerchief from his pocket and passed it to her. "See, Rose. You have ancestral strength in your blood. You're always going to be able to handle anything that comes your way."

Rube rubbed a hand over his eyes and cleared his throat. "Your aunt and mother had that same grit. I don't know everything, but I do know your mother endured a lot at the hands of Ezra Blaine. I never cared for the man and he never liked me."

"He was jealous of you and your success, Uncle. And he had an uncontrollable temper." Rose blew her nose and fought to gain control of her emotions. "These last five years since Ma died have been pure hell for us."

Jack nodded. "That's an understatement. But we have a second chance now."

Rose touched the piece of cloth again, imagining her great-great grandmother daring to put her life at risk for her beliefs. Something inside shifted. She squared her shoulders and sat up straighter. She was more than a lowdown moonshiner's daughter and now she had a chance to prove it.

Over the next few minutes she listened to Jack excitedly telling their uncle all his plans to return to the Martin farm, go to school, learn to weld, and explore everything life could offer.

The old man raised his bushy eyebrows. "I like it, Jack. You've got a clear path ahead and a good attitude." He turned to Rose. "I know living here might be a little scary, and I understand that. We hardly know each other. But my offer stands. You're welcome to stay, and I'll do my best to help you in whatever way I can. Your aunt worried a lot about you kids."

Rose twisted the handkerchief in her hands. "You'll never know how much I appreciate your offer, Uncle Rube. I have a lot to think about. As Ma used to say, whenever there's a question, it's always best to sleep on it."

"Wise woman." The old man pushed to his feet with a groan. "I had my housekeeper make a pot of soup earlier today. I think it's time for some supper."

So, that's why the house was so clean and well-tended. Rose tried to imagine having someone to do household chores. She pictured a rotund, gray-haired woman with a white apron and her hair twisted up into a bun. "Point me to the kitchen and I'll be happy to get supper on the table."

She picked up the piece of tartan cloth and brooch with reverence and placed them back into the box with the story of its history underneath, then wrapped it exactly the way she'd found it.

How she'd loved to have known her ancestors. She regretted that her grandmother had died before she was born. No doubt she would've had stories like these to share. She wondered for a moment why her mother never mentioned any of this. Perhaps she didn't know the story. Yet, she remembered how much her mother loved *The Little Prince* book and would read it to her at bedtime. Perhaps she was saving the real story for when Rose was older, only she never had a chance to tell her.

After re-attaching the ribbon, she gathered their tea glasses and pitcher and stood. Uncle Rube directed her toward the kitchen, then dropped back into his chair with a groan, fatigue written on his face.

Taking in the spotless counters, modern stove, and icebox, she tried again to imagine living in such luxury. Would she be a fool to return to Crossett with Oliver and give up this opportunity?

She had a lot to mull over. Perhaps she should make a list of the good and bad aspects of staying. If the good outweighed the bad, it would make the choice easier.

Yet, knots formed in her stomach at the thought of Oliver and Jack driving off without her. She'd be losing Jack, regardless. But Oliver? He'd done so much and been so good to her. And he'd said he cared about her. His actions backed up those words. Truth be told, she had come to care deeply for him, too. Could they possibly have a future together someday?

What to do?

She opened a cabinet and pulled out a canister of cornmeal and set about making cornbread to accompany the soup.

The soothing effects of doing something familiar helped to settle her thoughts. She'd sleep on it. Thank goodness she didn't have to decide right this minute.

---

Rube Livingston climbed into the Woody Wagon with Oliver the next morning after breakfast. They were to meet with Bill DeWitt at ten. While Jack expressed an interest in going, he finally chose to stay with

Rose. Oliver was thankful that he put his sister before his own curiosity. He vowed to take Jack to Sportsman's Field before they left St. Louis.

He'd struggled to sleep the night before. Thoughts ran like an open faucet through his mind. He'd had to pinch himself to make sure he was awake and not dreaming that he was lying in a bed in the home of a baseball legend he'd followed and admired for years.

Eventually, exhaustion had overcome him, and he dreamed of pitching the perfect knuckleball.

But now, as he put the Woody in reverse, he didn't attempt to quell the excitement. He was so close. The raven of doubt perched on his shoulder and began squawking. *What if you're not good enough? What if you mess up? What if you say or do the wrong thing or the man just doesn't like you?*

He forced the thoughts away. He'd spent his entire twenty-two years living and breathing baseball, waiting for this moment.

If he wasn't ready now, he never would be.

Following Rube's directions, he drove to the baseball field where they were to meet Bill DeWitt in the field house.

He pulled into the almost empty parking lot and shut off the motor. His heart pounded and his palms sweated.

The sheer size of the stadium left him speechless. He could imagine the roar of the crowds and the crack of the bat. Everything in his being longed for a chance to play.

Glad for the quiet moment to take it all in while Rube got out of the car, he took a deep breath.

What would happen over the next few minutes could change the course of his life forever.

Forcing himself to slow his steps so the older man could keep up, his heart raced with excitement and anticipation.

This was it!

His dream lay just within reach of his tingling fingertips itching to hold the bat.

He could feel it.

# CHAPTER 37

Oliver stepped into the field house, and the distinct odor of leather and musty clothes hit his nostrils. Even though it was off season, a few uniforms with Browns in orange and brown lettering still hung on nails. His heart ratcheted at the thought of putting on one of them. Several bats leaned against one wall, gloves lay in a stack, and a bucket of balls sat waiting like anxious children wanting to play.

Bill DeWitt. To finally meet him…it couldn't be real. Yet it was.

Rube called out, his voice echoing off the walls. "Bill. You in here?"

"In the office," a deep voice replied from down a corridor.

Oliver let Rube lead the way and followed behind, not missing a single detail as they went. He noted the rows of lockers, benches, concrete floors, and walls that could use a fresh coat of paint. When they passed by a window, he glimpsed the playing field, the distinctive diamond, and beyond that, empty stands. Thrilled was not a large enough word to express what vibrated through his being.

They walked into the office, where a clean-shaven, round-faced man wearing wire-rimmed spectacles sat behind a wooden desk.

He pushed back his chair and stood. "Rube, old friend, it's good to see you." He rounded the desk and clasped the old man's hand. "You're looking fit."

Rube chuckled. "Fit as an old geezer can be, I reckon." He motioned toward Oliver. "This is the young man I talked to you about. Name's Oliver Quinn."

Oliver stuck out his hand. The manager's handshake was firm and confident. "It's a real honor to meet you, sir."

The man motioned toward two wooden chairs. "You wouldn't by chance be related to the boxer, Patrick Quinn, would you?"

Oliver gasped. "That was my father, sir. You knew him?"

"Saw him fight a guy from Puerto Rico once in Kansas City and never forgot it. Had a future in the ring. I do hope he's doing well."

"He passed away when I was twelve. Sawmill accident. His boxing days ended when I was but a toddler, but he had a passion for baseball and passed that on to me." Oliver couldn't believe this man knew of his father. What were the odds? He sent up a silent thank you to the man who sired him for helping pave the way.

"I'm sorry to hear that he passed away. Helluva boxer." The man motioned toward two empty chairs. "Please, sit. Tell me why you want to play for the Browns."

Oliver cleared his throat as he perched on the edge of the chair. "Well, sir, I've been playing ball since I could walk and I've followed your team for years. I can tell you every game won, lost, and tied, and it's my dream to play for you."

"I see." Mr. DeWitt shuffled some papers to the side and placed his elbows on the desk. "Rube, you seen him play?"

"No. But he's knowledgeable. That much I can vouch for. Said he's studied my knuckleball method." Rube chuckled. "Anybody that knows about that is a player in my books."

"You do realize I cannot offer you a position on the team without seeing you in action, don't you?"

"Of course, sir." Oliver picked at a hangnail. "All I ask for is a chance."

"Tryouts aren't until next spring." He removed his spectacles and polished them. "You live around here?"

"Arkansas, sir. But I'm willing to move."

Rube leaned forward. "The boy can stay with me."

Oliver swallowed hard at the bold declaration. After all, the man didn't know him from Adam. "Thank you, Rube."

The old man leaned on his cane. "Say, are any of the boys around? Maybe someone could hit a few balls with Oliver?"

"For you, Rube." Mr. DeWitt stood. "I'll be right back."

Oliver turned to Rube. "I know I wouldn't have gotten in the door like this without your influence. You have to know how much I appreciate it."

Rube waved him away. "What else is an old man going to do but help younguns?"

A few minutes later, the manager stuck his head in the door. "Found Whitey and Jones hanging around. Come on, Oliver, let me see what you can do."

Oliver removed his paddy cap and ran a hand through his hair before he jammed it back on. It was happening. He jumped to his feet, then waited for Rube to get his balance with the cane.

They followed Mr. DeWitt out to the diamond, where two men tossed a ball back and forth.

One of the men threw a ball to Oliver without any warning, and he caught it with no effort out of pure instinct. The man who'd pitched it grinned. "Nice catch."

Mr. DeWitt called out, "Let Quinn pitch a few to you."

Oliver stepped onto the pitcher's mound. Surely he was dreaming. He couldn't possibly be standing where Walter Brown, Dizzy Dean, and Cliff Fannin had stood. Sacred ground. He focused on the batter.

He wound up and released the ball as soon as the batter stepped up to the box and settled the bat over his shoulder. The batter missed, and Oliver caught the ball when the other man tossed it back to him.

Twice more, he pitched and twice more the batter missed.

"Switch places," Mr. DeWitt called. "Jones, you pitch. I want to see Quinn in the batter's box."

Oliver nodded to the man when they passed. He took to the batter's box and tipped the bat on the ground. Keeping an eye on the pitcher's stance, he could almost read his mind and was ready when he let go a hard fastball.

The bat connected with the ball, sending it into far left field. He glanced at Mr. DeWitt. All it took was an almost imperceptible nod, and he sprinted for first base. He slid into second, before the other player reached him.

The three men played for a few more minutes before Bill DeWitt blew a whistle. "Okay. That's enough." He motioned to Oliver. "Come back to my office."

He took time to shake hands with the other two men and dust off his pants, before following Rube and Bill back inside. How he wished he could read the look on the manager's impassive face.

Did he play well enough for an invitation to try out?

The team manager took his place back behind the desk. "As I'm sure you know, Oliver, our boys had a pretty rough go last season. I'm looking to recruit talented players and hoping for a comeback next year."

Oliver waited until Rube settled back in a chair before sitting. He leaned forward. "Yes, sir."

"I like what I saw. You remind me of another player that recently retired. Maybe you've heard of Frankie Hayes?"

"He played for the Red Sox."

"They beat us pretty bad last year and part of that was because of Frankie." He adjusted his glasses. "Tell you what. Tryouts start on April 25th. Think you can be here?"

Oliver all but jumped from his seat. "I sure can." His heart ratcheted, and he blew out a breath he'd been holding. He slapped his thigh. "I'll be here, sir, and I won't let you down."

Mr. DeWitt chuckled. "I like your spunk. You just might be what the team needs. But I won't be the only one deciding. You'll have to prove yourself."

"I understand, and I promise I'll work hard."

"That, I believe, and with Rube in your corner, you just might make it."

The old man leaned on his cane. "I don't know about that, Bill, but I think Oliver won't have any trouble proving he can play."

The manager stood and extended his hand. "Then, I'll see you in April, Oliver Quinn."

Oliver pumped his hand enthusiastically and turned to Rube. "I can't wait to tell Rose and Jack."

The old man gave a lopsided grin. "They'll be thrilled for you. The league needs more outstanding players. Just happy I could help. Not much more I can do at my age." He struggled to get to his feet, and Oliver placed a hand on his elbow to steady him.

Once they returned to the car, Oliver sat for a long minute staring at what might be a bright future.

Rube clapped his shoulder. "That was promising, young man. Very promising."

"I'm on cloud nine right now." His throat clogged, and he choked on his words. "It's everything I've dreamed of for so long. I never imagined when I first met Rose that she would be the one to help me get here."

"Life's a funny thing." He propped his cane against the door. "The most unlikely meeting can bring about things you can't imagine. I remember when I first signed. I was walking on cloud nine then, too. And don't you worry. If you hadn't impressed Bill, he wouldn't have invited you to the tryouts."

Oliver couldn't wait to get back to the house with Rose and Jack. And he needed to make a phone call.

"Rube, do you mind if I use your phone to ring my mum when we get back? I'll happily pay you."

"No pay necessary. Of course, call her and tell her the good news." Rube directed him back the way they'd come, and Oliver memorized the route. He couldn't wait to treat Jack and Rose to a visit to the iconic stadium.

Back at the house, Rube excused himself, saying the excursion had tired him, and he needed a short nap. "Beatrice will be here to fix a meal, Rose, so don't worry about fixing anything." He shuffled toward his downstairs bedroom.

Once Oliver shared every detail with Rose and Jack, he picked up the telephone receiver and gave the operator the request to connect with the bakery.

"Mum, it's me, Oliver," he said when she answered.

"Where are you son? When will you be home?"

Over the next few minutes, he shared the details of the past few days, including Sara Beth's new baby and his plan to return home after dropping Jack back off at the Martin farm.

"Will Rose be returning with you, son?"

"I don't know yet. She's still trying to decide, but I've assured her she is welcome in our home." Rose raised her eyebrows.

"Can I please talk to her for a minute?"

"Sure." He turned to Rose and held out the receiver. "Mum wants to talk to you."

She dropped her gaze and spoke into the black receiver. "Hello, Fiona. It's so good to hear your voice."

While Oliver could only hear Rose's side of the conversation, no doubt his mother was letting her know she would be welcomed with open arms if she wanted to come live with them.

"Thank you, Fiona." Rose wrapped the phone cord around one finger. "I truly do appreciate your offer."

A moment of silence followed before Rose said, "Yes, ma'am. Here's Oliver."

Her eyes misted when she handed the receiver back.

"Okay, Mum. Barring no problems, I should be back home in a couple of days."

"Just be careful. Can't wait to have you back under my roof, and congratulations on getting a spot in the tryouts. I never doubted that you would. I know your father is smiling down on you. I love you, son."

"Love you, too. See you soon. Kiss the girls for me."

"I will."

The click told him she'd hung up, and he replaced the receiver on the hook.

Rose touched his arm. "Will you come out to the porch with me? I need to talk to you."

Oliver nodded.

His heart sank.

She wasn't going back with him.

# CHAPTER 38

Rose tugged a sweater around her shoulders and stepped out onto Uncle Rube's front porch as Oliver held the door open. The midday sun went behind a cloud and a gust of north wind ruffled her hair.

Oliver leaned against the porch railing and crossed his arms. "You've made your decision."

Did she imagine it, or did disappointment ring in his voice? "I have." She took a seat in a nearby rocker.

"Well, spill it. What have you decided to do?"

"I thought about it all through the night and played out every scenario in my head." She glanced around at the immaculate lawn and pristine houses that lined the street. Such a far cry from the moonshiner's shack she'd left behind. "It's so nice here. Everything's so clean and modern."

Oliver cleared his throat. "It's a very nice place. I'm sure you'll be happy here."

"Who said I'm staying?" She met his gaze as a flicker of surprise flashed.

"What are you saying, Rose? Spit it out." He shoved his hands in his pockets.

"I'm not staying here. If the offer still stands, I'm going back to Crossett with you and your family."

Oliver leaned forward and jerked off his cap, his eyes aglow. "You mean it?"

"Yes. While I think I could be happy here with Uncle Rube, it just doesn't feel right. The town is too big and I wouldn't know a single soul besides him. I don't feel ready for that."

He let out a whoop. "I'm so glad. I didn't want to influence your decision in any way. It needed to be completely your choice, but I happen to think you made the right one."

"I just think I'll do better in a small town with people I know than this big city."

"I couldn't agree more."

"But there is one stipulation." She met his steady gaze. "When you come back for the tryouts in April, I want to come with you. Perhaps spend a few days on the farm, then a few days here with Uncle Rube. By then, I'll know for sure if I want to stay."

"You've got it." A wide grin covered his face, and his green eyes sparkled with golden flecks. "I have to admit, I'm thrilled with your choice. And your uncle will understand. He only wants what's best for you all. And so do I."

"I haven't told Jack yet, but we talked a lot this morning." A red cardinal flitting from tree to tree caught her eye. "He has big dreams, and knowing Jack, he'll make them all come true."

"Jack has a great attitude. He'll accomplish whatever he sets out to do."

She chuckled. "Told me he's got an itch to pan for gold. I think it's far-fetched, but who knows? Maybe there is gold in Missouri. If there is, Jack will find it."

"I can picture him living out in the woods panning for gold. But I know he wants to finish his education first, and I hope you will, too."

She nodded. "I plan on it. Think I can go to school with Elizabeth and Margaret?"

"I'm sure of it. What was the last grade you finished?"

"Seventh. That was the year after Ma died."

"We know all the teachers in Crossett. When we get back, we'll have a meeting and see what they recommend. Maybe some tutoring to get you caught up."

"It's a little scary, but when I read the story about my great-great grandmother and how she risked everything for what she believed, I made up my mind. I can do anything and be brave like her."

Oliver lifted his hands, then dropped them. "I really want to hug you right now, Rose. May I?"

Meeting his steady gaze, she nodded and got to her feet. When he wrapped his arms around her, she sank into the embrace, taking comfort from his strong arms.

Maybe someday there would be more for her and Oliver, but for now, she'd cherish the deep and lasting friendship they'd formed. She returned the embrace, then stepped out of his arms.

"That was nice, Oliver. Thank you for believing in me and my brothers."

"Not hard to do. Just happy I get to be a part of it." He braced one hand on the porch railing. "I'm thinking we should get back to Layken's farm this afternoon. Would that suit you?"

"It would. I hate to leave Uncle Rube. He's so old and frail."

Oliver nodded. "He is, but he might just be stronger than you think."

A rotund middle-aged lady hurried up the walk, pinning her hair up as she went. She stopped short when she reached the porch, then with a warm smile, stepped up. "You must be Rube's niece, Rose. He's talked non-stop about you kids for days now. So glad you made it." She put a hand over her mouth. "Oh, sorry. I'm Beatrice, your uncle's housekeeper. Don't mean to ramble. I tend to do that." She chuckled.

Rose stuck out her hand. "It's nice to meet you, Beatrice. Uncle Rube speaks highly of you." She pointed to Oliver. "This is my friend Oliver, and my brother Jack is inside."

Beatrice shook Oliver's hand, then he opened the door for her. "It's nice to meet you, Beatrice."

After saying hello to Jack, she made a beeline for the kitchen. "I'll have some food whipped up in two shakes of a lamb's tail. Is Mr. Rube napping?"

Rose followed her into the kitchen. "Yes. He and Oliver went to the baseball field earlier this morning and I think it tired him out. Can I do anything to help?"

"Not a thing, but keep me company. It's not often I have a lovely young lady to visit with while I work." She bustled about the kitchen, opening cupboards and taking leftover meatloaf from the icebox. "I hope you kids like meatloaf sandwiches."

"Yes, ma'am, we do." Rose leaned against the counter. "Sure there's nothing I can do?"

Beatrice slid a loaf of bread toward her. "Here, you can slice the bread. How long are you staying?"

"We're heading out right after lunch. It's been such a wonderful visit for all of us, but me and Oliver will be coming back next April because he's going to try out for the St. Louis Browns baseball team."

"That must have made your uncle very happy. He's a legend, you know. Folks stop by often to see him and talk about his career in baseball." Beatrice placed a kettle of water on the stove. "And he's a pleasure to work for."

"I'm so glad he has you."

"It works both ways."

Rose laid the evenly sliced pieces of bread on a platter and Beatrice added the meatloaf and opened a jar of home canned pickles.

Uncle Rube stepped into the kitchen, his white hair sticking up in all directions. "I thought I heard you, Beatrice. I see you met my company."

"Yes, I did, Mister Rube. And they are delightful."

Rose moved closer to him. "Uncle Rube, we're going to head back to the farm after lunch." She laid a hand on his wrinkled arm. "It's been so wonderful to get to see you, and I cannot thank you enough for everything, especially saving the box Aunt Katherine left for me."

He patted her hand. "I'm just glad you came. And while I'm sorry you've decided not to stay, I understand you have to do what's best for you. But before you go, I want to give you some of your aunt's clothes and shoes."

Rose gasped. "Oh, I couldn't take something so personal."

"Please. You'd be doing me a favor. I haven't had the heart to get rid of them and she was just about your size."

Beatrice turned the burner off when the kettle whistled. "Dinner will be on the table in five minutes."

"Beatrice, you are a true blessing."

"As are you, Mister Rube." She poured boiling water over tea leaves and picked up the platter.

Uncle Rube took Rose's arm, and they walked to the dining room to find Jack and Oliver already seated.

After eating their fill, Oliver accompanied Rose upstairs to her aunt's bedroom, where they found an empty valise under the bed, as Uncle Rube had said they would.

She couldn't believe her good fortune. Aunt Katherine had stylish clothes and shoes that must have cost more than she could fathom. She blinked back unbidden tears as she touched the dresses.

With Oliver's help, she soon had the leather valise full. She wouldn't have to be ashamed of wearing rags when she went to school or to a job.

She hoped it would be both.

Oliver pointed the Woody wagon toward the highway leading to Layken's farm after a quick stop at the stadium. Jack and Rose's enthusiasm matched his own.

The mood was light and full of hope for all three of the travelers, and Oliver pulled into the driveway at the Martin farm a little after four o'clock.

Before they could get out of the car, Layken pulled in behind them and jumped out of his pickup waving a paper. "We did it! We paid off the bank note."

All three dogs surrounded him, barking and prancing, as if they understood.

Sara Beth stepped out onto the screened-in porch, holding Henry. A huge smile spread across her face. "Wish I could've seen Homer's face." She opened the screen door. "Oliver, Rose, Jack, so good to see you. Everyone, come in."

Oliver slapped Layken on the back and leaned down to pet Pirate and the girls before going inside. "That's great news, Layken. Sounds like a call for a celebration. And we have some things to celebrate, too."

Rich chocolate odors drifted from the kitchen as Tab and Uncle Seymour stepped into the living room.

Greetings, laughter, and lots of smiles went around the group. Rose held out her arms for Henry. "I need to see my godson."

Sara Beth placed the baby in her arms. "I can't tell you how happy I am to see you, Rose. I thought for sure you'd stay in St. Louis."

Oliver peered over Rose's shoulder at the cherub-faced infant. "She'll have to tell you all about it."

Rose glanced up at him, her violet-blue eyes twinkling. "And Oliver has news to share, too. He's been invited to try out for the Browns next April."

"Oh, my goodness. You were only gone for a short time, but it just goes to show how much can happen in forty-eight hours." She brushed back a strand of hair that had escaped. "But paying off the bank loan is tops for us. I can't tell you how relieved I am."

Layken took her in his arms and twirled her around. "I wish you could've been there, sweetheart. Homer had little to say. Mostly just blustered and took his time canceling the note. I thought he'd find a way to go back on his bargain, but he didn't. Maybe there's a shred of decency in him yet."

Sara Beth laughed. "I doubt it, but we're finally free of him. We did it, Layken."

Oliver couldn't help but share the couple's elation. He knew what it felt like to accomplish the impossible.

Jack shook Layken's hand and hugged Sara Beth, then took off out the back door with Tab, while Uncle Seymour built a fire in the fireplace to stave off the cool fall air.

Seeing the light on each of the faces warmed Oliver's heart.

Everything was working out for each one of them.

And for him, it went beyond anything he'd dared to hope for.

With a chance to try out for his favorite baseball team and Rose joining their family, things couldn't get any better.

Tomorrow morning, they would head home, toward a bright future filled with hope, love and certainty.

And they would spend all the days following, building on that future.

Who could say what lay ahead? But Oliver was more certain than ever he wanted Rose in his life as they both moved forward.

And maybe someday, when she'd achieved her deepest dreams and desires, she'd want to be more than just a friend.

A man could hope.

His father used to share a quote he loved and believed in, and it came to mind as Oliver contemplated where life was taking all of them.

*Hold fast to dreams, for if dreams die, life is a broken-winged bird that cannot fly.*

He took off his paddy cap and ran a hand through his hair. It took loads of courage to follow one's dreams, just as it took bravery for Rose's great-great grandmother to risk her life for what she believed in.

Rose sank into a rocker with the baby in her arms and smiled up at him with twinkling eyes the color of violets that had first mesmerized him.

Someday, that would be their child in her arms.

He just knew it.

Everything in its time.

# ABOUT JAN SIKES

Jan Sikes writes compelling and creative stories from the heart. She openly admits that she never set out in life to be an author, although she's been an avid reader all her life. But she had a story to tell. Not just any story, but a true story that rivals any fiction creation. She brought the entertaining true story to life through fictitious characters in an intricately woven tale that encompasses four books, accompanying music CDs, and a book of poetry and art.

And now, this author can't put down the pen. She continues to write fiction in a variety of genres, and has published many award-winning short stories and novels.

Jan is an active blogger, a devoted fan of Texas music, and a grandmother of five. She resides in North Texas.

For more visit JanSikes.com

# Fresh Ink Group
### Independent Multi-media Publisher
Fresh Ink Group / Push Pull Press
Voice of Indie / GeezWriter

&

Hardcovers
Softcovers
All Ebook Platforms
Audiobooks
Worldwide Distribution

&

Indie Author Services
Book Development, Editing, Proofing
Graphic/Cover Design
Video/Trailer Production
Website Creation
Social Media Management
Writing Contests
Writers' Blogs
Podcasts

&

Authors
Editors
Artists
Experts
Professionals

&

FreshInkGroup.com
info@FreshInkGroup.com
X: @FreshInkGroup
Facebook.com/FreshInkGroup
LinkedIn: Fresh Ink Group
Instagram: @FreshInkGroup and @FIGPublishing

# Book 1

## The Bargainer Series

**Jacketed Hardcover**
**Softcover**
**Ebooks**

*A Beggar's Bargain* — The Bargainer Series — Jan Sikes

Fresh Ink Group
FreshInkGroup.com

A shocking proposal that changes everything. Desperate to honor his father's dying wish, Layken Martin vows to do whatever it takes to save the family farm. Once the Army discharges him following World War II, Layken returns to Missouri to find his legacy in shambles and in jeopardy. A foreclosure notice from the bank doubles the threat. He appeals to the local banker for more time—a chance to rebuild, plant, and harvest crops and time to heal far away from the noise of bombs and gunfire. But the banker firmly denies his request. Now what?

Then the banker makes an alternative proposition—marry his unwanted daughter, Sara Beth, in exchange for a two-year extension. Out of options, money, and time, Layken agrees to the bargain. Now, he has two years to make a living off the land while he shares his life with a stranger. If he fails at either, he'll lose it all.

# The White Rune Series

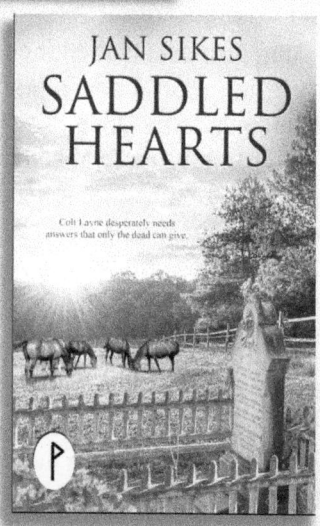

**JAN SIKES — GHOSTLY INTERFERENCE**

**JAN SIKES — JAGGED FEATHERS**

**JAN SIKES — SADDLED HEARTS**

# More by Jan Sikes

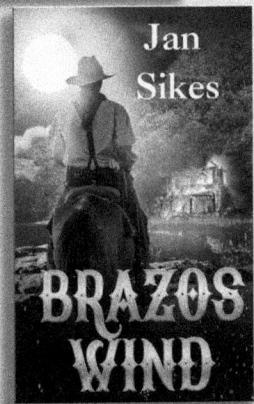

# True Story Series

## Flowers and Stone
**JAN SIKES**
BOOK 1 TRUE STORY SERIES

## The Convict and the Rose
The cold iron bars and forty foot walls of Leavenworth prison could not separate the rebel from his rose.
True Story Series
Sequel to Flowers and Stone
**JAN SIKES**

## Home at Last
True Story Series
2016 First Place Texas Biography Fiction
Award Winning Author
**JAN SIKES**

## Til Death Do Us Part
True Story Series
Award Winning Author
**JAN SIKES**

# Shorts by Jan Sikes

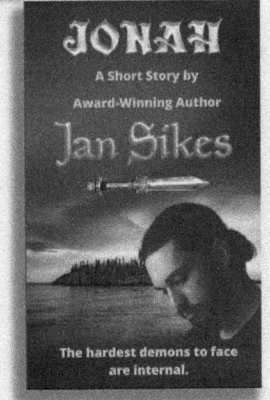

# Music by Rick Sikes

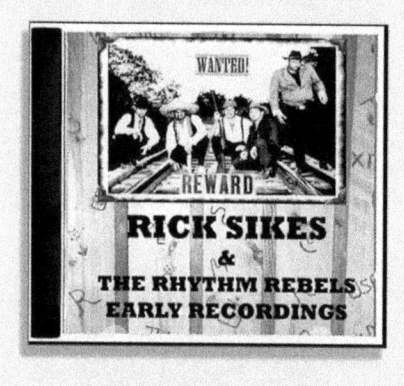

### Download/Stream Everywhere

Milton Keynes UK
Ingram Content Group UK Ltd.
UKHW030905141024
449705UK00012B/545